The E
in the Forest

by Michael Eaude

The Clapton Press

The Clapton Press Limited
38 Thistlewaite Road
London E5 0QQ

www.theclaptonpress.com

The Bones in the Forest © 2024, Michael Eaude

ISBN 978-1-913693-40-4

Cover design by Gruffydd
Cover photograph courtesy of Thomas Griesbeck

For Marisa with love

Era tremendamente injusto. Como si los hubieran matado dos veces. La primera, con una bala, y la segunda, quitándoles la identidad.

It was enormously unjust. As if they'd killed them twice. First with a bullet and then by stripping them of their identity.

Antonio Ontañón, President of 'Héroes de la República', Santander

Chapter One

The man who was not yet a killer climbed the mountain track with long strides and the tension in his mind eased into the pleasure of physical action. Each step trod lightly over the rough ground. This was the pulse of life, of the heart, to walk with steady rhythm over the cold hills.

The anxiety that had made his throat dry and breath come fast as he left the house melted away as he walked. He had slipped out the back door, across the yard and the two fallow fields fringed with stones and into the pine forest that surrounded the village. Then it was simple. He followed the dark path he knew as well as the rooms of his own house.

He had waited for the winter night to start rolling across the land. The smell of wood stoves drifted over the steep, slate roofs and smoke trailed up into the last light above the ridge. Berta's dog had barked and he paused a moment. The dog stopped, although it may not have been barking at him. The dogs sometimes barked at wind in the trees or a mouse in the grass. It was said that they howled the night someone was going to die. Today this did indeed seem to be the case.

He had half-hoped he might meet someone, for then he would have had to postpone his plan for another day. His life would have trundled on along the familiar grooves, as it had since he came to the village. All his concentration was reserved for the path, being careful he didn't turn an ankle on a loose stone. Despite the freezing temperature and the silent breeze that slid down the mountain like a serpent and chilled his cheek, his back was warm underneath his rucksack. He carried the shotgun in his left hand, balanced easily at its point of equilibrium, rather than on the sling over his shoulder.

Now, he sat waiting and his mind had to adjust to the imminent situation. It was no longer in the future, at the faraway end of his steady walk, but here and now. He had come to destroy Enrique, the man who had betrayed him. He loved this land and he wasn't going to let Enrique continue to ruin it with his constant bye-laws, his trampling over others, and what was worse, all done with that firm, frank handshake and smile. But it was a false smile. He had learned the hard way Enrique was false.

He concentrated on breathing deeply to calm himself and listened to the sounds of the night. Dry grass crackled under the bushes as animals crept or hunted, small darting mammals like shrews or stoats, a fox maybe. Even a hedgehog might snap a twig or rustle leaves as it snouted for grubs. An owl hooted across the valley and a light breeze moved like a sigh through the needle-thin leaves of the pines behind and below him. Then he heard an engine change gear: way down the mountain road, a car was climbing the hair-pin bends.

He had reached the spot in good time. He placed his bag and shotgun carefully to the left of a rosemary bush, so he would not lose them in the dark. For there was no light. The stars and the thin, curved moon were hidden behind cloud.

Though he had struggled to loosen the stones on the hillside, he had succeeded in getting them to crash down the slope, one by one. One boulder bounced straight across the road into the ravine below and was lost. Another came to rest perfectly in the middle of the road. The others he had helped into position.

The car's noise disappeared, then appeared again louder. He could picture its progress through the sound of its gears on the bends, where the road turned and almost doubled back on itself before the short straight up to the next corner. Then he saw its lights flash across the pines planted in rows fifty years ago and point along the straight below him. The headlights lit up the stones in the road. Then they shone for a moment downwards as the car braked sharply and dipped forward. Beads of sweat stood out on his forehead despite the frost. He stood up, knowing he was hidden in the pitch dark, pushed his gloves deep into a pocket and gripped the chilled barrel of the shotgun.

'These bloody rocks are going to sweep someone away one of these days,' a man complained, getting out of the car. Someone inside said something he did not catch. Then he caught a swirl of blonde in the dim light that had come on inside the car when the driver opened the door. It wasn't Enrique, it was that blasted, stuck-up Dutch woman married to Fernando, the lanky lawyer from Zaragoza. Why the hell had the idiots chosen today of all days? They hadn't been up to their house in the village all winter. He crouched down carefully as the two of them together heaved one of the boulders aside, and a twig snapped under his shoe. He froze, but the couple just carried on with their work.

'Shit,' he heard the lawyer say. 'That weighed a ton.'

'See if you can squeeze through here,' the Dutch woman said. She stood in the headlights and directed the car as it inched forward into the space they had cleared. Then she turned and looked straight at him. He could only see the profile of her head against the road, but he was sure she looked straight at him. Her nose seemed to lift like a deer sniffing scent on the breeze. 'It's a really weird feeling,

9

I mean a rock could break off and tumble down the slope at any moment,' she said.

'Funny, now you say that, that there's a rockfall when it hasn't been raining,' the lawyer said, as she got back into the car. *Fucking legal mind*, the man on the hillside thought, *never off duty*. Finally he exhaled, as the lawyer also got into the car and they drove off.

He waited a long minute while the total dark filled the mountainside again. He waited till his eyes had adjusted so he could just pick out the line of the ridge opposite against the sky. He put his gloves back on, placed the shotgun on the ground alongside the rucksack beside the rosemary bush and stepped down the slope to the road. He heaved the boulder back into the middle. To check the rocks' position, for an instant he switched on the torch he wore held by a strap round his head. When he finished, he heard another car climbing the hill. Or was it the lawyer's disappearing, further up the road over the mountain pass to Valeria?

Ten minutes later the second car rounded the corner. Travelling faster than the first car, its wheels skidded slightly as it stopped. The door opened and slammed shut. He heard the occupant's irritated steps on the road. He knew it was Enrique before he saw his broad shoulders and the tilt of his head in the car lights. He heard him swear: '*me cago en...*' and trail off into a mutter. Enrique was alone, as he was certain he would be. He stood up and began to ease his way down the slope as Enrique bent to roll the boulder aside. As he reached the road, he switched on the torch on his helmet.

Enrique whirled round and raised an arm. 'What the hell? Turn that thing off, will you.'

His mouth was dry and nothing came out when he opened it. He swallowed, then said, 'Hola Enrique.' Enrique peered forward into the dark.

'Oh, it's you. But what the hell are you doing out here?'

'I was out walking,' he said.

'*Hombre*,' said Enrique, 'on a night like this. Help me shift these damned rocks, you old bastard, and I'll give you a ride back.' Even then he could have calmly got into the car and travelled back with Enrique. He wasn't offended by Enrique's words: 'old bastard' was no insult, but a term of endearment.

'No,' he said, more to himself than in reply to Enrique, and pulled the trigger. As the recoil jerked him backwards and his torch flashed up into the sky, he heard Enrique scream. He stood still, trying to bring his breathing under control. Why did the stupid sod have to scream like that? He listened intently. There was no sound but the scream rebounding inside his skull. The scream seemed so loud and to linger in the thin air, but no-one else could have heard it. He bent his head slowly and found Enrique with the light. The body lay on its back, arms and legs splayed out like a dead man in a film. The killer pulled his gloves back on and approached the body. Enrique was dead in real life.

It was then, as he stepped across the lights of Enrique's car, that he jumped. He heard another car change gear as it rounded one of the mountain curves. And it was already close: he had not heard it start the ascent over the noise of Enrique's engine. He couldn't believe it. Some winter nights, not one car passed this way and he'd had three in half an hour. He froze, colder than the icy air, now unable to move.

Then urgency staved off panic. He acted fast, improvising with his mind fully alive. He laid down the shotgun carefully at the side of the road. He checked Enrique was dead with the side of one finger on his neck. He dragged the heavy body the rest of the way across the road and heaved it over the edge of the ravine. It started to fall, but then stopped. Already the lights of the climbing car were swirling across the pines. He ran back to Enrique's car and shut the door. There was room enough for another car to pass. He positioned himself in front of Enrique's car.

The other car came to a stop beside Enrique's. A man got out, held on to the open door and said: 'Excuse me. Anyone there?'

He turned on the torch, knowing it was shining straight at the man and said gruffly: 'No problem, carry on, carry on.'

'But what's the matter, man, do you need help?'

'No, you go on. I've just cleared some boulders off the road. You can get through here.' The man put up a hand to shield his eyes from the light.

'But... can you move that damned torch away? It's shining right in my eyes.'

'Sorry,' he grunted.

It was Miguel, the doctor from Zaragoza. He had seen the man's bald head and recognised his voice. The fool showed no sign of driving on. He thought he'd have to kill him too.

'Let me help you with the boulders.'

'No, no, really. I've finished actually. I was just about to drive on myself,' he said chattily.

'Do I know you? Are you from the village?'

'Just visiting.'

Then a voice came from inside the car. It was the doctor's daughter: 'Daddy, it's cold. Why have we stopped?'

12

Whiny little brat, he thought. *Have to shoot her as well.*

'Yes, darling, coming,' the doctor said, then turned back to the light shining down at his legs.

'Are you sure you're alright?'

'Really, really, I'm fine. You carry on,' the killer said. 'I'll be following you.'

The doctor still hesitated a moment, then got back into the car. It drove slowly through the gap Enrique had cleared in the moments before his death. He had turned off the light and crouched down in the shadow. He willed the car to accelerate away and it did, but slowly as if in doubt. The doctor would be puzzled not to know who it was he'd met on the mountain. He just hoped he'd disguised his voice well enough.

Now there was no point in pursuing his plan. He turned off Enrique's car's lights and engine. He heard the doctor's car driving up the winding road. The owl hooted again. Two long, tranquil calls. He wished the bird would just shut the fuck up. He moved carefully to the edge of the ravine and switched on the torch. He started back in shock: Enrique seemed to be suspended in space right in front of him. The body had snagged on a scrubby oak, little more than a bush that had sunk its roots into a cleft of the rock. Perhaps he could climb down and loosen it. If he had a long pole, he could reach it.

There was no time. The first car that had passed would report the rocks fallen onto the road. The second might report the suspicious man in the darkness who had ordered them on. The doctor might be calling even now on his mobile. The killer had planned to put Enrique back in his car and push it into the ravine. With luck it would be lost for days, even weeks. A couple of kids had driven off this road one night coming back from a village *fiesta* a few summers before. Despite teams out searching for them at dawn and helicopters flying up and down the valley, the car and their remains were only found two weeks later when vultures were spotted beside a clump of trees at the bottom of the ravine.

A good plan was to know you had to change the original plan. He recovered the shotgun and his rucksack from the hillside. He found the ejected shotgun shell. He forced himself to look for a further ten minutes to see if he had left anything behind. Then he climbed down to the road once more and began to walk very fast away from the village down the twisting road the three cars had come up.

A few hundred yards further down, a stream cascaded off the mountain, bouncing from rock to rock. Normally, it ran under the road through the enclosed culvert, but sprayed water across the asphalt when it was running full. It was a spot well-known to everyone who drove habitually up the road over the pass to Valeria, for on winter nights after rain the edges of the spray turned to ice. He himself had skidded there more than once. He took off his boots and socks. He packed them away in a plastic bag in the rucksack. Barefoot he began to climb the stream. He knew it was possible, as the last time he had driven along the road, he had stopped and studied a route up through the water. Take it slow, despite the cold, was the answer. The danger was the moss and ferns that had formed round the pools. He gripped the wet rock with his toes. All he needed now was to slip and twist an ankle or break a leg.

Ten minutes later, he sat down on a rock at the top of the waterfall. His feet were frozen and his hands in sodden gloves were chilled, yet sweat poured down his back and he couldn't stop shaking. He dried himself off with the small towel he had brought. He put away the towel and gloves in another plastic bag. He rubbed his numbed feet for a long minute. He pulled on the pair of woollen socks and boots again. He had a three-hour walk ahead. Slowly, the rhythm of his stride along one of the old sheep paths across the moor calmed his mood. Slowly too, his body settled. He heard the wind in the trees, a tawny owl's two sharp hoots, the small animals scuttling away through the undergrowth. Sometimes he brushed a bush, savory or thyme, and released its scent. A night jay cackled, but raised no smile in the long-striding killer.

Once he caught the whiff of a fox. This was the life he loved, this was the country that was eternal, worth a hundred times more than petty human concerns. As he stepped forward, he listened to all the noises, identifying each one, and no longer needed to think about anything else.

Chapter Two

She turned the brush sideways to fit between the plant-pots, which she pushed apart with a foot. Sometimes, she bent to drag a heavy pot a few inches across the bricks. Briskly, she brushed the dead leaves and soil that the blackbirds had scratched with their claws or pecked with their beaks out of the pots in their search for worms into a pile and swept it all into the dust-pan. Then she emptied it into the compost, careful to pick out the dog-ends, ear buds and rolled-up sweet papers that people had tossed over their balconies. These she put in a big silvery dustbin. Total cleanliness in the home, chaos outside: that was her neighbours' philosophy of freedom.

She had watched the same family of blackbirds for several years, while they sat on the surrounding roofs and aerials and watched her work. At dusk, one sang with an exquisite melody for so common a bird. Common, but beautiful: sleek-feathered, questing and stern with its yellow-rimmed eye. There was more beauty in the world than humans allowed you to think.

As she moved the plant-pots, there were often live, wriggling worms in the damp patches underneath. Wriggling, she imagined, in the pain of having the pot dragged over them. She crouched, picked up the worm by rolling her fingers gently across it and dropped it back on top of the pot. The Californian red worms specially bred for composting had arrived in thc post from Albacete in a grey cardboard box-file labelled 'About 1,000 worms'. Now they had multiplied and their pale little offspring like wisps of white thread were all over the garden. It was a garden of pots on a brick patio built on top of the garage of the block of flats.

She watched a blackbird sitting on the TV aerial of the next building along, the sun catching its feathers like light on burnished armour. Two worms wriggled in the blackbird's beak, as it held them firm. It would be taking them to the nest to drop live into the chicks' outstretched mouths. She fancied it had stopped there in the morning sun not just to rest, but to show her its triumph.

Then the phone began to ring. She cursed: she'd forgotten to bring it down with her. She ran up the metal staircase two at a time and flung herself on the phone before the answering-machine could click on.

'Yes,' she panted.

'I rang earlier and you didn't answer,' the voice said accusingly, as if she had gone out deliberately to avoid the call. It was her mother.

'I was shopping. How are you?'

'Not well at all, no. I've got a pain here in my neck so that I can hardly move.'

'I thought the pain was in your back'. Julia was a science teacher and couldn't stop herself trying to be precise.

'Oh, there too. Some days I ache from the top of my head to the bottom of my feet. I said to the doctor, "Doctor, it's not worth living with pain like this." This new one's no good. She answers, "Where exactly does it hurt?" How can I tell? That's her job, to find out what's wrong. I ask her to send me to the pain clinic, but she doesn't think it *appropriate*, she says. Then, the other one, thinks she's so clever, tells me I have to tell the doctor exactly what the matter is or how can she know what to do.'

The other one, Julia knew, was her sister, who received no gratitude for usually accompanying their mother to the doctor's. 'What does she know? When she gets to my age, then she'll know what it's like, won't she, but I won't be around to hear her.'

'How was the visit to Charo?' Julia asked. At the age of 82, when she felt inspired, the various pains dropped off her mother like clothes on a wedding night and she got on the bus to travel across the city to visit any one of myriad relatives or people from the village who, like her, had emigrated to Barcelona fifty or more years before.

'Ah, the poor woman. She puts on a brave face in a rough sea, but she's frightened, I can see. She lays the table with a lace cloth and serves coffee in little blue cups with saucers and with biscuits on a matching plate. As for him, he's not working, so he's sitting around, a useless package in the way, and the father-in-law's deaf as a post. If you want to say anything to the old blockhead you have to shout. He was never any use either, like his son. Before she died, she was as good as gold and work, she worked and he had to do what she said, she was in charge, but when she went, the stupid dolt and his son spent it all in carousing, eventually lost his flat, he never had an ounce of sense, but look there's no justice in this world, he's sitting there with cutlery and three meals a day on a clean table and a room of his own with the sheets changed every week while she's out cleaning offices at 6 o'clock in the morning.'

Julia had heard all this before. And sometimes she told her mother she'd heard it all before. But it made no difference. Her mother had to go over her grievances and her stories like a miser counting her dulled hoard of coins before finally reaching the point. If there was one and if she ever did. Talking was life for her mother. If she had someone to listen, she could go on for hours. It didn't matter if she'd told the story before. Her listener could put on a sour face, stare at the floor with her mouth severely closed or, head down, flip through a magazine, but her mother would go on talking. And if the listener got up to go, then her mother would clutch her arm to pull her back into the room and still not stop talking.

Julia placed the phone between her left ear and shoulder while she picked up the bowl full of wheat and took it into the living-room. She sat down and began to pick out the bits of stalk and even squashed insects mixed up with the hard oblong brown ears. She made her own bread with her own wheat which she ground in her own milling machine. The bread you bought in the shops nowadays tasted of cardboard.

'What's Charo frightened about? Isn't she alright now?'

'No, she's not. Not at all, they've told her she's got to have another operation, down there, down below. It seems to have come back and of course she smiles and she gives me coffee and biscuits, but I can tell she's frightened.'

'Well, who wouldn't be? Poor woman.'

'She told me that now they're digging people up from the war. She was talking about poor Uncle Rogelio. I remember the other one who died in the village, he was so playful. In the spring when the grass was long and green by the gully, he'd tear it up and throw it over the kids. We'd roll around laughing and he'd shout and toss the grass over us. His mother, *la tía* Nieves, never got over it. She came in without even knocking and her eyes were staring into space as if they were seeing nothing and she said to my mother, "They've killed my Néstor." Just like that.

My mother said, "What are you saying, woman, sit down." She wouldn't sit down. She said again: "They've killed my Néstor" and then she threw herself down on the floor screaming and banging her head against the wall. She wanted to knock herself senseless. My mother told me to run out and get the men in to hold her down and it took my father and another man who was working with him in the kitchen garden, you know, that lazy blockhead who had no

19

land of his own and if he'd had any, he wouldn't have known what to do with it. *La tía* Nieves was completely gone. She bit my father and kicked her legs up in the air so everyone could see her petticoats and she was a very respectable woman, but she was out of her mind with grief.

It turns out that Néstor who was very good-looking and liked to go to all the village dances, he'd taken the mule and gone down to the dance at Collado. Some say he had a girlfriend there, but I don't know whether that's true or not, but that's what they said afterwards, that he'd already made a lot of people jealous. There was a lot of rivalry between the lads from different villages, who didn't like it if someone from another village danced with a girl from their village. I remember one year there was a gang from Los Santos, and they lay in wait by the ruins of the old monastery, near where *la tía* Mercedes used to live. They'd picked up stones and attacked a group from Alpuente who were going down to the summer *fiesta* because they thought they were after the village girls. One of them ended up with a broken arm and everyone felt their bruises the following day. Then, the next year, the others had to return the favour, naturally enough, and there was another bust-up. Who knows exactly what happened, only those involved know and they're not going to tell you when now they're old and respectable, that's if they're still alive, but it seems that Néstor liked a girl from the village and danced with her the whole evening. In the morning, his mule was still tied to the ring in the wall and when they looked for the owner, he was found hanging from a beam in the front porch. The doctor came and certified it as a natural death, it was the time just before the Civil War and if you belonged to the side of law and order, then the reds would stop at nothing to get you.'

'It worked both ways.'

'What would you know? You weren't there,' her mother shouted. 'I'm telling you, they hanged Néstor out of envy and then got one of their red doctors to sign it off as a natural death.' She stifled a sob at this story of events from 70 years ago that she had told hundreds of times and that Julia had heard dozens of times. 'Poor boy. And the day before, he was laughing by the stream and throwing grass over us. That's how I remember when it was, in the spring when the grass grows strong and green. Why would he commit suicide?'

'And what about Uncle Rogelio?'

'Charo says someone phoned her from the, what do you call it? Those people who want to remember the past.'

'Historians?'

'That's it, the Historical Memory, and said they were planning to excavate his grave.'

'Uncle Rogelio's grave! But where is it? I thought no-one knew what happened to him.'

'It seems they've found his name in some papers, I don't know where, Charo knows the name, and now the relatives of the other people in the grave with him are trying to get the Council to dig them up and give them all a proper burial and they wanted Charo to sign. It seems right to me, that he should have a decent burial in the cemetery. Just imagine all these years not knowing what happened to him and someone rings up out of nowhere—'

'—but hold on. I thought Uncle Rogelio had gone into exile in France and was never heard of again.'

'He was never heard of again and that's what they said, that he'd left Spain and must have taken up with a woman, you know how people gossip, they're malicious and they like to tell stories whether it's true or not, because nothing was ever heard of him again. Of course, he was in Barcelona and he got mixed up with those, you know, not the communists, the other reds.'

'The anarchists.'

'Anarchists, that's it, the ones who burned churches and killed all the priests, but I don't believe Rogelio was involved in all that, he was easily led astray but he was a good man. He was too good, which made him easily taken in, but he wouldn't do anyone any harm. People aren't like that in my family and I knew him.'

Julia had put down the bowl of wheat and got up to walk around the flat while she listened. Her mother incessantly explained the anecdotes of her family and village in obsessive detail, so that her three children, various grandchildren, neighbours and shopkeepers had learned to think about other things while she talked. Telling the same story a lot didn't make it any more true. Many stories were 'official' family stories, true only because they had been repeated so often.

Julia noticed that, as her mother grew older, different aspects of stories emerged. Whether these amounted to fresh embroidery or were actual memory floating up to pierce the smothering blanket of the traditional tale, she could not easily tell.

For many years, Rogelio, one of her mother's uncles, had been the interesting black sheep of the family. Like Julia's father, he had emigrated to Barcelona from the village in the 1930s, working in factories or construction during the winter, then returning to work on the land from spring to autumn. Rogelio brought back strange ideas to that remote Aragonese village of impoverished smallholdings. They did not have to be poor. If they banded together in cooperatives, they could pool their labour. The key thing, though, was to do away with the middlemen, who came to the village to buy the corn and became fat by doing nothing except forcing the prices low in the village and high when they sold the corn in Zaragoza.

'And how will you do that, Rogelio?' teased the villagers, sceptical because they had always been poor. They had always helped each other anyway to build houses, to thresh the corn in August or to kill the family pig in November. 'Who will take the corn to the city?'

'When the workers take over the factories, we can deal directly with them. Peasant to worker, worker to peasant, without any need for parasites like bosses or middlemen, you'll see,' said Rogelio. These conversations took place in the short midday breaks when the women brought lunch out to the men in the fields in baskets covered with white cloths, then left and the men stretched out on the soft grass under an oak after eating. No-one disliked Rogelio, he was friendly to everyone, and as hard a worker as any of them. No-one could fault him on that count. He wasn't like that Communist prick, Jorge Llanos, who drank too much and talked a lot in order to work less. The others who sowed, reaped and cut back the long grass beside the paths that bordered the fields saw Rogelio's ideas as impossible day-dreams, like marrying a Duchess or winning the state lottery.

The priest, Don Lucas, didn't take it like that, though, and in the years before the war, he preached sermons against the godless creeds of the cities. There, the foreign ideas of liberalism had allowed the atheist creed of anarchism to flower. Anarchism preached against property, which meant that anyone could go into someone else's house and take whatever he wished. If a man had a cow because he had worked hard for it, like Manuel in Vallanca, then anarchism preached he should share it with his lazier neighbours. Anarchism preached against authority, but without authority and structure, who would work? Everyone would lie around drinking and the result would be no food for anyone. Anarchism preached free love. Men would come and steal your daughters and you could do nothing about it. Women would be shared around. It would all end in madness and the collapse of society. That's what Don Lucas told the villagers on Sundays.

Many in the congregation thought of Rogelio, who was handsome with a frank and ready smile. They knew he wouldn't help himself to anyone's property, but they could picture him in Barcelona dancing with other men's daughters. Good luck to him, the men thought without saying so. Don Lucas' sermons struck fear of the unknown into many hearts. News of strikes, killings, churches burned, barricades and imprisonment drifted through from the cities like pollen on a spring breeze. The sermons made some, though, wonder whether Rogelio was not right. If plump Don Lucas preached against the anarchists, then perhaps the anarchists had something when they said men and women could live with No God, No King, No Boss.

It had filtered into Julia's childhood consciousness that her mother had an uncle, poor Rogelio, who had disappeared in the war. It was never clear where, why or on what side. Under Franco, it could be dangerous to be known to have a relative who had fought on the other side. She had gleaned from her usually silent father that Rogelio was with the anarchists. She assumed he was in one of the anarchist militia groups that had fanned out from Barcelona to take Zaragoza as the first step toward taking the world, but never reached Zaragoza.

There was a woman, Susana, in the village who had never known her father. She was only a baby when he had left for France in 1939. Susana's mother, *la tía* Alberta, had reared the children on her own. She had worked as a maid at the inn, taking great baskets of sheets and nappies to wash in the stream, even in mid-winter when there was ice on the puddles, her two toddlers tottering behind her, cheeks red from the frost and snot hanging like glue from their noses, Julia's mother told her with a catch of emotion in her voice. Julia herself could still remember Alberta, bent double and dressed all in black, like a witch in a child's story-book, gleaning ears of corn from the edges of the field after the harvest. Under the trees, among the grass, the reapers often left a few stalks. Sometimes, Julia's mother gave Susana and her brother a meal. They were the poorest in a village where everyone was poor. Then, in 1977, Susana's father turned up. He drove a foreign car and wore a grey suit, a tie and polished black shoes. Their neighbour Matilde said she had seen him that afternoon, he was a tall white-haired man in a trilby hat and he was smoking with a gold cigarette-holder. No-one knew exactly what happened, but the interview with Susana was brief.

Afterwards, she boasted to people: 'If he didn't want to know about us when we were starving, now when we have enough to eat, I don't want to know about him.' They never saw Susana's father in the village again. It was about that time that Julia's mother started talking about the possibility that Rogelio was alive and living in France. Speculation in her mind turned into fact. If became when.
'When Rogelio comes back from France, we won't treat him like Susana, the stuck-up fool, treated her father. If my uncle went away, it was for good reasons and I'll welcome him back to our family.'

As the years passed, her mother stopped talking about him, except the occasional lament, when the war was mentioned in conversation, about her uncle who was lost in France and she would never see again. Now she said on the phone: 'Charo wants to go to this village where they say Uncle Rogelio's buried, but she can't with this cancer she's got. They want someone to sign the papers.'

25

Chapter Three

Julia squashed her nose against the glass, as she'd liked to do as a child on the bus journey to her parents' village. Sometimes, the road ran beside the small river. Once, she thought she saw a kingfisher, but its bright flash glimpsed through the poplars might only have been a scrap of yellow paper caught on a reed. Bare, crumbling, red cliffs climbed each side of the green valley. A backcloth of sterile majesty to the fertile plain.

The bus to Valeria ran along the river valley, where old men sank mattocks into the black soil, their bicycles resting against a tree beside the road. They were the few who hadn't emigrated to Madrid or Barcelona. Those who survived their childhood were tough and lived to a great age. Throughout the countryside, you saw them riding out of the villages on bicycles little younger than themselves, cardboard boxes tied with cord behind the saddle, mattocks like rifles on their shoulders.

The bus stopped in Villa Baja, the capital of the *comarca*, the county, spilling out most of its passengers. A couple of women got on. One, elderly and fat, pulled herself up the three steps of the bus.

'Ay, *hijo mío*,' she said to the driver in a near-shout interrupted by hoarse panting. 'When you get to my age it's no joke.'

'It would be worse not to get there,' said the driver and the woman roared with laughter at the old chestnut, her face turning pink and her whole body trembling.

Although nearly all the seats were empty, the woman plopped down directly across the aisle from Julia. The woman settled into her seat and sighed, 'Ay, *hija mía*, I've been down to see the doctor and he's given me some pills and told me I've got to go and see the specialist at the hospital in the capital. I haven't been breathing right, it tires me out just to walk from my front door to the hen-coop. Before, I had no problem on my feet all day, well you have to when you have four children, don't you? You can't just stop and say, I'm tired, I've got a headache, come back tomorrow, if you've got one bawling in front of you who wants his nappy changed or is hungry.' She paused for Julia to make some assenting comment, but Julia said nothing and was looking out of the window.

'Where are you off to? I haven't seen you on this route before and of course all of us who use it regularly know each other.'

'To Valeria. I'm tired and don't feel very well, I think I'm going to sleep,' Julia said coldly.

'You go right ahead, dear, I can understand if you have a headache. We all have our problems, mind. My husband died when we all thought he was perfectly alright. One day he came in from the field, put his mattock against the wall and sat down by the stove to pull his boots off. "Oh, I don't feel too good today," he said. I should have taken more notice because he wasn't one to complain, but I was cooking the dinner, turning over the sausage in the pan, so I didn't even look round. When I did, it was because I heard him falling off the chair and blood was coming from his head. "What have you done, Eduardo?" I said, thinking he had banged his head. When I knelt down beside him, he was stone dead. It was blood from his mouth. One of his boots was half off. It was the effort that brought it on. "There was nothing you could have done, *señora*," the doctor said, but I did blame myself and I was depressed and took tablets. I always thought I should have turned round when he said he wasn't well. But I didn't and my Eduardo died with me right there but not even looking at him.'

Julia knew she'd be trapped here the whole journey unless she took action. She had little sympathy for garrulous old ladies. Her mother was enough to cope with. She didn't see why she should cope with other people's mothers too.

'I'm sorry, *señora*, about your troubles. But your husband was old. You know, my daughter died when she was eight years old. She went out to visit a friend and she was knocked down by a motorbike. Then my husband left me for a Cuban tart twenty years younger than me.'

She hadn't meant to say anything. As the words popped out, she knew they were self-indulgent and cruel. 'Oh, life is a valley of boulders,' the woman sighed and leaned across the aisle to squeeze Julia's arm. The woman was silent for a bit, but then she went on. 'There was a woman in the village whose son died when he was 18, driving off a bridge into the icy water on New Year's Eve. It must be the worst, it's not right that your own children go before you.' Julia shut her eyes as the woman drivelled on compulsively. Language was comfort and Julia, as she dozed with the rain of indistinct words drizzling in the background, was despite herself not uncomforted.

The bus climbed towards Valeria, leaving the river valley behind and zig-zagging up the side of one of those red hills. Once you got into the hills, they were not so uniformly bare as they seemed from a distance. There were bushes, little valleys with trees along a gully, stone huts to corral sheep.

The bus stopped and the woman who had been talking got off in what seemed the middle of nowhere. 'God bless you, pretty one,' she said to Julia and let herself down the steps backwards, her hands gripping the rail. There was no house visible, just replanted pine woods and open scrub.

Julia peered back to see which way the woman set off, but she stood by the side of the road waving at the bus as it moved away. Julia waved back. *I'm not a very kindly or pleasant person*, she thought to herself.

As the bus climbed, the road ran between brown rocks with seams of white, red and yellow. At one stage, the rocks hung over the road, with steel netting draped up the cliffs to catch any boulders that might fall in a storm. Then the countryside opened out again, with gorse bushes, low trees forced close to the ground by the wind as if they were listening to the soil, abandoned dry-stone huts with their wooden roof-beams rotted and their lichen-covered brown tiles fallen in and the occasional cultivated field with heaps of stones around it. The land here was harsh and dry. It had taken hard labour generations ago to drag rocks aside in order to clear a field for spindly corn. Harsh terrain, tough people, her father used to say of their own village and this Valeria, where Rogelio had died 70 years before, would be no different.

The square in Valeria was empty when she got off the bus. She watched the two other passengers, women with full wicker baskets on their arms, bustle across the cracked cement. The driver scurried into the café. When she looked back, the two women had disappeared. It was 5 o'clock on a February afternoon and a sharp wind blew straight off the mountains through a gap in the houses on one side of the square. Just three streets led off the square. She could see a few houses with their sheds, vegetable plots and hen-coops behind them. Beyond the houses, mist or low cloud cut off the tops of the trees rising up the hillside. She took in the bar, the church with a stone bell-tower and the Town Hall beside it with a ragged red-and-yellow striped flag stretched out in the wind. Along the side of the square where the bar was, a short arcade showed signs of former prosperity: pillars supported the houses and one of these had a coat-of-arms below twisted window casements and eaves with ornamental brickwork under the roof. Julia needed no more than 30 seconds to take in the whole scene of apparent abandon and decline. Two *Guardia Civil* cars were parked outside the Town Hall, alongside a wooden bench. Dogs made up for the lack of people. They wandered towards her, thin, scrawny, dirty dogs without the energy to wag their tails. One nuzzled its nose into her groin. She swatted it away with a grimace and followed the driver into the café.

She noticed a black ribbon nailed to the lintel. The door itself stuck. She pulled it, then pushed and she followed it in suddenly as it opened. '*Buenas tardes,*' she said. Four men played cards at a table at the back. Four other tables were empty but for ash-trays. The four men all drew their cards against their chests and raised or turned their heads to stare at her. Julia nodded at them. A bottle and four glasses stood on their table. Behind the men, against the wall, a wood-burner with logs piled beside it filled the bar with heat. In the corner, a shotgun leaned against the rough stone wall, whitewashed sloppily. Spots of white spattered the dirty floor of cracked tiles. The four men did not return Julia's nod and said nothing, but continued to stare back at her till one of them said, 'Come on' and they returned to the game. She shuddered internally at their harshness while she looked calmly, with a still face, back at them. *Get a grip*, she said to herself.

The bus-driver was sitting at the bar and he did nod at her. She regretted now not having chatted to him on the way up, but she had wanted to soak up the landscape, so different from, but reminiscent of her grandparents' village where she had spent the summer holidays of her childhood. *It's like stepping 50 years back in time, but we're only 50 miles out of Zaragoza*, she thought, knowing that her thought was a cliché, yet was true. Another man, lean and tall, was sitting on a stool at the end of the bar. He too stared openly at her as he drew on his cigarette. The whole place was full of cigarette smoke that swirled like mist as a result of the door opening: they were doing their best to escape from the pure, thin mountain air that might damage their health.

The only information she had on the village was the name of Charo's contact from the Association for Historical Memory. She had rung him a few weeks before from Barcelona. The line was crackly, but she understood that the permission of descendants of the people dumped in an improvised grave in the woods would assist in their exhumation. Could she send the permission of Rogelio's closest living relative, duly witnessed before a notary?

'I can come up for a couple of days,' she said on impulse.

'Ah, even better, then we could go to the Town Hall and submit the papers,' Jaime said with a slow, easy courtesy. She had started to tell him when she could come, but he interrupted her: 'We're here all the time.' And he repeated: 'Nowhere to go, we'll be here. If we had anywhere, we'd be in the city for the winter, like most people.'

'Was it three people in the grave, you said?'

'We think so. There's Rogelio, your uncle, you say, there's Evaristo, Raimunda's grandfather, and my aunt.'

'Aunt?' Julia said, surprised.

'Those bastards respected no-one.' She couldn't think of what to say, startled at the sudden ferocity in his voice as he spat out 'bastards'. Then he added, in his calm still voice: 'They still don't, of course,' and laughed. She wondered how old he was and whether he was still all there in the head, or if the loneliness of village life had worn him down.

'No, they don't,' she replied. Jaime told her there was a *posada*, an inn, in the village.

She thought of walking straight out again from the unwelcoming bar, but it might very well itself be the *posada*. She approached the counter. 'Cold out,' she said.

'Hwuf, if you think this is cold, *señora*, you should have been here last week,' the bus-driver said, rubbing his hands theatrically and shivering in memory. 'And for eight days before that, we couldn't get up here for the snow.'

'This is a cold village in the winter,' the lean man at the bar said slowly. 'Are you a reporter?'

'Reporter. No, why?'

'There have been a lot of reporters.'

'Reporters don't ride the bus,' the driver said.

The lean man thought about this. He took a sip from his glass and a drag on his cigarette. His face, sunken under the cheek-bones, was covered with little brown spots and his hand shook as he moved it towards the glass. It was hard to know his age, but he didn't look too healthy. She wondered whether to say who she was. If she didn't tell her story, she knew she'd never win anyone's confidence, but the atmosphere felt not just guarded, but hostile. The feelings from the Civil War, she knew, were not dead, even if the killings had stopped. Those *bastards*, as Jaime had said, were still very much alive. She held her tongue.

The driver banged with his knuckles on the counter. 'Hey, Pilar,' he shouted.

A woman bustled in from the back, drying her hands on her apron as if it were a habit rather than because they were wet. 'I was just finishing off the potatoes, sorry to keep you waiting. And you *señora*, *buenas tardes*, what will you be having?'

'*Buenas tardes*,' Julia replied, 'a *cortado* for me. Is this the *posada* too?'

'Heavens, no, we've got a spare room and in summer when the village fills up, we can put people up. No, it's down the street on the right, Toni runs the *posada*. You'll find him there, I imagine. If not, go round the back, he might be out feeding the hens. He's been busy with all the reporters here. Our misfortune's quite a bonus for him out of season, and for us of course. Not usually a soul up here in the winter.' The woman, with a round, red face and plump arms whose flesh shook as she put Julia's and the driver's *cortados* on the counter, had broken the ice with her chatter.

'Reporters? I don't understand. What do you mean, your misfortune?'

The lean man said in a deep voice with clearly enunciated words: 'She could be an embedded reporter.'

Julia realised he was blind drunk. He just managed to stay upright on his stool by leaning sideways against the wall. He carefully took another drink, placed the glass back on the counter and wiped away some wine that had dribbled down his stubbly chin with the back of his hand. 'Like in Iran,' he added.

'Iraq, Ambrosio,' Pilar the bar-woman said without looking at him. 'You don't know?' she went on to Julia. 'Our mayor, poor man, may he rest in peace, was killed three weeks ago. It was in all the papers and on the telly. We were all interviewed. Several TV channels filmed this very bar.'

'Oh, no, I missed it, I'm sorry. I mean, I haven't been watching the news much.' The truth was she didn't watch television at all, but she'd learned that to say that made her too much of a freak. Free time was with her plants, reading or trying to prevent her mother going on at her sister too much.

'The place was buzzing with reporters for days, we've never had a winter like it. The police are still up here every day questioning people.'

'Killed, you say? What happened?'

'Yes, he was killed,' she said and her voice dropped in respect for death. 'Murdered, no doubt about it. He was shot. He was found on the mountain road and no-one knows who did it. It's an unsolved mystery.'

'The police interviewed me,' the drunk informed them.

'Not for the first time, Ambrosio,' shouted one of the men at the card-table. They had been of course following the conversation whilst ignoring Julia and flicking their cards down on the formica table as if it were green baize in a Las Vegas casino.

'What a business,' Julia said. 'It must have affected the village very badly.'

'Nothing ever happens here and even less so in winter, when we're sometimes cut off for days on end. Normally the only time any official comes up here is when they want our taxes,' Pilar was chattering.

'Not everyone,' said Ambrosio. He tapped his nose as Julia looked at him. She did what he wanted and asked: 'What do you mean?'

'Not everyone. Not everyone was affected. Not everyone talked well of the mayor. Me, I can't say I had any problems with him. But in this bar I've heard people talk, talk poison of the dead mayor.'

'Don't take no notice of him,' Pilar said, wiping the counter fiercely as if she wanted to wipe away Ambrosio's words. She tossed her head. 'It's just tittle-tattle.'

As Julia walked off the square with her overnight bag over her shoulder, the wind ran through her coat like a knife through water. Even the dogs had disappeared. The cracked layer of thin cement that covered the earth as a token to modernity gave way to an unpaved street, running uphill. The earth was packed down with flagstones set into the clay. There was just one car parked ahead on the street. Most of the houses were closed, their shutters drawn. The black slate roofs were damp as if someone had hosed them down. Cloud swirled over the pine-forested hill in front of her when she looked up. When she looked down again, an enormously fat woman with a blanket round her shoulders was staring at her from the door of a house.

'*Buenas tardes*,' Julia said. The woman just stared. Maybe she was deaf, perhaps she'd lost her mind. It wouldn't be surprising to go mad if you were confined to a place like this. Then she reached the end of the street. A few more houses were dotted along a track that followed a contour in the hillside up into the woods. Patches of snow nestled against logs and in a ditch. On the right of the track, the ground had been cleared of bushes and levelled. Lamp-posts lined a paved road, with the kerb-stones in place, and the foundations of houses were visible. Where the village petered out, it looked like a small new estate was being built.

She turned back and then saw the *posada*, a two-storey house like all the others. She had walked right past it. The windows were unshuttered and above the door, on a twisted and splintery plank, 'PENSIÓN' was painted in white letters. She pulled a worn cord and a clear musical note rang out. No answer. She pulled again. She pushed at the door, pushed again and it opened, the bottom scraping across the big brown tiles of the entrance hall.

'Hello?' She shut the door behind her, enjoying the sudden silence of being out of the wind. Brown-varnished wooden roof-beams crossed the ceiling, with concave white plaster sections between. The walls were whitewashed. A

35

trunk, like the ones past generations kept their clothes in, with polished brass corners and embroidered yellow cloth along the lid, stood opposite the door.

'Hello?' she said again. Then, 'Toni,' she shouted, but her voice was lost in the entrails of the old house like a stone falling into a deep well. She walked on into the house, along a dark corridor and pushed open a door into a large room. A big hairy dog lay in front of the stove on a mat. She shivered, realising how cold it had been outside. She shut the door behind her. She noticed a sunken sofa draped with a thick red blanket and, to her surprise, shelves of books along one wall. More books and a jumble of papers occupied a long, wooden table. The smell of a meat stew cooking added to the smell of dog and the warmth of the wood stove. The dog opened one eye, raised its head slightly and gave two loud barks before dropping its head back onto the mat. Unexpectedly, a woman stepped out from the kitchen adjoining the living-room. She was short, white-haired and smiled through thick spectacles at Julia:

'*Buenas tardes*', she said, then stood rubbing her hands. 'Good afternoon'. 'I'll fetch Toni'. The woman went out the back door. Suddenly, Julia felt tired after the tension of the trip, the bleakness of the mountain village and the tense atmosphere in the bar. She sank gratefully into the deep softness of the sofa.

Julia heard an irregular sound like thick drops of water splashing into a pail. She opened her eyes wide, squeezed them shut against the light and, rubbing them, saw it was dark outside. By the stove, a man was peeling the yellowing outer leaves off small, firm sprouts, which dropped into a colander on his lap. He was dressed in corduroy trousers, a thick wool jersey and an unzipped padded waistcoat. The top of his head was bald, with straggly curls hanging down the side. 'I'm sorry,' she started. 'I came in, then I must have fallen asleep.'

'Don't worry,' the man said in a deep voice with a slightly strange lilt she could not place. 'After the journey and the mountain air, coming into the warm sends you off. It happens to lots of people.' He looked round and grinned. He had a deep vertical cleft that ran up one side of his face like a knife scar. He looked more like a sailor than a mountain dweller.

'I'm looking for a room for two nights.'

'No problem. There's no-one staying here. We hardly ever get anyone in the winter. Of course, it's been different this month, but they've all gone now. The vultures from the media,' he added without animosity. 'I'll show you a room, and you can sort yourself out before supper.'

Julia's room was large with a round paper lampshade, a floor of long, wooden planks, walls painted ochre and a double-bed piled high with patchwork blankets. It reminded her of student flats in 1970s Barcelona. All it lacked was a reproduction of Van Gogh's *Sunflowers* or a poster of Che. The window gave onto the street, but here she would not be disturbed by traffic. She went along the corridor to the spacious bathroom, with a brick wall to shoulder height separating the shower from the rest of the room. It gave onto the back yard, where rabbits, shining white in the dark, lay on the frozen mud inside a wire enclosure. Vegetable refuse and droppings covered the yard. Chickens roosted in a hen-house against a stone wall. Beyond, a few abandoned stone huts and then the hills, bare on the ridge, with snow lying bright like forgotten bed-sheets in the shaded hollows halfway up. She rubbed her face hard in cold water. She could not escape the feeling she had stepped out of her life into a fairy-tale.

She and Toni ate at the wooden table, the books and papers pushed to one end. The lamb stew was thick, the sprouts and potatoes tasty, with brown bread and a rough fruity red wine.

'This is great,' she said.

'Home-made, even the bread. Not the wine, though.'

'By you?'

'The bread, yes. Amparo who you met when you arrived comes in and cooks for the guests. Then when there are no guests, she comes in and cooks for me, though I tell her not to.' He laughed, wiping his lips with a chunk of bread and sipping wine without leaving any gravy mark on the glass. He was not as rough as he appeared.

'I came to see a man called Jaime.'

'Jaime? There are two Jaimes, one who lives on the side of the village closer to the mountain, a retired shepherd, Jaime Rodríguez; and the other on the other side of the square. He's called *El Moreno*, the dark one. So which will it be?'

'I'll have to tell you why I'm here. It's about the excavation of a Civil War grave.'

'Oh, the bones in the forest. I'd assumed you were here because of the murder.'

'A *vulture*. They did in the bar, too.'

'Don't take it to heart. People are fed up with everyone asking questions. Apart from the shock of the murder, it's done a lot of damage, with reporters fluttering around like wasps at jam-making. We had a woman from the village paid to go on a reality show. She didn't have anything to say, she was just the loudest and chuntered on about ETA terrorists. Just a load of mindless gossip. The murder's deepened the divisions in the village. Anyway, that's another story. Your man's Jaime *el Moreno*. His aunt was killed by the fascists and he's been trying to get the grave

38

exhumed and the people reburied. What's your connection?'

'My great-uncle.' He nodded and went on eating and chewing. 'I'm Julia,' she said.

'Toni.' He put down his spoon and offered his hand across the table.

'And how much is the room?'

'Twenty euros plus five for the meal.'

'That's cheap.'

'You can always pay more, Julia.'

She grinned and shook her head. 'You're not from here.'

'You guessed!' He swept his arm towards the rows of books. She resisted a sudden desire to reach across the table and run her finger down the line carved in his face. 'No, I'm from England, but I've been here on and off for ten years and permanently for the last four.' She followed his gesture and now saw that many of the book spines had titles in English.

'Why?'

'It's a long story.'

'We've got all night,' she said, then put her hand to her mouth in an involuntary gesture of embarrassment. 'I mean—'

'—I know what you mean. Don't worry. Briefly, I've always liked Spain. I disliked England. Not just Margaret Thatcher, though she was bad enough, but English society. My marriage in England broke up, I lost my job and so I came here.'

Another one, she thought. Everyone's marriages were breaking up nowadays. 'All this way to escape a broken marriage?'

'You'll be surprised, Julia, there's a lot of foreigners with second homes in these semi-abandoned villages. All

39

these houses you've seen shut up belong to people living in the cities: mainly Spanish people of course, many with roots in the village who emigrated to Valencia or Barcelona, but in addition there's a Dutch woman married to a Zaragoza lawyer, a German/Spanish couple, an Argentinian from Barcelona, several exiles from the Basque country, and there's me. But in winter there are only thirty or so of us. It's pretty bleak, all we have to do is play cards, watch TV and tell malicious stories about anyone not in the room at that particular moment.'

After eating, she sat by the stove and Toni, while he washed the dishes, told her about the murder of the Mayor.

'In some ways, it's a classic clash of incomers and old residents. Enrique had some sort of office job in Zaragoza, but chucked it in about ten years ago and came to live here with his wife. He wanted the rural life, fresh air, long walks. He was a bird-watcher and knew his stuff: he told me all the little I know about the birds in these mountains. He soon got on the wrong side of the locals, the *jamón de pata negra*, quality ham, as they say round these parts. Enrique wanted to clean up the tip, where people just tossed their rubbish into the ravine. When he was elected Mayor, he had several people fined for illegal dumping. There was also a dispute with the shepherds who'd always driven their sheep through the village. He insisted you couldn't have a modern village that aspired to live off tourism, if sheep were shitting in the main square and goats were eating the roses that incomers had planted in front of their houses. The future lay in rural tourism, according to Enrique, for bird-watchers, hikers and nature lovers in general, people from Madrid or Germany, executives with money who wanted to unwind in the wild mountains. Outsiders like me were encouraged: we bought abandoned houses for a song and provided employment to local kids who did them up. Kids with no education who would have otherwise been shepherds tramping the mountains suddenly found they were 'builders' and earning the sort of cash you'd get as a bricklayer in Barcelona or Madrid, though they hardly knew how to mix the cement to hold one brick on top of another.

'None of this was particularly objectionable, but then there was a group of people, friends or acquaintances of his wife, who wanted to register Valeria as their primary residence. Obviously they were going to vote for Enrique in elections. But there were others from local families who'd emigrated a generation ago to Barcelona and now wanted to return or their children wanted to return, and some of these he didn't let register. Of course, none of this smelt good, especially because his wife, Carmela, ran the restaurant-hotel they opened a few years ago.'

'Jaime told me to come here, as if it was the only inn in the village.'

'It is now because of the murder and also because it's winter, the hotel's shut.'

'It doesn't look as if you liked the poor mayor much.'

Toni had finished the washing-up and sat down. With a few glasses of wine in him, his face reddened—or perhaps it was just the heat of the stove. The line from the edge of his lips to the edge of his eye was pale. It wasn't a scar, but a crease. His eyes were brown and soft. He scratched his forehead:

'So, are you interested?'

'Of course. It's fascinating.'

'I ramble on sometimes. Living alone too much.'

'I'll stop you if you do.'

Toni grinned. 'Easier said than done.'

'The mayor...' Julia prompted.

'How can I explain it? In fact, I did like him. He was a

41

friendly guy. He often sat at this very table to eat with me and the guests. He was usually the life and soul of the party. But he had a stubborn, inflexible side, you know? Of course it's a good idea that people stop tipping their old domestic appliances and rubbish by the entrance to the village, but he shouldn't have insisted on fining people who had dumped stuff there all their lives. It all came down to education and offering an alternative, rather than imposing the law. Other things were less important. What does it matter if sheep walk through the village from one pasture to another? I like it. And if you want rural tourism, someone who comes from London or Berlin will be delighted to see a flock of sheep in the streets.'

'But to kill him, because of one of these disputes...'

'It's incredible. Of course it is. Incredible. I don't know if the village can recover from it. In one basic thing Enrique was absolutely right, that if the village continues to lose its working population and no new people are attracted, it will die. Many villages in these mountains prettier than this one are already deserted.'

'So no-one knows who killed him?'

'Someone knows, of course, but no-one's saying, no. But it must have been someone local and that's poisoned the whole village.'

It wasn't till she was lying in bed, the shutters open so that she could enjoy the privilege of seeing moonlight and the stars, bright in the frosty night, that she realised Toni had told her the background to the murder of the Mayor of Valeria, but had avoided telling her anything much about himself. Nor had he asked her anything. Was that because he was just another egotist rambling on or because there'd be time enough the next day? She realised he was the first new person she'd met, talked to and liked in years. She'd wanted to touch his pale crease, so vulnerable.

She heard bells tinkling, clear in the pure air. She could picture the half-dozen bearded goats with a bell hanging from the leather collar round their necks that led the flock of sheep returning from the pastures. Chewing the incomers' rose thorns and flowers. She fell asleep and dreamed vividly, being in a new place with new people. Firmly opposed to her dreams having any meaning, she was woken by a cock that crowed as if in triumph and the mindless dawn chatter of hens.

Chapter Four

All at once, the village streets lost any pretence of being urban and petered out in mud tracks with isolated houses and barns on the slope. The one-time threshing floors in front of the houses were now either parking places, packed earth little different from the street, or gardens. Jaime's was roughly concreted. The weather extremes had opened weed-filled cracks in the cement, too thin and too poorly mixed. A battered four-by-four was parked beside a row of dead-looking plants in broken pails or in large olive oil or fertiliser cans with their tops cut off. Unlike Toni's, Jaime's house had no bell-cord or knocker. She banged with her fist on the wooden door, but like Toni he didn't answer. There was a plank resting on two stones beside the door, where people could sit and while away the summer evenings, she supposed. She walked round the side of the house and found a sprawl of single-storey sheds, the wire enclosure for chickens and a yard laid with big slabs of grey stone. Beyond, the slope ran upwards into the forest through scrub and scruffy trees huddled close to the ground.

From his voice on the phone a month before, Julia had created a picture of Jaime as an elderly, querulous and stubborn man. Thin and balding to accompany his persistence, she imagined. Her view was somehow reinforced by his shambolic front yard. But now a large man in his fifties stood up, leaned on his shovel and stared at her when Julia said his name. His belly swelled like a proud sail in front of him and the belt pulled through the loops of his trousers failed to keep his shirt fully tucked in. White-streaked hair tumbled over his face. He struck his forehead with his fist when Julia explained who she was.

'Ay, my head! With all this fuss and bother of the murder, I'd completely forgotten you were going to come. Of course, everything about the reburial's halted now, but come in, come into the house'. He dropped his shovel, stepped towards Julia in his manure-covered boots, grabbed her by the elbow as if concerned she might flee and pulled her inside. He smelled nice, of sheep-shit and country work, she decided. Relieved to find him nicer than her mental picture of him, she was happy for once to be pulled. He sat her in a kitchen chair with a cup of coffee from the black pot on the wood-burning stove that heated the room.

'Excuse the mess. My wife's away, she's a *golondrina*, a swallow. There's not many of us who live here all through the winter.'

'A swallow?'

'It's what we call the women from the village who left to work in the city. Like the swallows, they fly away in the autumn and return in the spring. It's not the same now of course. Aurelia's not working, she just spends the coldest winter months with her sister in Barcelona. But we still say 'swallow'.' He laughed. 'So here I am, with my chickens, sheep and rabbits, abandoned by my swallow.'

For a few seconds, they sat without saying anything and Julia listened to the silence of the mountains.

'Today's not a bad day for winter. It can be bitter here, with temperatures of minus 6, minus 8 and then I have to break the ice in the hen-house so the hens can drink'.

'And don't they freeze?'

'They've got their feathers.'

'I'm not sure I'd fancy spending a winter up here.'

'Most people don't. That's why there's hardly anyone left. When I was a kid there were 200 people living here all year round, now there's only 20 or 30 left and when we old

45

ones die off, the village will die too.'

'And now you've got this death of the Mayor.'

'It's turned the whole village upside down. There's some bad blood and jealousy and there's no entertainment here, so people amuse themselves with gossip and rumours. We all know each other, even if we don't talk to each other. We know about everyone else, and who their sisters, brothers, mothers and grandparents are. This murder's stunned everyone. It's one thing to complain about the Mayor, but to kill him, that's something else.'

They were silent again, the weight of death in the air. The silence of the mountains was alive with the noise of the wind in the pines and in the poplars along the stream. Sometimes a crow cawed or a dog barked. There was always an undercurrent of malice and envy, thought Julia. Life had not given her a positive view of human nature.

Jaime broke the silence by jumping up: 'No time like the present. Come on, I'll take you up there.'

Jaime's car was a four-wheel drive, once white, now streaked with mud, dented and scratched by stones as if he had driven it in rallies. Julia had to pull herself up into the high seat. They drove back across the empty square and down a slope to a sharp curve across the bridge over the stream, which ran fast in its deep gully below the village. All the high-mountain streams were like this, fast-flowing with snow and storm water and cut deep into the rock. They took a track up the hill behind the street where she had slept. She peered out, but couldn't distinguish the back of Toni's inn from the other houses in the street with their scattered dry-stone out-houses. She saw the outline of the new estate. Then they were bumping up through the wood, first replanted pines, then into an original forest of twisted, mossy oak.

Jaime cleared his throat. 'The problem in our village

46

was that the fascists lived here alongside the relatives of the people they killed. These past three weeks, you know, thinking about all the tensions with the Mayor, it's brought home again how terrible it must have been after the war. Each time you crossed the square you might bump into one of the bastards, excuse my language—'

'No need.'

'—who'd killed your sister or daughter. That's what my grandmother told me. And he might smile at you, spit at you or make some comment, and there was nothing you could do except try and stay indoors as much as possible, because there was a fascist dictatorship in place and the local Falangists could do what the hell they liked, from teasing you to beating you up, shaving a girl's head because her father or brother was a red or making you drink castor oil until you vomited, shit yourself or pissed in your knickers. I think my mother, and like her all the other women, were constantly afraid of being abused, raped or even murdered, although the extreme abuses were less likely after the first couple of post-war years, because there were even regime bigwigs who didn't like this kind of immunity the Falangists enjoyed. In fact, about 1942 when Teodoro Pérez came back from Russia, things got more controlled.'

While he spoke in this fierce flood of words, Jaime drove slowly by necessity. The track was rutted and he tried to run the wheels along the ruts, but occasionally the vehicle jumped across a frozen ridge of earth packed with stone or bumped through a pot-hole. The ice cracked like breaking glass and Julia was flung up and down in her seat, so that she rode clutching the metal handle above the door. Patches of snow began to appear in hollows under the leafless small oaks, twisted into shapes that too easily reminded her of torment, as the road slowly rose. The sun

47

that had lit the wood like a Christmas card disappeared suddenly behind cloud and Jaime was driving in a mist with his yellow headlights picking out the tree trunks.

'Shit...' He braked and Julia was flung forward. When she raised her head, a man on the track in front of them was reining back his black horse. Julia saw the horse's pink gums as the bridle pulled it round and the fog of warm air pouring from its nostrils. The rider walked the horse toward the car, then leaned down from the saddle and spoke into the window that Jaime wound down.

'You shouldn't be driving up here.'

'Who says?'

'I do. As you well know, I'm the authority in the forest.'

'It's a public right of way. I can go where I like.'

'Under the regulations, you're not permitted to drive a 4-by-4 vehicle along a forest foot-path.'

'You know as well as I do that everyone has always driven this way to get to the clearing.'

'Times change. New regulations have been introduced to protect the forests.'

The forest ranger leaned down further from his horse, whose brown teeth blew out steam as he pulled its head sideways, and stared into the vehicle at Julia. She looked back. She thought she could win a staring game with most. The trick was to concentrate on a detail. She stared at the big milky buttons on the horseman's sheepskin coat.

The horseman gave way first. 'Ah, paying respects, are we?'

'That's right.'

'You know what I think, Jaime,' the horseman said, his tone apparently relaxed, like the use of Jaime's first name. 'Pity a few more weren't dumped in the glade. Might have saved us a few problems later, eh?' The horseman spat sideways and laughed like a stage villain as he wheeled his horse away into the mist, one hand on the rein and the other jauntily on the stock of the rifle behind the saddle. Jaime made to open the door and go after him.

Julia caught hold of his arm. 'No,' she said sharply.

'Bastard...'

'Let it go, he's just winding you up.'

'It's because you're here. He wants to frighten you off.'

'I know.'

'Did you hear what the son of a bitch said?'

Julia knew that the forest guard's verbal violence was, at least in part, a revenge at her having outstared him. A man of the forest on horseback would not take kindly to a city woman facing him down.

She was more shaken than she let on. The forest was exactly the same as it had been five minutes before, as indifferent to them as all nature was. Yet the encounter had invested it with danger. It was as if the fog had suddenly thrown them back through 70 years of mornings to the day Rogelio had been driven up here for the only time in his short life. The bare twisted arms of the oaks looming in the fog now clutched at them, as if in the most clichéd ghost story. Primeval fears of the dark forest were not so easily eliminated by reason, she thought. Jaime's ruddy face was as white as the unmelted snow in the ditch as he drove on.

'You see what this village is like,' he muttered.

'So who was he?'

'What a bastard! I've known him since he was born, Arturo must be ten years younger than me, the second son of Eulogio and Herlinda, who'd turn in their graves if they heard him. He went away to study in Zaragoza and came back some years ago to be the forest ranger. All this land running up to the mountain peaks and over toward Mas de las Matas is public forest belonging to the Community of local town councils and they employ a ranger to manage it.

Keep the paths clear, stop poachers, direct the summer fire-fighting brigades to clear the undergrowth.'

And then the path opened into a bright clearing. The sun had cleared the mist. The ground steamed gently as the dew evaporated. They could see the forest running on up the mountain towards the peaks of bare rock and snow. Here the pine forest surrounding the glade kept out the wind, though they could hear it roaring like ocean breakers through the tree tops. The ground was clear of snow, too, and last year's withered grass and flowers made it light and springy to walk on.

Julia followed Jaime across the glade to the far side, where a stake had been hammered into the ground and a piece of wood nailed across the stake had been painted in red with the legend:

31/8/1936
Here three victims of fascism
were vilely murdered.

'What a beautiful place! And this notice? It's new—did you put it up?'

'That's another story. Some years ago, after my mother died, when I first applied for the grave to be opened and the victims to be reburied in the cemetery, I put up a similar notice. On several occasions, someone smashed it. The last time, some mindless idiot like the horseman we've just met had painted out "victims of fascism" and scrawled "red murderers" and instead of "vilely murdered" they put "executed".'

'Christ! And does this track go on anywhere?'

'Not really. You can walk up through there right over the mountain pass in summer, but this is as far as the track goes.'

50

'So someone came up here specifically to smash your notices and deface the previous one?'

'It's not a happy village, *señora* Herrero.'

'Call me Julia.'

'Julia.'

'After all, we're on the same side. And the man on horseback?'

'Arturo. Like the Mayor, who didn't want to give us permission for reburial, you see he's on the other side.'

Jaime wandered away into the undergrowth. Julia thought he'd gone for a pee and was left alone to wonder about her great-uncle's death in this cold, clear place. Of course, it wouldn't have been cold then, in August, even in the early morning. She glanced over to where Jaime had disappeared. She stood to attention, feeling ridiculous yet compelled, then raised her right hand with its fist clenched before Rogelio's grave. She had never in her life given the clenched-fist salute and while she was standing in the raw air, her breath misting as she exhaled, she wondered if it was only a communist salute, not an anarchist one at all. But she didn't stop doing so, not even when she heard the dry branches snap under Jaime's feet as he approached through the undergrowth.

He was carrying a long, early-sprouting, green branch. 'No flowers at this time of year, but I found this.' She laid it in front of the wooden post.

'Thank you'. Jaime hadn't gone for a pee, but to leave her on her own. She felt suddenly close to this rough, chubby, obsessive man.

'It would be good to put their names on the monument,' Julia suggested. He nodded. 'Who was the third person?'

'Evaristo. He was an old guy from the village. It appears he spoke out of turn.'

'And his family?'

'His wife died. Of a broken heart, they say. Their children left the village, sold their house. I wrote to an address someone gave me. Their grand-daughter Raimunda, who's my age, sent me back a signed statement requesting the exhumation, but she didn't want to get involved. It's too painful, even now.'

'I can understand that.'

'A lot of families left the village after the war. Those who could. They didn't want to know, hear or think about what had happened here and went on happening after the war. Most of them never came back.'

They drove back down the track, back into the mist and through the wood, back through the square with its lazy, impertinent dogs, two police cars and stone church. She felt exhausted by the journey. She had been thrown up against history in the clearing. And she had come face-to-face with the hatred that endured.

'I'll tell you what I know about your uncle and the murders in the village,' Jaime said back in his sitting-room while he fed the stove with more wood and put the smoke-blackened coffee-pot to heat on top.

'My mother's uncle, my great-uncle.'

'Ah yes. You know, this entire Movement for Historical Memory is a movement of grandchildren, not of children. The children had to live in fear right through the Franco decades. It was only a few years ago, not long before she died, that my mother told me the story of her sister Juanita, Rogelio and Evaristo.'

Chapter Five

Rogelio sat on an old fruit box under one of the plane trees that lined the Avenue and watched the men on the other side of the wire fence unloading boxes from a ship. They swung the boxes hand to hand down the line from the ship onto the quay. He'd arrived at the dock gate before dawn along with hundreds of other men in brown jackets and caps, waiting, with their midday bread roll wrapped in a twist of cloth.

'Looks good,' a fellow he didn't know muttered to him as they watched the supervisors come out of the gate. 'Here come the supers. Arrogant pricks.' The fellow spat sideways, barely moving his head. 'Word is there's six ships in today.'

The supervisors in their long, grey coats and felt hats pointed at men and the chosen ones stepped forward and gave their names to the clerk who stood behind each supervisor. The clerks entered the names in the book, gave the men a brass tag and the security guards let them through the gate. They picked the fellow who spat beside Rogelio, but that was it. He was left with several dozen others in the street as dawn began to lighten the sky over the sea. As they moved away down the Avenue, Rogelio, like the other union members, chatted with some of the unemployed men.

Once they were out of sight of the dock security guards, the union activists pulled the rest together at the mouth of an alley and Sánchez, a burly bearded man with a honeyed voice, stood up on the wooden fruit box he'd brought with him and spoke, just as he had been doing for several mornings: 'Look, brothers, we can't go on like this, day after day. We've got to get stable employment on the docks.

53

We're not donkeys, to be used one day and not the next. We've got to eat and we've got families who have to eat. Even a donkey gets fed when it's not working. We have to stand together. We need a collective agreement that employs all dock workers on a decent wage. We're making plans for a strike one day soon. You have to be ready. If we stick together, we'll win and things will be better for everyone.'

That's all he said and then the well-known union organiser disappeared up the alley. The men had listened in silence, then dispersed. Rogelio took Sánchez's box and strolled back down to the dock. His task was to watch movement in and out. There was nothing that could arouse suspicion about an unemployed man watching the dock at work. The lines of men unloaded boxes of fruit, bundles were hoisted out of the holds and swung on the crane onto the quay, the lorries backed up, and everyone had to shout above the noise to make themselves heard. The action. There were always several men with no work greedily or lazily watching the action inside the dock's security fence.

The security guards were nervous. Several stood by the gate and several more went in and out of the wooden hut inside the gate. When the gates opened for the lorries to enter or leave the quay, which was a steady stream most of the day, the guards held their rifles at the ready, nervously watching anything that moved. Rogelio studied one whose head twitched like a rabbit's as he glanced constantly from side to side. The guards sensed something was going to happen, but what or when they didn't know any more than Rogelio did himself.

Before dawn next morning, the several hundred workers were back again. Someone tugged at his elbow. It was Germinal from the section. 'It's today,' he whispered. Rogelio watched Germinal go round some of the other comrades, then stroll away over the cobbles. He and half a dozen other men followed Germinal, all separate from each other without exchanging a clear look or a word, across the silvery tram-tracks, under the plane trees and up one of the narrow streets into the Barceloneta area. They ended up with Sánchez in a bar with the metal shutter half up to show it was thinking about opening, but hadn't done so yet.

'OK, comrades,' Sánchez, the coordinator of the Docks section of the CNT, said briskly, 'we're going for the strike today. As soon as we've got hold of the gates, we'll run an assembly, but the basic demands are: regular employment —no more casual labour, direct negotiation with us and a 20% rise in the basic wage. We all know the arguments and the importance of organising the waterfront. There are several fruit ships in today and the bosses won't want the produce rotting. Cops and soldiers are stretched with the engineering strike in Sants. It's as good a day as any. Rogelio, tell us what you saw yesterday.'

He coughed. 'There are eight or ten guards in the hut inside the gate, there's four more on patrol outside, all armed with rifles. Twelve or fourteen in all.'

'OK, we've got a car with a special unit that'll take care of the four outside. Action timed for 7 am. Your task is to get the ten in the guard-house. Once it's taken, Germinal uses his whistle, four blasts and the car goes in. Once the gates are secured open, we send in the guys who haven't been selected for work. They'll be the first pickets. Our men inside will be bringing everyone out. We'll make a show of strength on the gate. Nothing in, nothing out. We can expect rapid reinforcements from their side, but they won't have expected your squad getting in and disarming the guard-house. Remember, no shooting if you can help it. We'll have surprise and a bit of time on our side. Good luck, *salud*.' As he said *salud*, Sánchez clenched his fist beside his head. The others responded with the same word and gesture.

Clutching the cold pistol he'd been issued with under his blouse, sliding quietly through the narrow, cobbled streets of the dock quarter, beneath the washing hung from cords stretched across the street from window to window, Rogelio had no time to be nervous. They passed women throwing out water, men scurrying to work, all of whom made as if they hadn't noticed the special unit. It was his first taste of action, but he felt ready, he'd done arms training, he'd been on political courses, he'd been through the delivery boys' strike, been arrested, beaten up and dumped in the street 48 hours later. He followed Germinal, Ramón, Liberto, Paco, Jordi and Marçal along the street. He was watching the back, checking no unexpected cop car came up behind them. Again they separated, to cross the wide avenue between the narrow streets of workers' housing and the dock area with its windowless redbrick warehouses.

Sparrows and nightingales sang in the trees along the avenue as light touched the bottom of the sky. They reached the fence, where two guys waiting for them cut the wire, held it back and waved the squad through, a clap on the back for each one of them and a fiercely whispered, 'Good luck, lads.' One of the two guys climbed through the hole after Rogelio. He was carrying a heavy sledge-hammer and winked at Rogelio. The action group came together in a narrow corridor between two piles of planks that rose above their heads. In front of them there were no more than 50 metres to the guard-house, with a few heaps of wire and rubble between it and them. With hardly a word, Germinal indicated that two would go round one side, two round the other and Paco, Rogelio, Germinal himself and the man with the sledge-hammer who wore a cap pulled down over his eyes and a thick moustache so that even his mother wouldn't have recognised him were heading straight in through the back. All of them tied scarves round their mouths and pulled down their caps.

Rogelio had no time to think once they started running towards the guard-house, spread out and pistols in hand as if they were charging into battle. As they were. The early-morning breeze off the sea cooled his face. He felt exalted by youth, by action and by the sense they were taking history into their hands. He caught the eye of Paco beside him and saw he felt the same. The sledge-hammer crashed into the wooden wall of the guard-hut. They'll rebuild it of cement next time, he thought. His revolver butt crashed through glass. A scream, shouts. Chairs were knocked over, swearing.

'No-one move, drop your weapons,' Germinal said crisply. Then silence. Rogelio was covering two guards who stood against the side wall of the hut, their rifles already on the ground and arms up. One of them was no more than a boy. His hands were shaking and Rogelio was reminded to rest his own pistol against the wooden window-frame. Tension and excitement made his own hands shake too and it wouldn't do to be misinterpreted.

Paco stood in the door. 'Lay down your weapons, keep your mouths shut and no-one gets hurt,' he ordered rapidly. Then he jumped and swore, as outside there was one shot, then two more cracks and a scream. Everyone looked up.

Rogelio grabbed his pistol tighter in both hands. He too said: 'Stay calm, no-one move' and felt calmer for his words. He heard Germinal's whistle—four sharp blasts. The gates were open, with a lorry that had been coming in stalled in the middle. Rogelio saw one of the guards outside whirl round and run back toward the gate. Behind him, the

CNT car, with two men crouching on the running-board, one hand clutching a rifle and the other holding on inside the door where the window had been wound down, screeched as it braked. The guard running toward the gate and guard-house stopped, not knowing which way to turn. His shoulders fell, he dropped his rifle and stumbled back against the fence, his hands holding onto the wire, as the two anarchists from the car frisked him.

Inside the hut, they had the guards up against a wall. Germinal was explaining: 'OK, listen carefully, none of us want bloodshed. We're securing the gate for the workers' strike that's started this morning. The cause is just. We're not cattle to be picked off the street each day by the bosses. You're workers, too. Now, listen, I want you out of that gate in 30 seconds flat, but if any of us see you again working as a security guard or in any activity on behalf of the bosses, you'll have a bullet in your head.' He paused and stared into each guard's face in turn. 'Understood?' he shouted. The disarmed guards were struggling to their feet. Rogelio and his comrades stared hard at them too as if they were recording the guards' faces on their brains.

Outside the hut, things hadn't gone so well. A guard had been shot and lay groaning on the cement. It seemed he'd fired at one of the squad and he'd been dropped where he stood. As the guards were hurrying away, trying not to hear their fallen comrade's moans, the action group loaded weapons into the car, both their own pistols and the guards' rifles and ammunition. The wounded guard was carried into the hut. As Rogelio and Liberto strolled away along the avenue, they heard feet clattering on a ship's metal gangway, then saw the workers begin to pour down towards the gate. The CNT car drew away, the lorry was reversing out and Sánchez stood up on his box. The mass assembly was starting. The strike was on. Rogelio's face burst into a beam of laughter and he hugged Liberto, 'We're going to win, comrade.'

After the most exciting moments of his life, now Rogelio had nothing to do but hang about and keep out of the way. He sauntered up past the Post Office into the old quarter, through the narrow streets where the sun never warmed the pavement. Old women in black shuffled along in slippers, baskets hanging on their arms, towards the Santa Caterina market. Old men in vests sat by the doorways. The smell of reheated cooking oil and cracked sewers, rotting scraps of vegetables in the gutter, the cobbles slippery. Beggars, their legs twisted by disease (by poverty, as he had learned to say now he was an anarchist) pulled themselves along by their muscular arms on home-made trolleys on wheels.

He stopped to chat with a comrade carrying an orange gas cylinder on his shoulder.

'*Salut*, Rogelio,'

'*Salud*, Manel.'

'Have you heard? Docks are out. Mass picket on the main gate.' Manel's job in the street meant he was the repository of every piece of gossip that flew through the packed old quarter.

'I heard,' said Rogelio, dying to tell him his part in what had happened that morning.

'Troops not in?' Manel leaned towards him, lowering his voice and eyes flickering past Rogelio's shoulder. 'The civil governor's holding off. The little birdies say the bosses will talk.'

Rogelio walked on and crossed the invisible frontier from the twisted streets to the square blocks of the Eixample, from workers' tenements to bourgeois apartment blocks, from twisting, shit-stinking alleys with heaps of horse-dung kicked against the walls to wide, well-swept boulevards. Here, he had to step more carefully. The cops patrolled with confidence along the pavements and a workman not at work could easily arouse suspicion. Here maids in uniform pushed prams and ladies with umbrellas and long, pleated white dresses strolled together. Council workers sprinkled water on the paving-stones. In his six months in Barcelona, Rogelio had learnt enough about the city to walk fast as if he was on an errand.

He reached the house where Juanita worked. He rang the porter's bell. A man in a blue overall slid back his cubby-hole's window. 'Hey, Martín, can you get word to Juanita, if she's got a moment? I can wait an hour.' The house porter, a man from Juanita's own village, nodded and closed the little window.

Rogelio went up to the corner and squatted with his back against a tree, his eye out for cops who might have him for loitering. The house where Juanita worked fascinated him. It rose five storeys, like all its neighbours, but her employers' house had wrought-iron balcony railings in complicated twisting lines ending in ornate sculpted roses. When he got back to the village he'd tell the blacksmith. He hadn't imagined ironwork could be beautiful too. That was the bourgeoisie, of course, they had time and money to indulge in art. After the revolution, workers too could devote themselves to artistic labour, as everyone would work fewer hours and they would not have the dead weight of these parasites on their backs.

He thought he was watching, but his attention had drifted, for he didn't see Juanita till she was standing in front of him. 'Hey, Roge, I've only got ten minutes.' They squeezed hands rapidly and then set off walking without touching. She wore a starched white dress, her hair pinned up under a white cap. He never told her he found this uniform attractive, he just told her that soon when the

60

revolution came, she could leave that job and wear the easy red dress she had worn the night they'd met at a dance at the Workers' *Ateneu* in Barceloneta. She was attending an evening literacy class there, whereas he was taking an economics course given by a professor who looked every inch a professor with his little round glasses and long white beard.

'You know, the docks are out.'

'No! And you're not down there?'

'Sánchez picked me for a special job and I've got to steer clear, for today at least.'

Rogelio waited outside while the maid went into the pharmacy on her errand. If the maids had a task they could do any time in the morning, they waited in case word came from their boyfriends.

'Still free tonight?'

She grinned, 'Of course.' He grabbed her shoulders and kissed her.

She slapped his arm. 'Not here, stupid'.

It was too late.

'Juana,' a sharp voice made her pull back from Rogelio. Where his fingers had squeezed her shoulder, now the hand of the housekeeper pressed down into the stiff frill. 'I have warned you I won't have my girls associating with men during working hours. You are employed to attend to your duty.'

Juanita shrugged the housekeeper's hand off her shoulder and stepped back. Making a great effort to control his temper, for he'd have slapped this bourgeois bitch twice round the chops if he'd had his way, Rogelio tried to pour oil on the troubled water.

'It wasn't her fault, Madam. I came up to her in the street. My fault entirely.'

The housekeeper looked over Rogelio's left shoulder:

61

'You're nothing to do with me. If I see your face round here again, I'll call the police. Come on, girl.'

Then Rogelio spotted Martín the house porter hovering in the doorway behind the housekeeper and in a flash realised what had happened. It was him who'd brought the housekeeper out. The cheating bastard, paid by both sides. The porter saw him coming and darted back across the street towards the house, but he half-tripped on a tramline and Rogelio was too quick for him, grabbed him by the neck, spun him round and drove his fist into his face. He raised his arm for another blow, but other arms pulled him back. His cap fell off.

'Hey, hey, easy, lad,' one of the two coppers said and to back up his calming words, brought his night-stick down on Rogelio's skull.

Jaime interrupted his story to open the stove with a rag wrapped round his hand and throw in more wood. The day was dark with low cloud, uglier than when they had driven to the clearing, even though it was no later than 2 o'clock.

'I should get back to the *posada*, as I told Toni I'd eat there.'

'The story's long. Am I boring you?'

'No,' she said. 'Not at all. You're revealing a world I know nothing of. I wish I had a tape-recorder. But how do you know all this?'

'From my mother. Throughout the Franco regime and for some years afterwards, while the Dúrcal brothers were still alive, my mother never spoke about her sister. Though every year on August 31 she walked up to that clearing and laid flowers there. She never spoke, but she remembered everything her sister had told her. When the younger Dúrcal died, in 1995 or 96. I should know, I'm getting forgetful, but the date's on his tombstone, what does it matter? When Atilano Dúrcal died, she sat me down and told me the whole story.'

Julia thought she knew already, but had to ask: 'Who were the Dúrcal brothers?'

'They were the local *fachas*, weren't they? They came back with the Franco forces when they re-took the village, they took part in the murder of my aunt and your great-uncle. They were the ones responsible.'

'God, and all those decades your mother had to live in the same village with her sister's killers.'

'That's right.'

'And why didn't she tell you?'

Jaime, biting his lower lip contemplatively, looked at her. 'She was afraid.'

'It's natural that she'd be afraid of them, but what about after Franco died?'

'No, I don't believe she was ever afraid of *them,* and even less so towards the end of their lives. The older brother had a stroke long before his death and for ten years he was a wreck confined to his bed or a wheelchair. A living corpse, dribbling, unable to speak, dependent on his daughter for everything, eating, shitting, dressing, undressing. You couldn't be afraid of him. The only fear she might have had in that respect was fear she might pity him. She needed to continue to hate him and despise him for what he did. I think she was right, don't you?'

'Right? About what?'

'To keep hating him.'

'I don't know, Jaime. But what was your mother afraid of?'

'I think she was afraid we, or I, might kill them and if that happened the Dúrcal brothers would have ruined my brother's life and mine just as they had ruined her sister's life and hers.'

'She was afraid for you.' Julia leaned forward spontaneously, kissed him on the cheek and squeezed his arm. *Perhaps I'm not such a cold bitch after all.* 'I'll be back about 4.' Jaime nodded. Tears ran down his cheeks while he pulled open the stove and roughly tossed in another log.

The village was again closed in on itself as if it were abandoned. Only smoke crawling round a few chimney-stacks showed there were people living here. She wrapped the thick coat around her. The clouds bore down on the village even in the middle of the day. The only light as she crossed the square came from the bar. She noticed a curious painted sign she had not seen before and diverted from her diagonal path across the square to read it. In careful lettering, above the simple 'Bar Valeria' over the door, the sign read:

THIS IS VALERIA, NOT PARIS OR LONDON

She wondered as she turned off the square into the street of the *posada* if Jaime was mistaken thinking that his mother had been right in wanting to continue to hate the Dúrcal brothers. Hate corrodes the hater, she had learnt. When Ricard had left her and then gone to live with a Cuban woman with a ready smile, copper skin, hazel eyes and dark curling hair, whose main attraction was that she was twenty years younger and wore leggings two sizes too small for her, she had hated and despised him. Hated him for betrayal and despised him for such vulgar taste.

She'd chewed the bitter herbs of hate for several months, but if she was to get on with her life, she could not wallow in hatred for a person who had wronged her. Hate would destroy her. Now, she had seen him a couple of times at family events and she cultivated in herself indifference and superiority. She was sustained by superiority to this brilliant Professor of Economics in the Autonomous University, Ricard Clavell, who often spoke on the radio and television on questions concerning the economic crisis and was such an imbecile. Maybe Jaime's mother had been sustained by a sense of moral superiority to the Dúrcal brothers. Or maybe she accepted her life had been destroyed and she maintained her hate, as the only reason for her herself to continue to live decently. Julia realised the experience was beyond her. She had only been left by her husband; no-one had murdered her sister.

The sound of knocking on glass interrupted these thoughts. The door where she had seen the fat woman staring at her the day before opened and the woman who had then said nothing waved with a hand, arm outstretched and palm facing downwards, and hissed between her teeth.

Julia stopped: '*Buenos días*'.

'Come here, I have to tell you something.'

'I'm just going to eat.'

'It can wait.'

Julia looked at her watch and said loudly 'Five minutes', but the woman, who waddled with her feet turned outwards like a penguin, was already dropping with a groan back into her chair by the window. 'Ay, wait till you get to my age, then you'll know what pain is.' She said this in a voice of suffering, but didn't seem especially afflicted. She told Julia to shut the door and waved her to the other seat in the room, which opened directly onto the street. The room was chaotic. Piles of cloth were stacked in a corner, behind an old *Wertheim* sewing-machine on a wooden stand above its pedal and a vertical wheel. A wave of heat came from an open fire, ringed by a circle of white ash. Roughly split logs were heaped beside the fireplace. The floor was of stone or even beaten earth in one part— unlike the *posada* or Jaime's, the house had not been renovated—and from the once-white walls, flakes of lime like white soot sprinkled the floor. The woman settled herself down in her chair, dragged phlegm up from her lungs as if she was scratching her throat with an iron bar, wiped her nose with a hanky she shoved back in her sleeve and wound an old grey mule-blanket round her shoulders.

'So how do you like our village?'

'I hardly know. I haven't been here more than 24 hours.'

'This has always been a poor village. The people here have had to work from sunrise to sunset just to put a piece of bread in their mouths. Here no-one gave anyone anything as a gift. But the people aren't bad, you know. Even if we sometimes talk badly of each other, when it comes to an emergency, everyone helps out. Roofing a house or killing the pig, the people all work together. Everyone comes up here now because of this business of the mayor, it's even been on the telly. Imagine, they interviewed me, sitting right where I'm sitting now. I can't move about like I used to, you know, my legs are so swollen, so I said "If you want to interview me, you'll have to do it here in my house. I'm not going to stand out in the freezing street like some of them." You know some of these bitches would do anything just to get a camera pointing at them. Not me.' She shook her index finger from side to side. 'I said, "If you want me, you'll have to come to my house."'

Her hair was dyed jet black and her face was completely round, like a whole cheese, with lips painted red and shaved eyebrows pencilled in black. She wore two glittering golden studs in her ears and a golden cross round her neck. It was hard to guess her age, but she must be well over 75, thought Julia, though her fatness left her face unwrinkled.

'So, what did you want to tell me?' Julia interrupted. The woman stared at her.

'You should dye your hair, sweetheart. You'd look pretty.' Julia patted her white hair. Her ambition was to get it as snow-white and billowing as a woman she once saw serving lemonade in a cafeteria in Rome, but it obstinately maintained grey streaks among the white. She ran her hand back through it.

'Maybe I'll dye it white.' The woman took no notice of her sarcasm.

'You don't want to believe everything they tell you.'

'I don't.'

'That Jaime, you know, is not as saintly as he likes to appear, I can tell you.'

'How do you know I've been talking to Jaime?'

The old woman tapped the side of her nose. 'Never you mind how, dear! People here find out what's happening soon enough. We're not as stupid as they make out, those young know-all tarts with their plunging neck-lines and microphones on the television. *El Moreno* likes to go on about the suffering of his mother, but I can tell you we all suffered here after the war. He's a gramophone needle stuck on one track. There wasn't enough to eat then, the girls had to go to Barcelona or even France to enter in service. I was 11 years old when I was in a household in Barcelona and, picture it, I was hungry with what they gave me even though they lived in a five-bedroomed flat in the Ensanche. Five bedrooms! The men had to follow the harvest or take the animals down to the lowlands in winter, away for months at a time. Now his mother's dead and buried, her son goes on about how much she suffered, how we've got to bury the Civil War dead, honour the memory of the blessed Juanita. Damn it! The blessed Juanita was a whore, I tell you, a bitch in heat. That's all she thought about, getting something hard between her legs. There are two sides in a war, what's so special about his mother? My father knew Juanita, he was a caretaker in Barcelona, that's where I was born, she worked as a servant in the same house. He explained that those anarchist agitators were here to stir up trouble.'

'But if you were so poor, maybe things needed stirring up,' Julia said tartly.

'The reds want everything for themselves.'

'That's what the other side wants.'

'What do you know! You haven't lived through it like I have. I'll tell you. When the anarchists arrived, they ordered everyone to the square and said, from now on everything's going to be shared, all the animals will be held in common. I can remember it, I was only a kid, but we all had to go. My grandfather had a cow, which he'd bought by his hard work, but he had to share the milk with idlers who'd never lifted a finger in their lives. Of course, they were the reds' keenest supporters because they didn't want to work, did they? Then the father of María Gómez, he was one of those and he had a mule and he shouted more than anyone that property had to be, to be—'

'—collectivised.'

'That's it. But when they said to him, "What about the mule, Gómez?" the smarty-pants came back with, "Oh, the mule, no, this is mine. I need it for ploughing, don't I?" That's what the reds were like, dear, take away what the others had and everything for themselves. Do you think that's fair?'

'Not as you tell it, no, but it depends on—'

'What Jaime doesn't tell you, but I will although it

makes me unpopular, because I believe in the truth even when it hurts, is that the anarchists were shot when the national army came back, that's true, but before that they'd already killed the mayor and the priest, Don Silverio, a man of peace, a man of the cloth. A very nasty business, a religious man who never harmed anyone. So what do you think they were going to do when they came back and found the mayor and priest murdered and everyone's land stolen by those godless ruffians from Barcelona? Just smile, pat the murderers on the back and say, "Never mind, lads, it's just a misunderstanding". Juanita and her boyfriend got what was coming to them. I bet the sweet Jaime didn't tell you any of that. There's two sides to every story, darling.'

The woman placed her hands on her knees and stared at Julia. For the second time that day, she found herself in a staring contest. Twenty years earlier she'd have snapped back at this woman, mouthing these platitudes, an oral history at second hand, but similar monologues from women in her mother's village and from her mother herself had made her more circumspect. There was no basis for rational argument. These malicious old peasant women fed on rows like Peruvians delighted in raw chilli peppers. Suddenly Julia smiled beatifically at the angry round face staring at her, not ceding ground but stepping sideways:

'There are as many opinions as people, *señora*, but tell me, who's the guy on the black horse?'

'Black horse? That'll be Arturo, the forest guard. He stops poachers and people stealing the village's timber. He's a cousin of mine, my aunt Herlinda's son.'

'Lovely horse. I must be getting back to the *posada* to eat,' Julia added while she began to button her coat: 'I'm sorry about your bad business here with the Mayor.'

'A disaster! I've got my own ideas who did it, mind, but

no-one's interested in an old woman's opinion.'

She had switched from insulting belligerence to the weak old woman. Even her body posture changed, her shoulders slumped and hands now gently folded in her lap.

'Who do you think it was, then? I bet you know more than anyone.'

'That would be telling,' she said coquettishly, patting her hair. 'Come back and see me, dear. Where am I going to go, in my condition? I'm always here.' She left the old woman to her memories, and why not, that's all she had. Though the memories were probably false and Julia hated them, she didn't feel up to attacking them.

Reaching Toni's *posada* was like returning home, though she had been in the village fewer than 24 hours. She felt drained after her journeys into the past. He was a comforting figure with his uncombed hair and thick old wool sweater. They ate a single plate of stew, big white beans, potatoes and chunks of chorizo floating around in thick gravy they mopped up with slices of Toni's home-made bread. Toni laughed when she told him that Jaime had barely started the story of Rogelio.

'Yeah, he likes to talk. That's our speciality, talking. You spend all winter cooped up in the house and when you get an audience, it's like winning the lottery.'

'He seems a nice guy.'

'He's OK, yeah a decent man, obsessive about these Civil War dead, but you can understand why. His aunt murdered and his mother staying silent for over 50 years till the murderers had died.'

'He's told you the story?'

'He's told everyone who'll listen.'

'So why couldn't he get permission to rebury the bodies in the cemetery?'

'It's simple, really. For one, the village remains divided

along Civil War lines. There are still people who won't talk to each other because of events that happened 70 years ago, often before they were born. Then, it's a long time ago and there's lethargy about doing anything, you know, "Let sleeping dogs lie." And third, Enrique the mayor belongs, belonged to the PP, though he always seemed to me more liberal than that gang in Madrid or Teodoro Pérez, the regional *mafioso*. In the villages, political labels don't count for so much. Anyway, as you know, the PP's policy is hostile to digging up the Civil War dead.' He shrugged.

'This Teodoro Pérez, who's he?'

Toni said nothing while he finished chewing a chunk of meat and then wiped his mouth carefully with the cloth napkin.

'Teodoro Pérez was the Mayor under Franco in the '50s and '60s and then the first elected Mayor in 1979. I found it hard to believe when I first came here, but it seems it was not uncommon in these villages that the coming of democracy made no inroads at all in the local power structure. Now he's retired, but he's still a sort of local political boss. He doesn't hold any posts in the PP, but it seems he's behind most things that happen in the *comarca*. Put it another way, nothing happens without his knowing about it and probably his say-so. He was Enrique's political mentor, but he was also probably behind Arturo getting his job. He knows everyone. He's even eaten here, but I didn't know it was him until he'd gone and someone told me.'

'He lives in the village?'

'No, no, he did, but he lives down in the valley now. He owns a lot of land. If you saw him, you wouldn't take a second look, he's a short elderly guy in a woolly hat and sheepskin jacket. You'd think he was a shepherd, not a *godfather*. In fact he is a shepherd, I've heard he still takes his flock out to pasture most days.'

'So why did he come and eat here?'

'I suppose he likes to see for himself what's going on. I must have convinced him, because there were no objections to my opening the inn.' Toni laughed. 'I don't want to put you off. I support what you're doing. But I don't think you're going to get far with your reburial plans.' He rubbed his hand through his hair and stared into the fire. 'Don't think we live in a democracy up here.'

Chapter Six

Jaime lit a cigar and took a sip from his small white cup of black coffee. Though Julia didn't smoke and avoided bars and restaurants where smoking was permitted, here in Jaime's house the smell didn't bother her. It mingled with the smoke of the pinewood-filled stove, the mud and rabbit- and hen-droppings from outdoors and the sharp tang of coffee. When she came back from lunch, he had smiled at her without speaking. He knocked the coffee grounds into the red plastic bucket of vegetable remains, carefully filled with water the blackened bottom part of the percolator, holding it up to check the water did not cover the valve, screwed on the top and placed it with his plump but precise fingers on the griddle. While the heated water forced its way up through the grounds, releasing its pervasive smell just as the gurgling announced its arrival, Jaime stood by it as if supervising a chemical experiment. She watched all these everyday movements at peace.

'Good lunch?' he said, as he passed a cup to her and sat down.

Rogelio was grinning, though an improvised bandage crossed his head and was tied under his chin as if he had toothache. After being held for two nights, he had been released in the morning. Now, after escaping the police, it was the anarchists' response he feared and the excessive grin on his face without his even being aware of it was due to his fear of the anarchists' disapproval of him. He went at once to the *Casa Boix* to find Germinal, who embraced him and called for coffee.

'Eh, Roge,' he rebuked him with the affection you'd

73

have for a loyal but naughty boy, while walking him over to the corner of the bar with an arm round his shoulders. 'Not too clever, kid, getting into a brawl the day you're meant to be keeping out of trouble. As it happens, it helped you stay out of the limelight when the heat was on. You know, the injured guard died that night, and we've sent the rest of the action group out of the city for a few days. But you were lucky, man, you weren't identified by the police as a CNT militant.'

Rogelio had heard the story of the strike by word of mouth several times while in custody. He was pleased with himself for not boasting of his inside knowledge. Only now, with Germinal's arm on his shoulder, did he grasp the implications of the guard dying. Though he'd not shot the guard, that wouldn't matter if he was caught. He was one of those who'd charged onto the dock with a gun in his hand. If identified, he'd have been held on a murder charge. Shaken, he needed to hear the story again from Germinal.

'We screwed up, Roge. Our bit was all right. We weren't to blame for the guard's death, that's always a possibility in an action and the comrade was not wrong to fire back after the idiot had taken it into his head to die a hero for the bosses, as if they cared anything about the sustenance of his wife and kids, who'd be thrown out on the street at the end of the month if it wasn't for our solidarity fund.' Germinal spat into the sawdust flung over the floor of the bar, to get rid of the bilious taste of his contempt for the bosses and their dupes. 'The first day the bosses went along with us, promising to negotiate directly, you see. We thought they were on the defensive. Our pickets were strong and we had momentum. But that same night they brought in the army to smash the mass picket. One dead, crushed by a truck, three with broken legs, two hundred arrested and the rest had no choice but run for it.

Yesterday morning they got lorries onto the quay, had scabs and soldiers unloading the ships, so goods were in the markets at 6 am. They used massive force and a massive show of force. We calculated badly.'

Rogelio sat leaning forward, his forearms resting on his thighs. He loved the insider feeling Germinal's analysis gave him. Germinal shook his head and counted off their points of error by banging the back of his right hand into the open palm of his left. 'One, we didn't think they'd get the order from Madrid to use the army and two, we hadn't expected they'd risk a general strike with such a show of force, when there were already two other major disputes in the Barcelona area. That same morning, they occupied the streets of Barceloneta, raided several houses, picked up Sánchez and there was nothing anyone could do at the dock gates for the shift the next day. 'No work today,' the goons announced, standing there with two dozen soldiers at the ready behind them. Sánchez and most of the leaders are still inside.'

'And can't we up the stakes?' Rogelio asked, using a term he'd heard before in the many debates about tactics. 'Aren't we strong enough to bring off a general strike, Ger?'

'We've got to learn a lesson from this, comrade. We were wrong-footed. This time there was no spontaneous upsurge by the working class. Nothing's going to be happening just yet with this new Popular Front Government in power. Workers are waiting to see. The Government let out the prisoners from '34, not because they wanted to of course, but because of pressure from below. Obviously, it's a very popular move. We have to wait until people's expectations have been disappointed again. It will be quite soon this time, we think—look at how they authorised use of the Army in a strike, though Azaña will wriggle out of responsibility for that. If the Government introduces reforms, however slight, as they probably will, the military will be preparing. Azaña will make a real mess of it, as he always does. He'll provoke the military because you can provoke them just by daring to breathe, but he won't take any measures to prevent them organising. We have to wait, keep arguing and organising on our side: an opening will come sooner or later. Our mistake was we misinterpreted the workers' optimism towards the Popular Front. We've got to be a bit more patient: the revolutionary opportunity will come, comrade. When the military rise up in revolt, we've got to be ready for them.'

'What about you, Ger?' Rogelio asked.

'I've been sleeping away from home, moving around, helping hold the groups together till things blow over,' the anarchist leader said laconically.

'And Juanita?' he asked, as if casually.

'She's OK, Rogelio. She's staying at a friend's. Come back down at lunch-time. I'll get word to her you're out. Meanwhile go over to see Asensi *el Navalla* and ask him to look at your head.'

Germinal scribbled an address on a piece of paper and passed it to Rogelio. Then he took the piece of paper back, struck a match and burned it in the ash-tray.

Rogelio was disappointed not to meet Juanita straight away. He'd lain at night in the police cell and with dreams of hugging her isolated himself from half a dozen drunks arguing and farting. He was anxious she'd hold it against him that she'd lost her job. Germinal was ultra-security conscious, wouldn't tell him where she was, wouldn't leave him even with an address written in his handwriting and you couldn't argue with that. Just as he dreamed of hugging Juanita, so he plotted to get even with that bastard of a caretaker who'd ratted on him and Juanita to her boss. As he stepped out of the dark cellar into the sun, he swore to himself he would. Then he thought he better not, for if Germinal knew he was settling scores on his own, he'd be considered a liability and be chucked out of the action squad.

So the strike had failed. The time wasn't right, things hadn't gone their way, the Civil Governor had acted fast. 'It may yet prove a risky policy for him. We live to fight another day,' Germinal had said. 'Oh, and take that blood-stained bandage off, Roge, you look like a bloodthirsty anarchist.' This he'd shouted as Rogelio was going out the door and the barman and half a dozen others in the bar laughed as well. So Rogelio felt he had to laugh too, though he felt suddenly again on the outside. He knew he'd screwed up, however friendly Germinal was. Out in the sun, his head throbbed when he untied the bandage. Somewhere he'd lost his cap. He would have preferred to go and lie down.

He set out across the old quarter again, but this time cut up by the Estació de França to the Arc de Triomf and up the Passeig de la República to Gràcia. His route across the Eixample's wide streets wasn't through as classy an area as where Juanita had worked, but he still had to look sharp. Then Gràcia felt safe again, with more caps than hats. Every ground-floor premises in its narrow streets was a small bar or workshop, with men and women sitting in the doorways, plaiting rope, hammering nails into barrels or stretching leather over metal lasts before stitching shoes. The streets were full of delivery boys and you had to look out for the carters, bent forward and carrying their loads strapped to their backs. He crossed two of the nearly-linked squares, dodging the piles of mule-shit on the beaten earth. The mules carried heavier loads than the carters and in the narrower streets you had to squeeze into a doorway as they passed.

A block before he reached Asensi's barber-shop, he spotted its red and white pole, like carnival ribbons. The bell on the door rang with the clarity of a flute. A man was being shaved with an open blade, which the barber wiped carefully on the cloth at his waist before turning his neck towards the newcomer. 'Rogelio?'

'How do you know my name?'

'I recognised you.'

'Do I know you?' The barber laughed. The man being shaved with foam still covering most of his face turned towards him and another man reading *Solidaridad Obrera* while waiting on a chair looked up too.

'No, but someone hit you on the head, you have a bump the size of a boiled egg, you haven't shaved in three days, and by the smell of you, you haven't washed or taken off your clothes in three days, either.' Rogelio flushed and clenched his fists in anger as all three laughed out loud. Was everyone going to mock him from now on?

'Hey, don't take it like that, man.' The barber set down the razor on the counter, stepped forward wiping his hand on his apron and held it out to Rogelio. 'Germinal rang to say you were coming. It's a pleasure to meet you. The comrade said you had been beaten by the police after distinguishing yourself in the dock strike.' Rogelio realised how tense he was that he'd taken the barber's teasing amiss. He was feeling raw with anxiety that he had screwed up with Juanita and he was exhausted from his walk across town. 'I've got instructions to get you spruced up, a bath, change of clothes, shave, attend to your wound.'

'But I don't have a *céntimo* on me.'

'We don't charge comrades.'

Asensi *el Navalla* showed Rogelio through to the back, where a rosemary and a thyme bush, cabbages, sprouts and endives were growing in a little garden. Rogelio brushed his hand through the rosemary leaves, so similar to pine needles, and cupped a mountain perfume to his nose. The smell took him to his village and he felt a rush of anger at the thought of his parents working in ignorance and poverty from dawn to dusk.

Beside the garden, in a long whitewashed shed, Asensi told him to shower and get dressed in the blouse and trousers laid out on a chair. 'Give us a shout if they don't fit you.'

'But whose are they?' babbled Rogelio.

'Ours, yours, the movement's, comrade. A lot of our people get hurt in strikes or confrontations in the street. They often can't risk going to hospitals, so there are several places in the city where we treat them. As for your clothes, we'll wash your clothes and they'll serve for someone else. If they're torn, we sew them. Look.' *El Navalla* opened a cupboard at the end of the bathroom and there were stacks of working-men's clothes neatly folded, blue cotton trousers, grey shirts and cord jackets, with a number written on a piece of card stuck to the wood at the foot of each pile.

After his shower, Rogelio even found a cap that fitted him. Asensi sat him in the big, soft barber's chair and shaved him with the cut-throat razor. After each stroke he wiped the razor across a white cloth to remove the soap and bristles. Then the barber looked at the wound on his head, cut away the hair round it, pulled back the skin and hair to open the wound, while Rogelio's knuckles turned white as he gripped the arms of the chair. Then the barber cleaned the wound with a cloth soaked in iodine, washed it carefully in water and sewed it up with a fine needle.

'No brains spilled.'

'None to lose,' Rogelio said, his spirits raised by the shower, the shave, his ability to endure the pain of the wound being treated and the deepened sense that, whatever Juanita thought of him, he was part of this movement. With serious people like Germinal and Asensi, they were going to make the Revolution. In the village he had known good people, but he'd never met people like this. Rogelio watched everything Asensi *el Navalla* was doing in the barber's mirror. At the end he shut his eyes as the little pricks of the needle pulled the thread through his skin to close the wound again. While his eyes were tight shut, he felt a pang of guilt he was using the anarchists' service when he'd been flung in jail for being an idiot, not through any act of heroic militancy. Then he thought of Juanita holding his back in bed. He smiled when Asensi finished.

'Come back in three days and we'll have a look at it.'

'You know,' said Jaime, now looking straight at Julia, whereas he stared into the fire or at the ceiling while he repeated as faithfully as he could the story his mother had told and re-told him. 'You know, that's what the anarchist movement was like. Nowadays everyone talks against the anarchists, saying their dreams of equality and justice were violent, but my mother never did and nor will I. They were people ready to lay down their lives to free the poor from their chains. That's what my aunt and your great-uncle wanted.'

'Perhaps,' said Julia, 'they were ingenuous to think they could defeat the army.'

'Ingenuous, oh yes, but by God, Julia, they tried it. I'm not an educated man, but in recent years I've read books about the anarchists and maybe I've got it out of focus, I won't say I haven't, but they tried it, didn't they? They had guts, eh?' He stared into the shifting blue and orange flames behind the glass door of the cast-iron stove.

When Rogelio got back to *Casa Boix*, the comrades admired his clean, white bandage. Juanita was talking to a young man at the bar and when she saw him, she broke off in mid-sentence and, to his delight, ran over and embraced him right in the middle of the café and kissed him full on the lips. She didn't seem to resent his part in the loss of her job. She told him she'd started work in the Santa Caterina market that day with one of the women she'd met at *Dones lliures*, who ran a fish stall. She was learning to cut, gut and fillet sardines, cod, hake and there she didn't have the housekeeper on her back all the time, though the hours were long and her legs ached at the end of the day. Now she smelt of fish instead of starch.

Rogelio took her back to the room he shared with Paco, who was out of town lying low. He waited outside while she stripped down to scrub herself in the basin filled with the fresh water from the street fountain he had gone down to fetch in the long-necked, white, ceramic jug. Then they made love on the narrow bed, lying afterwards in each other's arms. She still smelt of fish, but he didn't mind.

'I'm proud to be part of this movement,' he told her. 'You know, today I saw in practice what solidarity is.'

'Of course. Me, I had nothing. I was just a servant girl from a starving village lost in the mountains. Now I'm someone.'

'I want to stay with you for ever.'

She kissed him, she stroked his bandage. Then she said: 'I'm not tied to you, you know.'

Later, Germinal put an arm round his shoulder and told him: 'Listen, Roge, you've got to work and you won't be able to get anything now on the docks. We can get you a few weeks on the buildings, because you'll need a bit of cash, but then you should head back to the village. I know you've always helped your family plough and plant in the spring. Do it again this year. We can expect conflict later on, but not a lot now. We'll be prepared. We'll send word in June or July, that's when we'll need you. There won't be any action till then.'

Rogelio was bright enough to know he was being pushed out of the way. Getting himself arrested on a stupid personal question meant he was marked by the cops. He worked on a site in Sant Martí for three weeks and wrote a letter to his mother to say he was coming back for the ploughing and sowing. Meanwhile, he danced with Juanita at the Ateneu and attended his economics classes.

Rogelio had a problem. He may have become an anarchist and be learning about political economy, but he was insecure and pestered Juanita to swear loyalty to him. The anarchists didn't believe in marriage, but they had ceremonies of commitment. He knew that women were no longer the property of their men, but he couldn't bear to think of Juanita with others. When she went to meetings of *Dones lliures*, he feared she was learning things that would draw her away from him. When she went out with her friends, he could not help thinking she might be meeting other men, though he knew she wasn't and though he knew it was her right to do so if she wanted.

And this confusion sometimes put him in a bad mood, even though he only had a short time before leaving for two or three months. At times, Juanita was reticent with Rogelio, resisting his jealousy. After three years in service, at the age of twenty-three she was suddenly growing. 'I love you, Rogelio,' she said. 'Swearing vows won't keep us any closer while you're away. We'll meet again when you come back, and if we still feel the same for each other, we'll carry on from there'.

Nor could Rogelio get that double-crosser Martín, the caretaker at the building where Juanita had worked, out of his mind. And maybe his feeling insecure with Juanita (which was the only thing that made their relationship insecure) led him to think obsessively that the blow he'd landed on Martín's cheek just before he was arrested was the job half-done. Perhaps Juanita would be bound closer to him if he finished the job.

It was a cold evening, with damp in the air as there usually is in Barcelona, hot or cold. A wind blew down the wide, straight streets of the Eixample. It was already dark, but half an hour before 10, when the *serenos*, the night-watchmen, come on duty. Paco rang the bell of the porter's flat beneath the stairs and Martín came out into the hallway, then opened the outer door in response to Paco's gestures through the lattice window. Rogelio, concealed flush against the wall, jumped into the gap and shoved Martín right across the lobby and against the wall.

Rogelio was a head taller than the caretaker. As he clutched him round the neck, he knew he'd give the cheating scumbag a lesson he'd never forget.

'You remember me, Martín? You think you can take tips off me and other guys for passing messages to the maids and then money off the housekeeper for sneaking to her.'

'Calm down,' the caretaker gasped, 'you're completely wrong—'

'Bullshit, I know your sort.' He swung his fist onto Martín's cheek and Martín's head banged against the wall and bounced back into Rogelio's shoulder. As he drew his fist back again, he heard a click of a door latch. He glanced sideways and saw a small girl looking at him. She was no more than three or four, barefoot in a grey shift. Her eyes were big and round in a round face as she stared at the scene. 'Papa,' the girl said and stepped forward, then thought better of it and scurried back inside the flat.

Rogelio suddenly felt ashamed. He was beating up a little girl's father and he was a head taller than the man. And now the whole family would be out and the alarm would be raised. He could already hear a woman shouting. As he hesitated, he felt a sharp pain in his arm. He gasped, loosened his grip on Martín's throat and jumped back. Martín, teeth clenched and blood running down his chin, was waving a knife at him.

'Oh yes, I remember you, you lout,' Martín muttered. Holding his wounded arm against his chest, Rogelio backed towards the door. Martín, twisting his face as he made sucking noises with his mouth, waved the knife from side to side. Rogelio summoned up the last of his dignity in the doorway: 'No more double-crossing, shit-face. You look out for me, I'll catch up with you.'

Asensi *el Navalla* sewed up the wound. Paco had to bang on the door to get him to open up. He told Juanita and Germinal he had been attacked in the street, but he didn't think they believed him. The truth would out, he feared, through Juanita's friends in the building, even though he'd sworn Paco to secrecy. He caught the train to Sagunto the following night, slept on the platform and caught the goods train to Teruel in the early morning. From there it was a day's walk, with occasional lifts on carts if he was lucky, to the village. His arm throbbed, but *el Navalla's* dressing and the dry mountain air meant it did not become infected.

'Yes, that fits. It's just what Rogelio did do, according to my mother,' Julia said. 'Every winter in Barcelona

84

working on the docks or the buildings and back in March to help his parents on the land. Like your *golondrinas*. My mother, who'd have been ten or eleven then, looked forward to him coming home because he was always joking and paying them attention, according to her. I wonder if she remembers the wound on his arm, he'll have had a bandage or a scar.'

'It wasn't a deep wound, but he did have a scar.'

'But, how can you remember Rogelio's story in such detail?' Julia thought how inept she was at telling stories, unlike Jaime or her mother. She could never recall such detail. Or did they just make it up? She knew that her mother's stories shifted from year to year, the past adapted to her own current perceptions and needs.

Jaime got up from beside the stove and stretched. 'As I said, it's what my mother told me in her last ten years. She died two years ago. If the mayor, may he rest in peace, had been half-way decent, we'd have buried Juanita in the cemetery along with her parents and brothers before my mother died. There's a place for her now, beside my mother. But my mother didn't live to see it.'

Julia took refuge in the bar while she waited for the bus. Several men were drinking their Sunday morning *café con leche*, chatting or reading yesterday's papers. Today's would arrive on the bus from the valley. First thing in the morning, the bar was a warmer place than most houses, before their stoves were banked up again. The same woman served Julia. She scooped the coffee-holder into the coffee bag, jammed it up into the machine and pressed the button for the hot water to hiss through the ground beans.

'*Valeria's not Paris or London*—what's the story behind your sign?' Julia asked.

85

'Oh that,' said Pilar, automatically wiping the counter with a dirty, damp cloth. Spreading germs everywhere, thought Julia, ever the biologist. 'The Mayor wanted to tax us an exorbitant sum for putting chairs and tables out on the square. No-one ever had before and there's only three months a year you can sit outside anyway.'

'He wanted to charge you Paris prices.'

'I thought of taking it down with, you know, him dying, but then we thought, well we'll leave it there for whoever the next Mayor is.'

'It must have been tough for you with the murder and all the publicity,' Julia probed.

'Tell you the truth, lady, we didn't have any time for the Mayor here, we didn't wish him dead of course, you wouldn't wish that on your worst enemy, though I made a lot out of all the journalists and voyeurs.'

'Voyeurs?'

'You'd be surprised, the number of people with nothing better to do on a Sunday morning than drive up the mountain and look at the scene of a violent crime. Then they all want a cup of coffee and a meal in a warm place so that they can talk about it. Human nature, I suppose, but who am I to complain?'

Whereas, on her arrival on Friday afternoon, Julia had been rescued by this woman from the oppressive silence of the four card-players staring at her; now she felt the woman was talking nervously. On both occasions she'd chatted away rapidly, but this time Pilar avoided Julia's eye, wiping the counter or arranging cups that needed no re-arrangement. It was then, taking the first sip of her coffee, that she noticed the man in a lumberjack shirt and a leather hat at the far end of the bar. It was the forest ranger she and Jaime had seen the previous morning, on his black steed in the white mist like a horseman of the Apocalypse.

86

At the very moment she looked at him, he turned to look towards her, uncannily as if he knew when she was going to look. When trapped, plunge forward, she thought, overcoming her first instinct to jerk her eyes away and down: 'Good morning.'

'So what brings you here to our remote village if you're not a vulture sniffing round the death of our Mayor?' His voice was resonant and ringing. He knew the answer perfectly well, she knew, as he'd seen her with Jaime on the road up to the clearing. He was trying to embarrass her or make her look evasive, but Julia had already determined to tell her story in the bar. It was the only way she was going to find out if she had any allies. She'd decided, she wasn't sure when, in the glade perhaps or while listening to Jaime, she had decided to follow the quest to rebury the three murdered people through to the end.

'Oh, *señor* Arturo,' she answered easily, more easily than she felt, but a school-teacher was accustomed to talking in public. 'My great-uncle Rogelio is one of the three who were chucked like dogs into a hole in the ground in the clearing in the forest. I want to see him decently buried, along with *señora* Juanita and *señor* Evaristo.' She took a sip of her coffee. 'What do you think?'

'You know what I think.'

'I don't recall what you said when we met.'

The several men reading yesterday's sports pages or stirring sugar into their coffee continued with exactly what they'd been doing, but she knew that they all gripped their pages a bit more tightly or stirred a little longer. Arturo Folches swivelled round on his stool, one leg on the rail along the bottom of the bar and the other stretched straight out. His arm shot out in front of him, its finger pointing at Julia.

'We've had enough trouble in this village, as you well

know. What we don't need is outsiders coming up and telling us what to do with our dead.'

'No,' said Julia, answering more calmly than he, trying to treat him just as she would an angry adolescent in class, 'but Rogelio is my relative. I'm here on behalf of my mother, a lady aged 82 never involved in politics in her life, whose opinions tend toward support for the former regime. I'm here on her behalf to support the campaign to rebury in the cemetery a man who was unjustly murdered.'

'You don't know the half of it, lady, or you don't want to know. For sure, *el Moreno* will have been stuffing your head full of the great injustice of the three bodies in the glade, but what happened here in the Civil War was this, I'll tell you. The anarchists came from outside and destroyed the peace and order of our village, killing in their turn. They reaped what they sowed.' And he banged his fist on the bar-counter.

Even deeper silence followed the noise of that violent action. Then, one of the men reading the paper rustled its pages and said: 'People are upset, *señora*, at the murder of the Mayor. This question you're talking about raises tempers. Better to let sleeping dogs lie for a while until the pain of this murder's receded.'

'No point in raking over the coals of the past. We don't want to revive old hatreds,' another old man muttered.

A man sitting on his own, his round red face dotted with white stubble, a straw hat on his reddish hair, said 'What the fuck!' and then grinned round the room.

At this moment, the bus driver, the same man who had driven her up to Valeria on Friday afternoon, burst into the café.

'*Buenos días.*' He slapped the pile of newspapers down on the counter. 'Not so windy this morning. Maybe we're in for some better weather.' Pilar slid his *cortado* across the bar. 'Don't fool yourself, Chema, there's a lot of winter still to come.'

Some of the men came up to the bar, put down their coin on the pile and took a newspaper. Folches didn't move, but continued to read yesterday's *Vanguardia*, leaning over the broadsheet opened out on the counter. While Julia was finishing her coffee, the blow of his fist on the bar reverberated through her mind still, like an echo of the Civil War past (or was it a threat for the future?).

The elderly man who had spoken after Folches' outburst came up to her and said: 'Never you mind us, *señora*. Everyone here's nervous. We've had a hellish three weeks. Once we have a new mayor, in a few months' time, we'll be able to debate the question of reburial more calmly.'

Folches had the last word. He pushed aside his paper, crumpling the page, and stood. He spun a coin onto the counter and jerked down the brim of his hat. 'I don't believe what I'm hearing, Cleto, we've already debated this question, fuck it. I'm sick of this question. Let the reds lie where they are and let today's reds be grateful there are no longer any honourable men like Antonio and Atilano Dúrcal left.'

'Time,' said the driver, draining his coffee in one gulp. Julia and five of the men in the bar followed him out. The weather did seem milder. The sun was out and Julia didn't button her coat on the walk across the square. The dogs stood around, too bored or hungry to move. Her heart still racing, though she was outwardly calm, Julia watched Arturo Folches stride away along the arcade, like a pantomime villain, his paper folded under his arm.

Chapter Seven

When she got back to Barcelona that Sunday afternoon, Julia went straight down the iron stairs to the patio. She swept leaves and emptied them into the big earthenware flower-pot where they mingled with the kitchen leavings and where the red worms hastened their decay. Then she sat on the wobbly bench against the wall under the balcony and out of view of any neighbours. She rested her eyesight by looking at the view of the Collserola hills beyond the garden behind. The blackbird sat on a TV aerial and sang its way into dusk with such pitch and melody that, if you hadn't seen it before, you would think it a rare and exotic species. The bright-green and yellow parrakeets croaked like hoarse, crude old men as they stared with one eye and tore nest twigs off a bare tree with their beak and one claw. In the dirty, bustling city, Julia crouched in her rural hidden corner.

The memories of the weekend filled her mind and she pushed the buttons of her mother's number: 'It's Julia, how are you?' This was never a simple question with her mother.

'Here,' she answered in a voice that made you think her best friend had just died. 'I've been coughing all day.'

'Why's that then?' Her mother's coughing attacks were often nervous in origin, Julia believed. The school-teacher part of her wanted to explain that they were caused by some concern, some stress, and sometimes her mother seemed to grasp this, but it was a lost battle trying to reform an 82-year old. It was hard enough with a teenager.

'What do I know?'

'What did you do yesterday?'

'That imbecile Dorita came by, she wants to go out to a

90

film, but what interest have I got in going to the cinema?'

'She was just being friendly, I imagine.'

'Her daughter's husband has cancer. He had to have an operation and they told him they'd cleaned it all out. Damned sawbones treat you like an idiot, now it's come back. He works in a travel agency, but because he had time off, they got rid of him, in the middle of the holiday season they had to have the office covered. He doesn't want to eat, she gives him everything he likes but he takes a mouthful and then spits it out. "You've got to eat," she shouts at him. He's so thin you can see his ribs, she says, as if his skin's transparent, and his hair's fallen out with the chemical treatment. That's what happened to *la tía* Amalia, she had to wear a wig after her treatment and she was a fat woman, not as fat as *la tía* Benedicta, but then when she was bad, she wouldn't eat either and her skin hung off her belly in folds like an elephant, when we helped get her into bed. She just sat in the corner in her wig and faded away.'

Julia knew quite well that her mother, scared of cancer, had wanted nothing to do with looking after her sister-in-law Amalia and took to scrubbing manically any plate or cup the dying woman with no appetite and a wig might have touched. History was there to be rewritten.

'You should have gone with Dorita. She probably needed the company.'

Her mother snorted. 'She's an imbecile and she's boring. Anyway, they have films on the TV for free if I want to see a film. What interest have I got in her son-in-law's problems? She just comes, sits down and wants to talk.'

'So if you're not interested, why tell me all about them?'

'It's what she said, isn't it?' Her mother started to cough again, deep, painful-sounding rasps that made you think something would have to be spat out. Though the coughing was real enough, she hammed it up too. Julia took advantage of a theatrical groan to say: 'I've been up to Valeria.'

'That's where you were. I rang you this morning and you weren't there. Did you find out about Rogelio? Poor man, I remember him now when he came back from Barcelona. He'd always have time to play with us, such a big, handsome, good man. And then we lost him, the war came and we never saw him again.'

'Did he have a scar on his arm?'

'A scar, you say? I don't remember that, but he did have his arm bandaged one time, maybe the last time he went away before he was lost in the war. And then we never heard anything more about him. People always said he must have escaped into France and married and raised a family, he was a man who liked children. But if he'd come back, even forty years later, I'd have known him and I'd have welcomed him, because he was family and who can blame him? Not like that Susana whose father came back and she, so proud, the damned fool, told him to get the hell back where he came from. After the war things were hard, there wasn't enough to eat and everyone worked all day. Who could blame Susana's father if he found a new life in France?'

'Anyway, Rogelio didn't get to France. It does seem pretty certain that he's one of the people killed in Valeria.'

'Ay, poor man, but perhaps it's better to know his fate.' Her mother sighed. 'So what's going to happen? Will we bring him back to the village, finally lay him to rest in the earth where he belongs?' Already her mother was imagining a long funeral procession through the village, led by the priest and an altar-boy carrying the cross, from the church down through the barley fields to the cemetery shaded by cypresses, with her at the front sighing and crying, poor Rogelio's closest living relative.

'I don't think so. They want to rebury him in the cemetery there, alongside his friends. I think we should agree to that.'

Chilled by sitting too long in the falling winter dusk, she climbed the iron stairs, her hand clasping the now-leafless vine that had curled up the rail, and put on the heating. Then she turned on the computer and typed 'Historical Memory' into Google. She clicked on the first entry at www.memoriahistorica.org and a picture of seven self-satisfied men came up. She recognised Fraga sitting in the front row beside the Catalan nationalist Miquel Roca. What the hell was that old fascist Fraga doing there? And then she scrolled across the page and read the page heading of the *Association for the Recovery of Historical Memory* 'Why did the fathers of the Constitution leave my grandfather by the side of the road?' Of course, Roca and Fraga were two of those who drafted the post-Franco Constitution. This Association didn't step lightly. They charged directly at the Fathers of the Constitution.

She had to sign in to read the documents on the site. She typed in ROGELIO where it said 'Nickname' and then for 'Password' she put JUANITA. Juanita and Rogelio, living their love affair in 1936, to end so brutally in Valeria. They had died together, at least. Or maybe not. It was likely one had been shot before the other and the other had had to watch their loved one being murdered. He or she would have died maddened, in anguish. The thought left her staring beyond the computer at the wall, painted pink in a distant weekend of optimism. She knew she would have to go back to hear the end of *El Moreno*'s story.

She began to read the documents, skipping around the huge web site at random. There were data on repression: she read that 80% of the more than 5,000 people killed in

Galicia during the war had been summarily shot, without any due legal process, their bodies left by the roadside. Or in beautiful clearings in the mountain forest, she thought, remembering herself, neither communist nor anarchist, standing where her mother's uncle's remains lay with her fist clenched and tears close to the front of her eyes. She must be as theatrical as her mother, she smiled to herself. But acting up and exaggeration didn't mean the emotions were false.

She read of dogged men and women who waited day after day at excavations. One man remembered that his father was wearing a watch that caught the sun when he, aged four and a half, had seen his father taken away from home, never to return. That day was carved in his memory because his mother sobbed and ignored him while he gripped her hand. He was waiting patiently beside the dig for a skeleton with a watch. There were other stubborn men and women who had devoted years of their lives to struggling against bureaucratic inertia, indifference, fear or downright hostility, in order to excavate a grave. Often these groups were led by just one or two tenacious people, which reminded her of the kindly, rough Jaime *el Moreno*.

She read a long article on Ciriego, a town she had never heard of where the cemetery of the city of Santander is located. During the eleven years from 1937 to 1948, 850 people were shot against the walls of the cemetery. For twenty years a small group, led by a now-retired bank clerk Antonio Ontañón, had worked to raise a monument 'To the Heroes of the Republic and Freedom'. Entered originally in the register of deaths as 'unknown', now the executed people had their names restored to them in the register and recorded on the monument. She turned her attention to the photo of Toni Ontañón, white hair, white beard, glasses, looking straight at the camera with the monument to the dead (and to his tenacity) behind him. He wore a red zippered anorak and black scarf. His hands were thrust with downward force into his pockets and his mouth turned down morosely at its two ends. Such long reflection on death and ignominy would make anyone morose. Ontañón was quoted: 'It was enormously unjust. As if they'd killed them twice. First with a bullet and then by stripping them of their identity.'

It appeared there were excavations and campaigns taking place all over the country. It was news to her, for they rarely got a mention in the papers. There were sensational figures of the numbers killed that she supposed she'd read at some time or another in the press, but they had never meant much. Now they connected like a wire wound round her wrist to that forest glade. And they were all over the country: in the common pit for unmarked deaths in Valencia cemetery (30,000) and in Málaga cemetery (over 3,000) and in places she had never heard of, Milagros (42 people killed by Falangists), Fontanosas (7 people for collaborating with the *maquis*). The *maquis*, she read, were national heroes in France, but in Spain they were shadowy figures, reds or bandits. Gurb (13 soldiers), Piedrafita de Babia (14 people), Puebla de Cazalla (some 200 victims in a town of 11,000), Villaviciosa (sixteen nurses), Melegís (18 soldiers).

At Santa Marta de Tera there was a photo of a completely bald old man wiping tears from his eyes as four farm labourers' bones were found. Outside another village, on a mountain road, they'd taken a picture of a woman, aged 86, tall and dignified, signalling with a still finger the ground where her betrothed had been murdered and had a few spadefuls of earth tossed over him. She had never married. Every year for 65 years she had had the guts to lay flowers there on the anniversary of his death. She knew who the killers were. They lived down her street.

It was late and Julia had to work the following day. She ate bread, cheese and olives rapidly, the tears running down her face. She thought about murder. When you thought of people shot or 'executed' in a war, you thought of sadness, but not of crime. But of course all these 'executions' were murders, with no legal process. And even if there was a legal process, it was summary and fraudulent and they were still murders. In 2007, over 120,000 corpses were lying in unmarked graves in Spain. Or skeletons, remains of corpses. Biologist and composter as she was, she knew too much about decomposition to think that these were recognisable corpses; they were bones in the earth. And even the bones would now be brittle and flaking as they too began to decompose. Some corpses had bones broken, signs of torture. Skulls were usually splintered by a bullet hole. Some skeletons had their arms tied behind them with rusted wire. Maybe another would be wearing the remains of a watch, but it didn't seem likely.

She set the alarm for 7 am, but lay in bed unable to sleep, though it was past midnight. All the events and conversations of her two days in Valeria whirled through her mind, but refused to lie down in ordered sequence. She thought of the short, yet epic bus journey into the mountains to the wind-swept square of the semi-deserted village, of Jaime *el Moreno* and Toni the inn-keeper, both of whom she'd liked. Was she just lonely for company, she wondered? Too easily swayed by first impressions? The sinister forest ranger, alone on his black horse in the mist, alone at the end of the bar, alone striding across the square, the evil spirit of the visit, the baddy in a cheap film. That was too simplistic. She tried to look at him from other view-points, but none came. She recalled the fat woman who'd invited her to come again. Just as Jaime had heard

96

his story from his mother, the fat woman had heard her totally different one from her father. Jaime had insisted she come back in a few weeks, when all the fuss of the Mayor's death would have died down. In the visit to the forest glade, she had sealed her commitment to return, with her gesture of identification with her great-uncle.

Julia taught Biology to pre-university students in a secondary school. In the brief intervals between classes that Monday, she asked a couple of colleagues if they had heard of the murder of the Mayor of Valeria. Both had. It appears it had had big TV coverage for several days. When she got home, she was on the computer again, this time typing in 'Valeria murder'. In *El Periódico*, she found a photograph of Pilar, captioned 'the owner of the only bar in this remote mountain village' and an article.

BRUTAL MOUNTAIN KILLING

Valeria, a picturesque hamlet, often cut off for weeks by snow in winter, was in a state of shock today due to the death of its Mayor, Enrique Jurado. His mutilated body was found beside a lonely mountain road, where he had been shot with a hunting gun the previous night.

Eva Galdós, Civil Guard spokesperson for the region, told *El Periódico*: 'The victim's car was parked undamaged on the access road to Valeria. Passing motorists had reported by telephone a fall of rocks onto the road and an apparently abandoned car. At first light a patrol located the Mayor's corpse on the edge of the ravine below the car. It appears the murderer callously hurled his body off the road. One motorist who had passed the spot that evening reported the presence of a man at the scene. We have a description and are looking for this individual and the murder weapon. We ask anyone with information on this vile crime to come forward or to call us anonymously on xxx.'

The owner of the only bar in this picturesque village of just 40 residents in winter, Pilar Cervera, 34, native of Jaén, told *El Periódico*: 'We're all terribly shocked here. Nothing can explain this horrible murder. It can't have been anyone from our village. This is a quiet and peaceful place. It must have been someone from outside the village.'

The bar, on the main square, displays a notice *'This is not Paris or London.'* Asked about this curious sign, *señora* Cervera, who is unmarried, told us: 'We were in dispute with the Mayor about him wanting to charge us an excessive sum for using the part of the square in front of the bar as a café terrace in summer.'

In this lost village, one of the smallest in Spain with rights to its own Mayor and Town Hall, Enrique Jurado was elected Mayor in the last municipal elections with 26 votes in favour and 15 against, with 18 blank votes.

'Many on the electoral roll do not actually live in the village,' a person who preferred to remain anonymous told *El Periódico*. 'The Mayor was widely resented by residents who'd always lived here for getting his friends with second homes here to register to vote. At the same time, he refused to register the summer-time residents who were opposed to his dictatorial measures.'

Julia found similar quotes in several papers. Either all the reporters talked at once to the same person or they just sat in Pilar's bar and stole each other's stories. Journalists were like lazy school-kids, copying their neighbours' exams, too stupid or uncaring to worry whether they were copying mistakes or not. A quote from the Regional President of the PP popped up everywhere. 'Enrique

Jurado was a loyal servant of his people, assiduous in his attempts to improve his village. This terrible murder deserves the condemnation of all democrats.'

And so it went on, *blah, blah, blah* in numerous papers. She was about to close the computer, when she clicked on another file and was given a jolt at a photo of the forest ranger, Arturo Folches. It illustrated something of a scoop interview in *El Mundo*. Folches, dressed in his thick woollen jacket and a fur hat that covered his ears and cheeks as well as his hair, which made him look like a Bolshevik Commissar in the October Revolution (only the red star was missing), was staring out at the distant peaks. This was dated February 16, three days after the murder, and was headlined:

FOREST GUARD TELLS OF TENSIONS IN MURDER VILLAGE

The forest guard who oversees the land that extends from the ill-fated village of Valeria right up to the mountain peaks where eagles glide, ibex perch on the crags and the recently reintroduced bears have been spotted chewing on the abundant wild strawberries was happy to open his door to *El Mundo*. Arturo Folches lives in an attractive, traditional stone house, restored with all modern comforts, on the edge of the village. He received us in his sitting-room, seated at a table piled high with papers, and with a splendid view of the wooded mountains.

'The paperwork in this job accumulates sometimes,' the guard shrugged by way of apology. His deep blue eyes and rugged skin testify to his life outdoors protecting the forests from poachers and pyromaniacs rather than filling in official forms.

On our asking what the last few days had been like

in Valeria, Folches shook his head in profound anguish. 'Really, it's been hell, that's the only word for it, with the village full of reporters and television cameras. Rumours flying around everywhere. This is why I am happy to give this interview. I think I owe it to the village and the neighbours to set the record straight. There have been so many lies stated as fact on the television that someone has to take responsibility. I am one of the few people here with a formal position, a certain educational background and who has belonged to this hard-working mountain community all my life'.

On the wall behind *señor* Folches, locked in a rack, we noticed two shotguns, which inspired us to ask about the murder weapon: 'Almost everyone in these mountain villages has guns, so potentially could have fired on our Mayor,' the forest guard told us. 'The police have interviewed me, as I assume they have everyone who was in the village that night, to take a preliminary statement. Even a cursory inspection of these guns shows they haven't been fired for some weeks. I've seen it here on the television' (our rugged interviewee flung out his arm in a vigorous gesture towards the offending box) 'that police entering people's houses means that that person is *under suspicion*. This is nonsense. It's obvious that in a proper investigation the police will interview everyone in a small village. They made quite clear to me that they were seeking information on what I had done and seen that day, on my movements on the night of the murder, but not that I was under suspicion. The same applies to everyone else interviewed.'

'We understand, *señor* Folches, that you yourself had some disputes with the deceased Mayor,' *El Mundo* inquired.

'Me and a lot of people. It's not right to talk ill of the dead, but it's no secret that the Mayor was a difficult character. If someone argues with most of the village, is most of the village wrong or is it him who's the problem?'

'But a majority elected him to office.'

'You have to understand that the last elections took place three years ago and since then a lot of water has flowed under the bridge. However, despite my disputes with Enrique, we had a cordial relationship. Here in this village people are not rancorous. He was not keen to give me a licence for rural tourism in the house I had prepared at some expense and wished to open. In fact, there were personal motives involved because he and his wife ran a hotel and saw my project as competition. This dispute didn't stop me chatting with him. Many of the initiatives he took had the support of everyone, such as the mobile telephone aerials that have given us coverage or getting greater allocations of money to improve the roads.'

'You suggest that people here are not rancorous, but we understand that many people were not on speaking terms with the Mayor. We've also been told that the morning after the murder, there were celebrations in the village bar, with bottles of *cava* being opened.'

'This is a complete and utter lie, just the sort of thing with no basis in fact that gives the village a bad name,' insisted Folches, his face flushing with anger.

'Were you there?'

'I was not, but I have spoken in detail with people I know very well who were present and they assure me this story is completely false. What is happening is that a lot of people are trying to make out that the people of this village are a gang of ignorant yokels. In fact, the main problem we've had here has been from incomers. Indeed, several of the people who've bought houses in the village over the last few years are Basques from a dubious background. Don't get me wrong, I have nothing at all against Basques, very fine people on the whole, and I am not saying they are members of ETA, but I personally have heard them making nationalist remarks and affirming, for example, that our democratic police are torturers. Classic ETA propaganda. If I were the police, I wouldn't be interviewing villagers and placing them under the spotlight of suspicion, but I'd be looking at Basque nationalist circles. The Mayor refused to allow some of these people to register as residents, in my view reasonably, so there was a clear motive for hostility.'

'We understand there was also conflict here about unmarked graves from the Civil War in the forest.'

'Oh, that. Nothing. The thing is there's a villager of extreme left-wing opinions who is always going on about it. Look, all this happened 70 years ago, as you well know. Everyone concerned in those unfortunate events is dead and right was certainly not just on one side. Raking over the past, exhuming and reburying the victims with all the fanfares and self-justification involved, can only lead to the reopening of old wounds, which left alone will slowly continue to heal.'

We asked our frank and outspoken forest ranger a penultimate question: 'Do you know, *señor* Folches, who might have killed the Mayor?'

'Of course not.' We then finished by asking the vigorous and friendly forest guard to clarify a final rumour:

'We've heard, in the course of our investigations, that there was a project to construct a golf course and a luxury housing estate, and that the Mayor looked on this favourably, while many of the villagers were hostile to this project.'

'The Mayor, despite his brusque way of doing things, was in favour of developing tourism, as the future of this village. Many villages bigger and prettier than this one have died, with everyone emigrating to Barcelona or Madrid. The only people engaged in agriculture or raising cows and sheep here are elderly. Their children only want to come here on their summer holidays, they have jobs in the cities. I agree with our poor Mayor's way of looking at the future, even though he didn't always go about his job with tact.'

Arturo Folches ended the interview by asking us to accompany him to the back of his house, where the chill breeze made us hastily button our overcoats. Here he had wire runs with chickens and rabbits and a beautiful black horse grazing the green grass in a paddock fenced by wooden stakes, but it was not this he wanted to show us. The forest guard swept his arm across his domain:

'Take a good look at these mountains, *señores*. Most of Spain is bare, because over the centuries the Government and villagers themselves have stripped off the forests for timber and firewood and then the rain eroded the land. Here we have the good fortune to have maintained our natural heritage. These forests run right up to the snowy peaks, they are home to an enormous range of biodiversity. It's this which we have to conserve. My greatest fear is that all the negative publicity of this unfortunate incident will lead to the death of this village. Tell the truth, sirs, to your readers, this village is not guilty and is not ready to die.'

We thanked Sr. Folches for his revealing words and left him to his lonely, but wholesome job of watching over the sacred heritage of our beautiful mountains.

'Unfortunate incident', Julia thought. A strange way to refer to the murder of your elected representative. Arturo Folches with his blue eyes and black horse certainly wasn't someone you'd like to bump into on a dark night in a lonely place. She hadn't liked bumping into him on a dark morning in company.

As Julia browsed on through the dozens of files the murder had spawned, she began to get a picture of a village riven by disputes and rivalry, and not just between two opposed factions, but with multiple rifts. She recalled an Isabel Coixet film she'd seen about gossip, where what you say was compared to the feathers in a pillow. It's easy to tear the pillow, so that the feathers float everywhere, all over the room, out of the window and down the street, but then it's impossible to put all the feathers back into the pillow. Once something was said, it was impossible to forget it, however untrue it proved to be. Perhaps it was ETA who killed the Mayor. Perhaps it was Folches himself. Some resentful shepherd. The owner, 34, unmarried, of the only bar in town. Perhaps it was just some chance, crazy mid-winter mountain walker. Who knew? The killer knew, but he, or she, wasn't talking. Did anyone else know? Did the fat old woman with a face as round as a buttock know? Maybe Teodoro Pérez knew. Toni had said nothing happened in the *comarca* without his say-so, but she had seen no reference to him in any of the articles.

After work on the Tuesday, she caught the metro down to the Old City, despite her tiredness. A purpose, a quest lifts tiredness. It wasn't a long trip, just twenty minutes and five stations from her school up on the hill into the city centre. She could live for months out in her quarter under the Collserola hills and then emerge into this huge square with the *Corte Inglés* like an ocean liner towering up one side and languages of every nationality plus the two languages of Catalonia surrounding her. Here, unlike Valeria, she was anonymous in the crowds. And unlike Valeria, here she could not walk at her own pace, but had to thread her way through the tourists, shoppers, gossipers blocking half the pavement and those on errands with sharp elbows chopping their way through in a straight line like a speedboat through white-capped waves.

Then she turned into a narrow street running slightly downhill, with so few people she could count them. A woman in a dirty housecoat mopped the street in front of her narrow door. A man smoked in the doorway of his picture-framing shop. A smell of glue mingled with the tobacco. There was no pavement, the former cobbles and narrow one-person pavement replaced by flat slabs of stone with no kerb. A restaurant had pretty blue tiles set into the wall behind a tub painted green with a dead-looking grey plant. The houses of pitted brown stone rose straight up five storeys, with plants cascading from tiny wrought-iron balconies, geraniums and long-stalked green ferns. Two young black men, light on their feet, strolled towards her. The city crowds barely touched this peaceful side-street.

'Hey, you're looking better,' said Xavi. Julia had climbed four flights of dimly lit, uneven stairs. Two tiny flats opened off each landing.

'You should move somewhere with a lift before you get old,' she said and hugged him and kissed him on both cheeks. He smelt good, not perfumed but with the slight tang of citrus from the soap he used. While she unbuttoned her coat with one hand, he led her by the other into his back room, dominated by a drawing-board—he was an architect—in front of a wide window that looked out over the jumbled roofs of the old city away to the twin towers of Poble Nou.

'But where else could I get such a combination of tradition and modernity as this?' he said sweeping his arm regally across the view. As always, when she admired Xavi's view or he admired it for her, her eye was drawn to the Picasso reproduction on the wall beside the window, a grey drawing of a jumble of similar flat roofs with huts, washing-lines, chairs and the hunched top of the stairs that every block had, with its door giving onto the roof. Apart from the absence of pigeon-lofts, the foreground of Xavi's view had changed little in the hundred years since Picasso. Then, beyond the old city, modernity soared in the shape of the two waterfront Olympic towers and, behind the towers, the high-rise of the new Fòrum neighbourhood. There, the lights coming on twinkled on the fancy, jagged blocks of flats as the winter day was coming to an end.

'What do you mean, looking better?' Julia said, throwing herself into the arm-chair. 'I'm knackered.'

'Well, you haven't exactly looked good these past few months.'

'I haven't felt good. It doesn't help that everyone treads around you on egg-shells. "Are you alright, Julia?" "How are you feeling, Julia?", as if I was suffering terminal cancer not a broken marriage.'

'It's inevitable."

'It doesn't help you forget.'

'And so, how are you feeling Julia? Are you alright?' She made to hit him. This studio-apartment was a haven in the middle of the bustling city-centre. Perhaps that's what she needed, to change flat, get away from where she'd shared her life with Ricard.

'Better, but—'

'But?'

'Well, I wanted to talk to you about my weekend.'

'Ah, that's it, then, you've had a good weekend, you feel better and you look better.'

'Don't make assumptions.'

Xavi's eyes glistened behind his glasses. He tugged at his scrubby beard. He was her nephew, her elder sister's elder son, only ten years younger than she was and someone she'd grown increasingly close to over the years. In their dysfunctional family and through these months of her separation, she'd relied a lot on him.

'Grandma tells me you've been looking for Uncle Rogelio's remains.'

'That's what I've come about.'

'So tell me.'

'In truth, I don't know where to start. My head's just a mass of disordered images.'

'Then we'll do what the shamans do in Costa Rica, you'll see. Close your eyes, empty your mind by thinking of a sleeping yellow snake—'

'—does it have to be yellow?' she mumbled.

'—breathe slowly to get over the fright of coming across the yellow snake—it's sleeping on a litter of leaves and you don't want to awake its wrath—and tell me what comes into your mind.' He stood before her, his hands lightly rubbing, caressing her temples. As a good scientist, she knew such mystic methods were well-based on experience.

She told him the details of her two days in Valeria, from the unpromising first moment when the thin-ribbed dog slavered and sniffed her crotch as she crossed the empty square. She explained the unnerving tension in the bar, then the fat woman staring from her door onto a street of otherwise empty houses and the ghost estate beyond the *posada*. Then the welcoming warmth of the *posada* itself and Toni who ran it. She realised only as she told Xavi— realisation was one of the reasons you told people events— that suddenly in a new place, previously hostile, the *posada* made her feel she could start a new life there. 'Foolish, but that's what I felt.' The next day, she had experienced the grandeur of the forest that wrapped around the mountains under the snow-touched rocks and the meeting in the mist with the forest guard, as ghostly as the abandoned estate at the end of the street of straggling houses. Then came the moment in the glade at Rogelio's grave. 'I realised I wanted to pursue this through to the end. I can't explain why I raised my clenched fist, I mean you've always been the left-winger, but it seemed and still does seem the right thing to have done.' She explained how Jaime *el Moreno* had begun to tell her the story of her mother's uncle, as he'd heard it from his mother. Like Toni, he was kind to her, respecting her privacy at the forest grave, later bringing her coffee. 'He's obsessed with the fight to get his aunt Juanita buried, but he wasn't boring, he doesn't let the past dominate his life. I mean, he was living in the present, he could laugh and chat. He wasn't like some of the campaigners I looked up on the Internet last night, who looked depressed out of their minds with the stress of dealing with death for so long.

'But Xavi, what I really can't figure out is the mystery surrounding the murder of the Mayor. You get a brutal murder, by all accounts carried out by someone in a small village, but everyone carries on leaving their doors open. What I wonder is whether everyone knows, they know who did it. Or, if they don't actually know, they know a hell of a lot more than they're letting on.'

'You mean, a murderer's on the loose and they don't even bolt their doors? Yeah, that sounds pretty weird.'

'In Valeria I got the impression you could wander into anyone's house. I even fell asleep on Toni's sofa without anyone around.'

'It'll just be habit, village life.'

'Maybe, or like I say, they know who did it and so they're not scared.'

'Or they know it was done for a specific reason and it's not going to affect anyone else.'

'But then there's other people on the Mayor's side who

might have good reason to fear the killer, like this forest ranger, for example.'

She lay on the sofa, while Xavi sat on the chair by the window, his curly hair slowly fading into the background as the light died in the sky, leaving the glow that rose from the city streets. There were two murder incidents tangled up, the killings in the glade seventy years before and the murder of Enrique Jurado a month earlier.

'As Jaime asked, I'll write a formal letter requesting Rogelio's reburial. I'll send it registered to the village Council and to the Regional Government. Even if they don't act on it, they'll have to file it. Will you draft it for me?'

'But you're the teacher.'

'I'm a science teacher; you did Humanities.'

'I could draw you a letter. Writing's not like building houses.'

'I made a list of other things that need to be done.' She pulled a note from her jeans pocket. 'I've talked to my mother. You draft a letter. Then I want to get in touch with the Aragon Association for Historical Memory. We'll ask their lawyer to add our name to Jaime's to the local courts for permission to exhume and re-bury. And I want to visit an exhumation.'

'An exhumation?'

'Yes, somewhere they're digging for the dead.' He looked at her and raised his eyebrows. He knew her too well to ask her what she meant. She opened her arms: 'We always bury the dead, hide them away while they decompose. I want to know what it feels like to disinter the past.'

They went out to eat in a nearby restaurant, *La Bossa Vella*. The diffused light of the yellow street-lamps bathed the thick mediaeval blocks of porous, pitted stone in a gentle glow. She knew the restaurant from previous visits to Xavi, days when she'd wanted to savour the bustle and energy of the city centre. The boss even greeted her, 'Good to see you again, *senyora*,' and though she knew it was only professional courtesy, it warmed her. The restaurant had ochre walls hung with blown-up photos of the old city pre-war. One showed a picture of a mass demonstration with the dock gates and cranes in the background. She peered at it, wondering if her great-uncle Rogelio was among the crowd of men in caps pressing forward at the gate. At the back of the restaurant, partly separating the dining area from the kitchen and toilets, a giant rubber-plant pushed its branches along the wall. The restaurant's ceiling showed the original beams, stripped of their paint and varnished deep brown like a ship's hull, with plaster curving, cellar-like, between each beam.

'There's another thing that sticks in my mind.' It was there in the pattern, like a stitch lost when you're knitting a jersey. 'Toni, the inn-keeper, you know, the guy I felt so good around, at the end when I was leaving, he said, with a big smile, "Be careful, Julia, don't come back too soon." I asked him what he meant and he said with an urgency unlike anything he'd shown before: "This is an unhappy village and this murder's just a thin layer of ice on the surface of a deep pool of conflict. Wait till this new murder's solved before you get on with your old murders".'

'Well, the question of the Civil War dead will just be put on hold until all the fuss has died down and there's a new mayor.'

'Yes, but I felt Toni's words were a warning.'

'It's strange they haven't found the killer,' Xavi mused. 'It's like an Agatha Christie story, where there's only a limited number of candidates, but stuck in a village not an English country-house. Why couldn't it have been someone from outside the village?'

'Or someone from the village who's not living there now or who hired someone to do it. But in all the articles I read, everything points to the fact that someone walked to the spot where the Mayor was killed. There's nowhere to park a car on that mountain road evidently and the killer didn't travel with the Mayor. People saw him leaving the meeting he'd been at on his own. He was worried about the snow warning, so didn't hang about for a drink as he often did. And if they went on foot, Xavi, they had to come from the village. You have to see the place, it's that remote.'

Julia rarely ate in restaurants, and even less so now she was on her own. In fact, the last time she had done so was with Xavi several weeks before. When she did, she relished the opportunity to order dishes she had eaten rarely or never. Today she ordered aubergines stuffed with mince on a bed of rocket, radish and celery, covered with a walnut and sherry sauce.

Xavi said: 'They say people kill for money or for love and love's shorthand for possession and/or sex, isn't it? It's hard to believe someone would kill the Mayor because he wouldn't let a shepherd drive his flock through the village or because he charged the café too much for putting their tables on the square.'

'They might, though, if he refused to give someone a licence for rural tourism, so the person lost their income; or if not being able to drive your flock through made having a flock non-viable.'

'Was he married?'

'The Mayor, yes. You're trying to *chercher la femme*. She lived with him. Toni says she's with her sister in Zaragoza now. Imagine, if it's someone from the village and you're living there, you might be meeting your husband's murderer every time you go out. In fact, it's like what Jaime's mother told him after the Civil War, that she would have to pass her sister's killer on the street. Except she knew who he was, but in this case the killer's identity's secret'. Whether it was the wine, the excitement of the weekend or the confidence Xavi gave her that she could say whatever she wanted even if it was stupid, she was chattering on. She felt her face was flushed and her gestures were more expansive. The people in the café at Valeria who had seen a stern and controlled individual, with her serious brown eyes, thin bony face and grey hair pulled back would hardly recognise this lively woman.

'So it's likely to be money. Property or power and influence in a tiny—', Xavi said and then stopped. Julia looked up and saw he was staring over her shoulder. She turned to follow his gaze and saw a tall middle-aged man standing in the doorway. He looked decidedly elegant and prosperous in his long brown overcoat. It took her a moment of staring to realise it was Ricard, her ex-husband. The restaurant owner glided across the floor towards him, shook his hand and helped his companion off with her coat. It was the first time Julia had seen her close up, the younger woman Ricard had left her for. Her skin was coppery and she wore a tight, short skirt and heels as high as a television news presenter's and she was a good 20 years younger than him. He still hadn't seen her and Xavi. Her first feeling, stupidly, was embarrassment for him, having so little elegance as to run off with such a bimbo. Didn't he realise? Then anger came, pumping like molten iron into her muscles, so that she turned back to her plate, fists clenched under the table. She took a sip of wine and saw the tendons on her wrist standing out tensely, like cables sustaining a bridge in the wind.

'Hello, hello,' Ricard was saying, 'why, what a surprise,' and Julia knew he was on edge too, though she sat looking straight ahead and neither rose nor spoke. She could interpret Ricard in less than a second, she knew him so well. Xavi was on his feet, replying to Ricard's greetings and leading him by the arm round the corner towards the back room. As the girlfriend followed them, she glanced across at Julia and that's when Julia looked up. The girl smiled tentatively and Julia stared back at her smooth face, then looked down at her flat stomach and then stared again into her eyes. *Little bitch*, she thought automatically, but she didn't mean it. Julia arched an eyebrow. It wasn't the girl's fault, was it? It was him she was cosmically furious with.

Chapter Eight

Ricard rang her a few days later.

'Don't—' and then his voice cracked, the cry of a bird caught flying into a wire. 'Sorry, don't hang up, Julia. No, look, I'm so sorry about the other night. So stupid. Obviously we would have walked right out again and left you in peace if I'd seen you sitting there.'

She sort of breathed out audibly, but she didn't hang up. After the chance meeting, she knew he'd ring. She had no desire to talk to him, but she was going to have to sort herself out. She couldn't live at the level of explosive tension she'd felt in the *Bossa Vella* restaurant and that had stayed with her all week, like a bruise fading too slowly.

'Look, Ricard, I asked you not to ring me. I really don't want to talk to you.'

'I know, I know, sorry, I just wanted to apologise.'

'And there's no need to apologise, for God's sake. We bumped into each other in a restaurant by chance. Well, that happened, it might happen again. I don't want you using it as an excuse to ring me.'

Ricard thought people should be civilised when they split up and get on with each other politely. 'After all, if we've lived together for twenty years and been through what we've been through, then there's no reason not to be friends,' he had said. 'Yes there is, you fucking dumped me,' she had replied and Julia who was not wont to swear found that saying a strong word helped keep her calm. *Been through what we've been through* referred to their only child, Anna. She had died several years before when she was eight years old, knocked down by a motor-bike driven too fast in the drizzle by some thin-arsed, short-brained adolescent. Anna was walking with her red umbrella the hundred yards from home round the corner to her friend Carla's house and didn't even have to cross a road. The bike had come round that same corner like a bat out of hell and slid, the devil's scythe, across the damp pavement. Julia heard the crash, then an urgent shout. In the silence that followed, she rushed to the window. Then she ran down to the street and had held Anna's head in her arms, though she was already dead.

'She didn't suffer, *Senyora*,' the kindly young doctor, who wore round glasses with silver rims, told her later in the hospital, rubbing her arm. At those words she burst out crying for the first time. She knew she was the one who was going to suffer.

She never could get too worked up about the bike rider. While she was sitting on the ground, holding Anna on her lap and stroking her hair, a group of people looked on anxiously, murmuring while they waited for the ambulance. 'I'm sorry, I'm sorry, will she be alright?' the kid repeated. He was jumping up and down on the pavement and rubbing his leg where the slide into Anna and the wall had scraped the skin off. Blood was running through his fingers. He looked in worse shape than Anna, who just lay still in her mother's arms, with no blood or cuts visible. The only words Julia had for him was: 'Please, just fuck off.' And he did, as far as she knew. She remembered little more, except the firm grasp on her upper arm of the ambulance-man who prised Anna from her lap, while a policeman helped her to her feet. She looked out of the window of the police car at her familiar neighbourhood, changed forever, as they drove behind the ambulance, its siren roaring, to the hospital. Then the kindly young doctor stroked her arm, Ricard was there, how she never knew, making phone calls by the coffee machine, and in the sad faces of all her family, friends and colleagues who flocked round her in the following days, she saw horror and heard the carefulness in their choice of words. The horror was her own stern face reflected back at her. The carefulness, she knew, was because they feared for her sanity. They worried she might kill herself. They did not leave her alone, but she wanted to be on her own. The one thing she really wanted, Anna's life, was not possible. The girl's death had cut her off from other people. She wanted to be on her own, so she swore at her sister and her husband. 'Leave me in peace,' she shouted at people's good intentions. She was rude and she didn't care. She even told Xavi not to visit her. He did anyway and sat around not talking. He read the paper, cooked omelettes or hoovered the floor.

She saw the killer once more at the inquest, but thankfully he didn't try to apologise. What interest could she have in his regret? Her anger had focused on Ricard. Urbane, sparkling in conversation, a man who fed off conversation and laughter in cafés and at dinner parties. They'd met in a café over bottles of beer; they'd laughed through a lot of dinner parties. She knew her sparkle shone with his attention. She too became witty and more attractive. After Anna's death, he was attentive and concerned for her, but she knew she soon bored him. She didn't want attention and concern. She wanted the impossible. 'Life goes on,' everyone said, but it hadn't, had it? It had stopped for Anna. After a few weeks, Ricard wanted to re-start his social round, but she'd lost interest. She went back to work after two weeks off and spent her free time in the patio, turning over the compost, growing plants from the seeds she picked up on walks through the Collserola forest. Often she just sat on the bench and watched the birds come and go. If you sat still for ten minutes, they ignored you and came down into the patio, pecking about for seeds, jumping and weaving in the air to catch mosquitoes or digging for worms. Sometimes a gang of red, green and yellow parrakeets screeched overhead as if Barcelona were Brazil. Gulls and wood pigeons mingled with the ordinary small garden birds, the yellow-breasted finches, a bird with a white head stripe and the simple, beautiful yellow-beaked blackbird. A raucous magpie sat in the branchless tree behind the patio. Once, a hoopoe, with zebra wings, long beak and its curling crown of orange feathers fringed in black like a burlesque dancer's feather fan, stood on her back wall.

So, she'd told him to get on with his life and he had. And she'd been permanently, subterraneously angry with him for doing what she'd told him to do. She was polite, even pleasant with him on the surface, but Anna's death had removed her interest in their life. She was undoubtedly unfair to him. He was probably right when he explained that she had just withdrawn from him, he wanted to help her, but she couldn't be reached. She was unfair to him, but that's how things were. Somehow, in retrospect, all his charm, all his dynamism seemed ersatz, fluff blowing on the wind. She found peace not in ripe laughter at a dinner table with a wine glass in her hand and sparkling in the light, nor in the post-party gossip about the guests over late Sunday breakfast. She found peace sifting through her organic compost made out of vegetable scrapings. She cut up the pieces as small as she could, she turned the compost, she checked the temperatures with her long thermometer whilst watching the blackbird sitting on the wall and watching her. Wondering, she fancied, when the hell she was going inside so that it could carry on digging for worms on its patio. Refreshingly, birds had no sense of property. Or of loss. They were practical. With care and work, she found she could lose her thoughts in these physical actions and sights. The smell of organic decomposition was profoundly comforting, the smell of country cycles and seasons, the rhythm of life she had lost with the death of her daughter.

Ricard told her, ever so gently, carefully, that perhaps she was withdrawing from the world too much, perhaps she should see a psychiatrist. He had a friend who knew a woman he swore by who was a post-Kleinian and hot stuff. She'd got this friend through a rough patch when his wife had died. Academic categories comforted him. A post-Kleinian! The compost and its cycles of waste rotting down in the dark and producing seeds again were perhaps, he suggested, wallowing too much in the mire. She disliked him for treating her ever so gently, as if she might kill herself or go mad at any moment. More than that, she was bored with him. He didn't tell her anything she hadn't thought of herself. She made a joke, holding up her grimed hands: 'It's post-Kleinian dirt.'

'Oh, Julia,' he sighed. 'It's not funny.' But she had no desire to comfort him in his sadness. She couldn't be comforted and part of that was that she could not comfort anyone else.

After she had left Xavi the night of the restaurant, she had not caught a taxi home. She needed to unwind and feared she might vomit in a car. She walked on through the old streets of the Born, many of them now with the grimy stones of the houses scrubbed down and lit by angled lights so that they looked like a stage set for a mediaeval epic. The area had 'come up' post-Olympics, meaning the old residents in their tiny flats and the shops selling groceries, fruit or hardware were priced out and it was now full of boutiques, wine-bars, pretty restaurants with red-striped awnings, tourist apartments and ochre stone scrubbed clean of history.

It was one of those suddenly warm evenings, when the wind from the south blows in from Africa and nudges winter northwards. She walked on past the old dock warehouses, now converted to a History Museum and restaurants beside the water, into the old fishermen's and dockers' quarter of Barceloneta. She thought of Rogelio, her great-uncle, who had taken part in a great dock strike here, according to Jaime *el Moreno*. The only strike that would be possible now would be a waiters' strike, she thought. It might be effective, it would bring the tourism industry to a halt. But she didn't think that the waiters would be organised in a union like Rogelio, Juanita, Sánchez and Germinal had been in the CNT.

Breathing the sea air deeply into her lungs, she set out to walk along the broad promenade built along the beach at the time of the Olympics. There were men hanging about, with nothing to do and, like her, unwilling to go to their lonely beds, but Barcelona was not an especially dangerous city, even at one in the morning. Since Anna's death, anyway, she had given up worrying too much about her personal safety. It wasn't bravado, she just couldn't be bothered to get too worked up about what might happen to her.

She thought about her weekend in Valeria. Another world, a new world, but one that was not unfamiliar, from her mother's stories and her own summers in her mother's village before she got married. She walked towards the twin skyscrapers with her hands thrust down, pressing the bottom of her pockets, hearing the wavelets roll onto the sand and knowing she wanted to see Rogelio's story through to the end. So when Ricard rang, she didn't hang up on him. He seemed surprised, he who'd been saying they should talk, surprised the line was still open and uncertain what to say.

'You could do something for me.'

'Oh, of course,' he said.

'You must know people involved in the Historical Memory campaigns. I want to go and see an exhumation. Can you put me in touch with someone?'

'I could talk to Ferran. You remember Ferran, the Professor from Contemporary History?'

'Aren't you going to ask me what it's about, this new interest of mine?'

'No,' he said. 'I wasn't, I mean I assumed you wouldn't want to explain anything.'

'It's my mother's uncle, Rogelio. Someone reckons we've found his grave and I want to know the best way to proceed to get him properly reburied when the Town Council is an obstacle.'

'Isn't he the one who was meant to have disappeared into exile? Where is he, then? How do you know?'

'I'll tell you another time. You're right, I don't want to explain anything now. Talk to Ferran for me,' she said. She hung up and could picture Ricard's hurt face looking at the receiver and saying, we were just starting to talk, then she barked at me and hung up. She laughed at her image of him, though she knew it wasn't funny.

Xavi came up to see her that Saturday. The day was cold, but they sat in the midday sun that warmed the back wall of her patio. She was turning over a big flower-pot full of decaying kitchen waste. Knots of red worms wound round each other in the damper corners. He picked up a squirming knot. 'Look at that, you've got a whole ecosystem going here, Julia.' She liked his genuine interest: he picked up the worms without a second thought. He'd always been interested in everything, quick, his eyes darting here and there, his mouth pursing up, rapid comments and questions. He'd been the son she'd never had and also the younger brother she could show the world to.

Most people looked from a distance or giggled awkwardly when she showed them her worms. 'Put them back, the sun's no good for them,' she told Xavi. He wiped his hands on his trousers.

'I think I upset Grandma this morning. I went round to help her with some Internet thing. My weekly Good Samaritan visit.' Her mother was studying the Internet, but at 82 was not making much progress. She usually blamed her mistakes on anyone who was helping her or on the machine that had 'done something on its own'. 'She was complaining about her life and I told her it's really admirable that she grew up in a village unchanged for centuries, without a cash economy and without electricity or running water and here she was on the Internet. But she took it wrong, not as a compliment, but as a reproach. She started going on about how she was respectable, how her parents were very good people and she wasn't ignorant and so on. I don't think I managed to calm her down. I imagine you'll be hearing from her about my sins.'

'I'll let you know.' Julia laughed. Her mother was a world-class champion at perceiving an insult in the most innocent comment.

'Ricard rang me.'

'To apologise for the restaurant.'

'Yeah,' she laughed. 'How did you know?'

'He would, he feels bad about you, he's not a bad guy. He doesn't want to live with you, but he doesn't want you to suffer.'

'He doesn't want to feel I hate him, so that he can feel alright screwing his little Cuban tart, everyone good friends, let's be mature, no need for resentment, we've shared so much in the past.'

Xavi held up his hand. 'You need to get over your rage at him, Julia.'

'I know, but you can't just order it to go away, can you?'

'You can decide either to feed it or to try to ignore it.'

'You think I feed it?' Her nephew put his arm round her shoulders.

'Yeah.' She shrugged his arm off. They sat in silence for a while. She looked at some long branches with little white flowers.

'Have you seen this honeysuckle? It always blossoms in February. It's the first thing to flower in the patio. It brings you optimism in mid-winter. That's the pathetic fallacy, isn't it? Having nature reflect human feelings. After Anna died, I told him to get on with his life and he did and, even though I told him to do what he then did, I'm furious at him for it. Does that sound twisted?'

'Pretty twisted.'

'And now,' she said, 'he's screwing some girl half his age. It's not her, you know, I'm not jealous, it's just so embarrassing for him, and humiliating for me I guess, that he's mixed up in something so undignified. What's more, she'll dump him as soon as she's got her Spanish residency papers sorted out.'

'Who knows? Maybe they really like each other.'

'Come on! What have they got to talk about? Just think of all those academic dinner parties we used to go to, you know the people too, Toni and Rosa Blanch, Neus and Robin White, Teresa and David, Alba and Vilis, Isa and Andreu, Maria Tostó and her girlfriend, Jordi Amat. God, I haven't thought of these people for ages. Anyway, instead of me, he turns up with her. I can just see their faces. 'Oh hi, by the way, guys, Julia's not with me any more, this is

122

my new partner.' It'll certainly liven up everyone's breakfast conversation the next morning. Better than reading the Sunday scandal sheets.'

'He's probably changed his life too, Julia. I doubt Estefanía much fancies uni dinners. I imagine she's got him out dancing cumbias in Latin American clubs.'

Julia was genuinely surprised. Perhaps Xavi was right that she fed her anger, dropping worms into its ever-open beak like the blackbird and its baby. She had just supposed that Estefanía ('Is that her name?' she muttered) would replace her in everything, but Ricard had changed too. She smiled at the thought of him dancing the cumbia.

'He was never a great dancer, too stiff round the waist, too self-conscious...'

Like most people her age, Ferran was overweight. A smallish, round man who'd been active with Ricard in *Bandera roja* in the anti-Franco underground. They met in his office in the Autonomous University, one of the new universities built of glass and concrete in the late '60s out in the country among the woods and vines, a modern leprosy asylum to isolate the revolutionary students from infecting the rest of society. To get there, she took a winding road out of Barcelona through the dense Mediterranean jungle that covered the Collserola range behind the coastal plain. Sometimes she came up to walk there and on silent paths of round-topped pine, ash and strawberry trees, with great lianas tangling round each other, she had seen rabbits and grass-snakes and, toward dusk, heard wild boar grunting and rooting in the earth, just four or five kilometres from the city centre.

History could not be escaped in this wilderness, either, for in the Civil War fascists, bosses or alleged fascists, and sometimes just enemies of a particular person, had been brought to this lonely road and shot. Their bodies were recovered by council workers in the morning. In the past, she'd often argued about this with Ferran. No killing was justified, she thought, and these killings just put people off the revolutionary cause, both in the war and ever since. He would concede that some of those killings were unjustified, that there were indeed uncontrolled elements, often murderers crazed or depraved due to capitalist oppression who had been liberated when the prisons were thrown open on the outbreak of the 1936 Revolution. But in any Revolution, a time of convulsive change by definition, such events always took place. In fact, Ferran would go on, in Catalonia the authorities, including the anarchist leaders, had very quickly halted these killings, unlike the Franco side that, both during and after the war, had encouraged such murders. In addition, Ferran would say, raising a finger, in addition he did not believe that these killings affected the outcome of the Revolution. Its opponents would always find 'excesses' to complain about. Those who supported the Revolution were not too worried about the deaths of notorious fascists.

'You cannot construct Durruti's New World,' a younger, fierier Julia objected, 'on the basis of murdering anyone at all. You can't condone killings without trial. Every abuse of human rights weakens your cause. If you do kill, you just carry on the ethics of the same old capitalist system you want to smash.'

'If only, Julia. Yours is an idealist argument. In the dirty real world these things happen.'

'But you don't have to like them, for God's sake.'

And that *liking* of taking justice into their own hands was what she sensed. She had hated the unimaginative student revolutionaries who treated such deaths trivially.

Now Ferran rose from behind his desk in his clean, well-lit office.

'Julia! How good to see you.' His practised voice caressed her. Like everyone, nowadays he wore glasses. She found herself crying as he hugged her and then stroked her hair while she rested her head on a shoulder.

'Oh, oh, I'm such a fool.' She hardly knew this guy, didn't particularly like him, but she'd known him a long time. As he comforted her, she thought of Toni, the inn-keeper in Valeria. She wondered at the wanderings of thoughts and the associations of bodies.

Yellow tape marked off the grave as if it were a crime scene, as they were quick to understand it was. 'But not a cop in sight,' Xavi said. The open hole was wide and shallow like an archaeological dig, not deep and narrow like a grave. From the road, despite the cold, half a dozen people watched the excavation. They were silent and one old woman, a yellow head-scarf knotted under her chin, held a hand over her mouth. Xavi and Julia stopped beside them and watched the work of the volunteer diggers from the Association for Historical Memory. They were standing and squatting round a skeleton, taking shape in the black soil. Unlike Valeria, here in Santa Maria de Descorcoll the burial site was at the entrance to the village. The brown, windowless side-wall of the first house was not twenty yards behind them.

Two people were brushing away soil with what looked like very soft-haired, thin paintbrushes. With a small chisel and hammer, another tapped lightly at the compacted earth before it was brushed. They were young, a man and two women. One woman's anorak and t-shirt had risen up as she crouched with her paintbrush and you could see the bare skin of the small of her back. 'How can she, in this cold,' Julia muttered. Two older men stood above the pit, watching a skull take shape as the earth was brushed aside. Further along, the bones of another skeleton were already visible, little tags with yellow numbers marking exactly where the bones lay. Dirty white buckets full of earth were waiting to be sifted, she supposed. Behind them, between the diggers and the watching villagers, archaeological tools were scattered, a sieve, spades and trowels, cloth and bags. On the far side of the site a blue tarpaulin had been rolled back.

'It's so small,' Julia whispered to Xavi. The woman beside her nodded.

'He was just a boy, we think. We think it was Agustí Rossell, who was twelve.'

'They murdered children,' Julia said.

'They were heartless bastards,' the elderly woman said, not turning her head and without raising her voice in anger. She wasn't arguing, just stating a well-known fact. 'They're going to do a DNA test. They took saliva from Agustí's sister's son Oriol.'

'My God,' said Julia. At least her child had not been murdered. She bent forward, dull pain running through her kidneys and intestines at this stabbing memory of loss.

'Alright?' Xavi said. She nodded, wordless. The pain of hundreds of thousands living with the memory of unjust murders for decades didn't make her own random loss more bearable.

The woman went on: 'When Franco's people got here, they were all fired up, weren't they? I'm too young to remember, but my mother told me all about it. We were the vicious Reds, the Catalans who wanted independence, the priest-killers and nun-rapists. They weren't worried who they killed. No, they weren't.' She shook her head sharply then went on staring at the skull emerging more and more clearly as the bone was tenderly brushed clean.

Julia didn't stop shivering until they were in the village café. They sat down with the people working on the dig, slowly warming up. Julia took off her gloves to wrap her hands round the tall glass of milky coffee.

'This one was easy to arrange,' one of the older men, Ferran's friend the dig leader, was explaining. 'The villagers wanted to take advantage of the new law to excavate the grave. They knew where it was and the Council, run by Esquerra Republicana, supported them.'

'Though the Council had never lifted a finger before,' said the young woman who had been brushing the earth so gently off the skull. Her face was thin, her nose and chin almost sharp, bony. Her hair was short, highlighted by one long lock of hair braided with a red ribbon that fell over an ear. She was no more than twenty-one or two and talked in an intense rush. 'I mean, it's always the people who have to make the running, isn't it? The politicians here only agreed 'cos they had to.'

The dig leader went on: 'So they got in touch with us through the Association for the Recovery of Historical Memory. We're archaeologists and we do these digs in our free time. We could only start this week-end because the weather's been so wet and we needed to wait till it had dried out a bit.'

'And if the Council opposes it?'

'Then you're screwed,' the young woman jumped in. She stared at Julia. Julia liked her passion. She complained, but she didn't just complain. She acted, too. 'None of the political parties are interested. Digging up the truth about the past just opens a can of worms, doesn't it? Makes people ask why the politicians hadn't done anything about it before.'

'But with the new law?'

'The new law?' The young woman tossed her head back in indignation. The ribboned plait flew from over her ear to the back of her head. 'Look, under the new law, there's no reparation for murder. Imagine a government that makes a law that has no consequences for killers. It's just a cynical manoeuvre to try to keep people quiet.'

'Well, it hasn't kept you or me quiet,' Julia said. The fierce young woman's lips twitched in a hint of a grin.

On the way back, driving in the late afternoon, the sun illuminating the backs of the cottony clouds that billowed up over the mountains, she felt they had wasted their time. She'd asked the excavation team if they'd work at Valeria. 'We'd be pleased to,' said Ferran's friend. 'But, as you know, we can't work without legal permission and permission depends on local political decisions.' Her mood felt dark. She could not see how they could get past the forces lined up against them in Valeria.

'We're not going to get anything out of the courts or the local politicians.'

'Don't give up yet,' said Xavi. 'We've hardly started. It's a slow process, you just have to try every avenue.'

'Oh, don't talk to me in clichés, of course I'm not going to give up.'

'Well, it's a cliché because it's true.'

Julia thought of the young woman in the café, so indignant and furious in her speech and so careful and tender in her work. Perhaps it was her forthrightness and directness, interrupting the dig leader because she felt so strongly, that made Julia say: 'You know, I suppose you only encouraged me to pursue the Rogelio case to take my mind off Ricard. You're all the same, you think I need to get over Anna's death and my separation as if they're chronic diseases. Well, they're not. Look, I got married to a man, we lived together for twenty years, we had a daughter, she died' (and her voice cracked on the word, *silly fool*) 'and then he wasn't prepared to suffer the pain with me. OK, perfectly logical, we separate, but what I feel is he treated me like shit and what it revealed was that if he couldn't care for me then, then he never had really cared for me in the past and our whole marriage was a sham.'

They drove on in silence. What she liked about Xavi was that he didn't argue with her, didn't tell her she'd had a stressful day, didn't tell her Ricard wasn't as bad as all that. Because she knew all that and he knew she knew, so she didn't need telling. When they said good-bye outside her flat, they hugged. 'I'll call you,' he said.

Chapter Nine

A wooden cross stood askew, a short plank tied by wire across a longer branch. It was held upright by large stones piled round its base. Wreaths and bunches of flowers lay wilted on the stones and earth. Julia stopped the car, got out and stretched in the sun after the drive up the twisting mountain road. Even in April, snow patches lay in the deep hollows below the mountain ridge in front of her. Above the ridge, in the postcard-blue sky, large birds turned, their wings beating slowly like long-distance swimmers treading water. She screwed up her eyes, then shielded them with her hands, but could not make out if they were eagles, vultures or buzzards. She was more familiar with the smaller birds of her urban wilderness.

She had driven carefully round the hairpin bends, some of which ran under overhanging rock where the sun never reached. This was the route Enrique Jurado had taken, as alive then as she was today, on his last night three months before. She imagined that round each hairpin corner she might have to brake, the road blocked by rocks. She crossed the road to look at the small cairn.

Enrique Jurado,
democratically elected Mayor of Valeria,
was vilely and cowardly murdered at this spot

The words were painted in three lines of black paint on the cross-piece of the makeshift cross. The paint had run from the bottom of three of the letters. The messages on the wreaths and flowers in front of the cross had been washed away by the rain and snow. She poked them. One still read "in loving memory" and "appreciation", though it was not clear who it was from. She peered over the edge of the road, where loose boulders lay on narrow ledges and bushes were rooted improbably in cracks in the rock. Just behind and below the monument was the stunted juniper where the Mayor's body must have caught when the killer had pushed it over the edge. Beyond the tree there was nothing that would have stopped the corpse from tumbling to the bottom of the ravine, just like one more boulder. Stones lay shattered all down the steep slope, hammered into pieces by the frost, snow and rain. She hugged herself as she turned to look up above the road, from where boulders might fall in storms and from where the murderer must have stepped down that winter night. The air was cold, despite the sun, or was it just the chill of knowing she was at a murder scene? A bird was calling. She could not name it.

It reminded her of the two other murder sites she had seen already this year, the communal grave at Santa Maria de Descorcoll, clinical with its volunteer archaeologists in jeans and pony-tails and its gentle, wild girl with her back bared and red braid in her hair, brushing the dry soil off the skeletons with shattered skulls; and the forest glade on the other side of the village, also marked by a makeshift wooden sign, though not a cross. She remembered the fierce emotion she had felt there. It was a completely illogical feeling and she was suspicious of it, for she had not known Rogelio, nor cared about him. She was wary of the danger of transferring the emotions she suffered in her personal life onto the search for justice for Rogelio and his comrades. And, as always, her mind returned to the first violent death in her life, but that had been an accident. She started the car engine again to drive quickly away from that memory, awakened by the loneliness of this murder scene.

She parked in the square. The tattered flag on the

Town Hall no longer blew horizontal at half-mast, but hung in windless air from the top of the flagstaff. There were no brown and green *Guardia Civil* cars parked in front. No dogs approached her, though one lay dribbling into the dust under the arches. Several people were sitting out in the sun at the red plastic tables in front of the café. A young couple leaned back in their dark glasses and loosened the silvery zips on their mountain anoraks. The sign protesting *THIS IS VALERIA NOT PARIS OR LONDON* still hung above the café door. That had not changed. Several of the houses on the square had their shutters open: the second-home owners had come up for the Easter holidays.

She locked the car, hooked her bag on her shoulder and set off down the street towards Toni's inn. Down this street too, shutters were open and cars parked. The fat woman she had talked to sat on a pile of plump cushions on a wooden chair at the door of her house. Julia had hoped to avoid her and she did. The woman stared as Julia approached, made no response to her '*Buenos días*' and probably stared at her back as she walked on down the street.

Again, Julia pulled the string on the bell by the *pensión* door, again she heard it tinkle, again there was no reply. Breathing in the welcome smell of treated wood in the old house, not lingering this time, shouting 'Hello,' she walked on through to the back room. There was no-one there either, nor out the back where the hens in their wire enclosure pecked the dust, jerking their heads from side to side like animated dolls. She left her bag on the settee where she had fallen asleep on her first visit and went back towards the café.

She had remembered the village in every single detail and it was strange to feel that the village had no memory of her. She sat down at one of the tables in the sun in the square. She had a couple of hours to wait until her appointment.

The man at the next table leaned across and said: '*Señora*, you'll have to order inside.' He boasted a thin moustache and wore round, metal-rimmed glasses, which made him look like a Falangist bureaucrat, and was leaning back, legs crossed, and smoking while the blonde woman opposite him finished her lunch. She was made up with mascara and rouge, her hooped ear-rings waved in the breeze and she wore a neat, pale jacket, as if she was sipping an aperitif on the Rambla de Catalunya.

'Is the food good?' Julia asked.

'It's good,' the woman answered. 'Simple, but good. Are you visiting?' She spoke with a foreign accent.

'Yes. You too?'

'No, no,' the man said. 'We're in the category of summer residents, though sometimes we come in the winter too. We've had a house in the village for six years and come up from Zaragoza whenever we can. This place is paradise, the mountains, the birds, the fresh air. We're great bird-watchers and you can see all the Pyrenean mountain birds here. Just this morning I spotted a Lammergeier floating on a thermal over there.' He waved his arm toward the mountain and tapped the binoculars on the table. 'What brings you here?'

'I've come to see the new Mayor. My great-uncle is one of the people killed during the Civil War and buried in the forest. I was hoping we could get him reburied.'

'Ah,' the man said. Perhaps she'd been too direct, she thought. After all, they were having lunch on a spring day and talking of pretty birds. They didn't want to be reminded of the dead. He drew on his cigarette and the woman finished her mouthful.

'I don't think you're going to get very far,' she said.

'Why not?'

'You know about our trouble, the death of our Mayor, Enrique?'

'Yes, I was here two months ago.'

'You know,' the man interrupted, 'it's a difficult question and I do sympathise with your concern. But it was so long ago. If you want my advice, I'd say 'let sleeping dogs lie'. This is a wounded town and no-one welcomes an outsider who might rock the boat.' He must be the lawyer, thought Julia. One of those pompous professions.

'Are you talking from experience?'

'I live here.'

'I mean, have you experienced not being welcome?'

Neither of them said anything. 'You see, I was rather hoping,' Julia added, 'that burying the Civil War dead might help resolve problems.'

A man tumbled out of the café, mumbling to himself as he shuffled across the square. Despite his unshaven, lined face and unsteady walk, his trousers were ironed in a military crease. Julia recognised him as the drunken man at the bar who'd confused Iraq and Iran on her first visit. 'Pinochet,' she thought she heard, then distinctly heard his muttered plaint as he passed them: 'Oh, what's to become of me, Pinochet? Poor Pinochet, all alone, who'll look after you, Pinochet, when you're old?' The man banged his chest with his clenched fist as he stumbled away.

'Did I hear right?' Julia asked.

The couple at the next table smiled. The man's dryness seemed to lift. 'Yes, he's one of the few who lives here all year round, Ambrosio, ex-Legionnaire, ex-jailbird, they say he used to be a pick-pocket in Barcelona. He's harmless now, to everyone except himself.' He stood up. 'I'm going in to pay. Shall I order you anything?'

'Yes, great, order me the set meal—what you were having and a bottle of water.'

As he went into the bar, the blonde woman leaned towards Julia. 'My husband always says it's paradise here and I always remind him, it would be if it weren't for the people. Personally, I agree with you, why not rebury those poor people? The relatives would have their peace of mind, wouldn't they? But now everyone's still shaken by this murder business. By the way, I'm Brigitte.'

'Julia.' They nodded at each other from table to table. 'Have the police made any progress, do you know?'

'They're worse than bloody useless, as far as I can see. Look at us. They've interrogated us three times, you know, but they just go round in circles. They've examined everyone's guns, inspected the soles of everyone's boots, taken down countless statements, poked around every corner of the village. Of course people gossip and everyone's got a theory about who did it.'

'What's yours?'

The woman laughed. She said in dramatic triumph: 'We were there that night, on the road where the murder took place.'

'You saw him!'

'No, we didn't see anyone, it was pitch-dark. We were driving up to Valeria that night and had to stop because there were rocks blocking the road. We got out of the car to move them. The killer must have been lurking nearby. They've been over our statements with a fine tooth comb, we're suspects of course, but there's nothing else we can tell them. Of course, my husband was one of many who had a dispute with the Mayor. We wanted to register as residents, because we were planning to retire up here and wanted to have a vote to make sure the new housing estate didn't go ahead. You know, they've started building a new estate on that side of the village.' She waved her hand towards the bar. 'There was something fishy going on there: the Mayor definitely had some kind of interest in it. Talk no ill of the dead.' She drew an airy sign of the cross, then leaned forward to Julia to talk ill of him. 'But I wouldn't be surprised if he'd taken a backhander to reclassify what was agricultural land for building. They're talking about 20 houses. They've already laid out the streets. A developer from Barcelona. You know, now they've cemented over the coast, they're starting on the mountains.'

'So you think it was an ecologist who killed him?' Julia said.

'An ecologist?' Brigitte laughed. 'Well, yes, I hadn't thought of it like that. It could be, I suppose, though the only real ecologist round here's the forest ranger and I don't think he's against developing the village. In fact, he wants to open a hotel himself. Half the village disliked the Mayor and had their reasons. I've just given you ours. It sounds bad, I know, but I really don't mind if they don't find out who did it, because finding someone will just make the atmosphere worse here. It's been a nightmare as it is.'

Her husband came out of the bar chatting to another shorter man, bald on top but with hair growing long over his ears. They came towards the two women. Brigitte, leaning forward, and the shorter man exchanged two kisses, with the normal greetings. 'Hey, how ARE you? When did you get here?... Drop round later on if you're free...' Then the new man was introduced to Julia. 'Just visiting. Julia Herrero.' 'Miguel Vázquez.' They shook hands.

The lawyer told Julia he'd ordered her the set meal, vegetable soup followed by beef fillet with potatoes, and put his arm under his wife's elbow to help her up. 'Are you here for a few days?' the blonde woman said. Julia nodded. 'Look me up if you've got nothing to do.' Brigitte waved coquettishly with her free arm without looking round as she was led away.

Miguel Vázquez sat down at the table vacated by Brigitte and the lawyer. He leaned back in his chair and said into the air, 'just waiting for my coffee.' The woman in a damp, dirty apron who bustled sideways out of the door, her fleshy arms bobbling as she walked fast with her feet turned out like a duck's, carried the paper tablecloth, the cutlery with a paper napkin wrapped round it, glass, bottle of water, Julia's first course and Miguel Vázquez's coffee all together on a tin tray.

'You know how to save yourself a journey, *señora* Pilar,' Julia said. The plump woman put the tray on Miguel Vázquez's table, gave him his small cup of black coffee and then shot a look at Julia while she clipped the paper tablecloth with red plastic pegs to the under-side of her table.

'Do I know you?'

'I was up here a few weeks ago.'

'We've had so many people since the Mayor's death.'

'Good for business, then.'

'You could say that, but who wants to make money from someone else's misfortune?'

'That's true. I was up here to see Jaime *el Moreno* about the people in the glade.'

'Oh, yes. When I saw you today, I thought you were a foreigner. We get a few walkers and bird-watchers in the spring. When we first had the bird-watchers with their binoculars, we thought they were French spies, imagine.'

'Why did you think I was a foreigner?'

'No offence, but because of your white hair. Most women dye it, don't they?'

'I guess, but why conceal your age?' Julia said. 'What about the Mayor's death? Is that sorted out at all?'

'No, Madam. I'll bring your second course in ten minutes.' And she left abruptly.

'Don't mind Pilar,' Miguel Vázquez said. 'The murder's put everyone on edge. I'm a doctor, work in a hospital in Zaragoza and deal with death every day, but I feel the same, it's put me on edge too. You don't want death in your social life, do you?'

'No,' said Julia. 'No, you certainly don't.' She took a sip of the minestrone. 'You were the doctor on the mountain road that night, weren't you?' He nodded. 'What a shock! I mean, he could have killed you too.'

'Don't believe I haven't thought about it. In fact, I was reluctant to drive on. There was something odd about it. The guy wouldn't identify himself and wore this funny lamp on his helmet, as if he were a miner or something. I think, if I'd been on my tod, I'd have walked up to him, seen who it was and set to helping him. If I had, I guess he'd have killed me too. But I had my daughter with me, she's only nine, and because of her I wanted to get out of there.'

'But you heard him talk. Couldn't you recognise him?'

'I've thought about it every day since. In fact, the police asked me to spend a few days in the village and, without appearing to, get round to talk to everyone to see if I recognised their voice. I took two days off work and did just as they asked, but I couldn't recognise the voice. It was disguised, you see. On the mountain, I mean. The man said very little and spoke hoarsely as if he had a cold. It could even have been a woman, because it was obviously a put-on voice: that was one of the things that made me feel uneasy at the time, I realised afterwards.'

'Some experience!'

'I find myself listening to everyone still. For instance, I listened to you when I heard you talking with Brigitte and Fernando just now and compared your voice in my mind with the voice that night. The problem is, the more I think about it, the less I can recall exactly what that voice was like. But I still think I might recognise it if I heard it again, despite the disguise.'

'I imagine something you've heard is not as clear as something seen.'

'If I hadn't been with my daughter, I probably wouldn't have got out of there alive; and if I had been alone and got out, I'd be a prime suspect for the murder. But no-one believes you take your daughter along when you're out to shoot someone.' He laughed. Julia had one of the abrupt flashes that overcame her after Anna's death, but that had slowly become less frequent. This was the second that day, a gut feeling of grief that expressed itself as a physical spasm. She bent forward over the minestrone. She could feel Anna cuddling against her shoulder and smell the freshness of her skin and hair. This was not *thinking* of her, with the attached self-pity of dwelling on tragedy; rather it was an uncontrollable, direct, physical *feeling* of memory.

'Are you alright?' Miguel Vázquez said, half-rising.

'Yes, fine,' Julia said. 'The horror of the situation just hit me.' She forced a smile to convince him. 'Fine, really.'

Julia was the last person having lunch at the half-dozen tables. Miguel Vázquez had wandered off across the square. The couple in new anoraks had picked up small rucksacks and followed the path Pinochet had taken down towards the river. The bar door opened and she heard chatter from inside as Pilar brought her little tub of yoghurt and her coffee.

'You've still got the sign up, Pilar.'

'To remind the new Mayor.'

'You're still paying the old rate, then?' Pilar nodded. 'Don't go. I'm sure you can spare me five minutes now the meals are over. I just wanted to ask your opinion. What do you think I should do? You know about everything that goes on in the village.'

'I am not the person you should ask, *señora*.'

O.K., nothing to lose, Julia thought. 'I read you celebrated the Mayor's death here in the bar, the morning after, that there was a little party with some of the villagers.'

Pilar leaned forward, placing her hands on the table. The paper tablecloth crinkled under the force of her grip. 'That's a lie. It's the shit they write in the newspapers.' She spoke with the vehemence of someone shouting, but the voice came out not loud but suppressed in a fierce hiss.

'I never believed it myself. You must have had a hard time of it,' Julia said as lightly as she could.

'Don't soft-soap me, *señora*. I'm not a complete imbecile.'

'I never thought you were. You know why I'm here, I just want to get my great-uncle buried.'

'Then why are you asking me questions about the murder?'

'For crying out loud!' hissed back Julia, banging her fist on the plastic table. *Two could play at this game.* The coffee jumped and slopped into the saucer, wetting the sachet of sugar. 'Because, don't you see? We can't move forward on the three poor sods in the forest glade until the business of the Mayor's death is cleared up. I thought you might help.'

'So where the police have failed, you're the clever-clogs who's going to solve the case, are you?'

When the sun moved behind the buildings, Julia got up and went in to pay. There were several people in the bar. *'Buenas tardes,'* she said in general. In the card game, at the same back table as in February, to her surprise she recognised Toni the inn-keeper. His striped shirt, the incipient bald patch and glasses, the straggly curling hair made him recognisable even from behind among the old men with their short back-and-sides. Her first instinct was to approach him, but she didn't. There was time enough later. She paid Pilar, leaving her the change of a ten-euro note on an 8.50 meal.

Town Hall was a grand name to apply to the building. Downstairs was the pharmacy office. She read on the door that the doctor visited every Wednesday morning. There was a line of ancient mismatched chairs in the corridor and a wall scuffed with years of the feet and dirty hand-marks of people waiting. Upstairs, she found a meeting-room with two stacks of chairs against the wall, a top table that was no more than a board on two trestles and, on the wall behind the table, a large photo of a young King Juan Carlos with a purple sash across his chest. The shelves to the left of the door were stacked with a medley of dusty tourist booklets and leaflets sent from the Regional Council, ash-trays and plastic cups. The top shelf held a row of cardboard box-files, like the ones her worms had been sent in from Albacete, probably with the minutes of Council meetings from time immemorial. Laid out on an old oak table, its knotted wood worn smooth and spattered with dark stains, were copies of the Spanish Constitution and the Highway Code. The only public room in the village, she imagined it had been the one occupied by the police during their investigation into the Mayor's murder. They had a good view at least, across the fields to the ravine and, beyond the ravine, to the forest coating the mountain's flank.

Two other doors announced their purpose with typed notices: *Secretario* and *Alcalde*. The Secretary's door was ajar, but unoccupied. The small room was little more than jumbled piles of papers around a computer. Who ever said computers would save paper and bring order? The building felt deserted, with something of the air of a place rapidly abandoned after disaster. She tapped her knuckles on the other door, with no confidence now that anyone would be there. A wasted journey. But at once a woman opened the door, extended her hand without smiling and said: '*Señora* Herrero, I assume. Please come in.'

This office was as ordered as its occupant. The Mayor was about 45, dressed in a brown knee-length skirt, high-necked white blouse with a brooch-clasp at the neck and a suit jacket in a rather lighter brown than the skirt. Her hair was shortish, practical, showing ears enlivened by a gold stud in each lobe. The conservative impression of a modern provincial lady was confirmed, when Julia glanced down at the tiled floor, by flat shoes with just a hint of a heel. Unlike most Spanish women in public life, who seemed to feel the need to dress like a strip-club hostess from the ankle down. There were a couple of slim, coloured files on the table, an armchair with a reading lamp, shelves with neatly aligned box-files and official-looking books and the inevitable photo of Juan Carlos, obligatory in every public office either out of insecurity that the monarchy might be forgotten or just to conceal the pale mark left when the dictator's portrait had to be taken down.

'I'm very sorry to hear about your husband,' Julia began, as the Mayor sat down behind her desk, her fingers touching together lightly in an attentive pose. The woman nodded and said nothing at all, so Julia went on. 'I was

142

surprised to hear it was you who had taken over as Mayor.'

'I was the Deputy-Mayor, señora Herrero, and general life goes on after the death of an individual.'

'Yes, of course. But it must be difficult for you.' Again there was silence, in which the Mayor shrugged almost imperceptibly. It didn't look like Julia was getting anywhere with the personal approach.

'You probably know why I'm here. The Law on Historical Memory has given certain powers to local judges to order the opening of improvised Civil War graves, the identification of people in them and their reburial. Me and my nephew have applied for the reburial of my mother's uncle, who we have good reason to believe is one of three people in the glade in the pine forest. As you know, these procedures take time, especially when there is a difference of opinion in the middle. I know your husband was opposed to the reburial in thc ccmetery of the three people in the glade. I was hoping to discuss it with you. If we had your support, everything would be greatly facilitated.'

'Don't think, señora, that things are as easy as you suggest.'

Julia fought back the impulse to spit out, 'But of course things are easy.' Instead she just said to herself without moving her lips: *But of course things are easy. You just say, "obviously they should be properly buried. Let's get it done."* She looked out of the window onto the square and did move her lips to say:

'Nice view. How long were you deputy-mayor, señora?'

'Three years. I stood with my husband at the last election, though I don't see the relevance of the question.'

'It probably has none, but I was just wondering why your husband was opposed to reburying what remains of three bodies murdered and dumped in the wood seventy years ago.' She looked quickly back at the Mayor, but the deliberate crudeness of Julia's phrasing didn't make her twitch or blink. Instead, she sighed before delivering a speech with the apparent patience of a lawyer explaining reality to a deluded client.

'It's easy to pass a general law sitting in the comfort of the Madrid Parliament, but when you're involved in a particular local situation, a responsible mayor has to take into account the effect of any action on the town as a whole. As you probably know, if you've read anything in the papers about my husband's death or talked to any villager, Valeria is divided. Half the village is at loggerheads with the other half and there's not one fault-line, but several. It's not just one question, such as the property development or the Civil War deaths, but several questions that divide people. In this situation, the utmost discretion is required when dealing with difficult problems. People do not take kindly to an outsider coming in and just demanding his supposed rights. It's my responsibility as Mayor to seek to smooth over any rough edges, and not to allow provocative behaviour to damage our peaceful coexistence any further.'

The Mayor almost got passionate with this last sentence. Her voice rose a pitch and her fingers separated half an inch as she reached its climax. Julia's mind jumped to three or four responses, but all of them were 'provocative' and she kept her mouth shut. She felt like punching the complacent bitch on the nose, but she needed to find a way to win this woman to her side, or at least to neutralise her.

'I can understand your problems. After just a couple of days here, I've experienced some of these divisions.'

'You can't begin to imagine. They are fault-lines that go right the way back, right to the Civil War, and now they've ended up in murder.'

'You think your husband's death has something to do with the Civil War?'

'I didn't say that. Don't twist my words, *señora* Herrero. I meant that the village has had multiple divisions ever since the Civil War.'

After a pause, Julia asked: 'So how do you think you can... smooth over these divisions, these rough edges?'

'My late husband gave everything for this village. And it's not just a phrase, as he gave his life. He was an open, frank man and said what he thought was good for the village. I'm proud to share his vision,' and she nodded towards the silver-framed photo on her desk. 'We have to look to the future. There are new people coming in. The older generation, living in an isolated mountain community with its set ways and festering hates, is dying off. The old economic activities, livestock and agriculture, are in decline. It's tourism that represents the future. We have to exploit the fresh air, the natural beauty of the village, the wildlife and scenery. In our hotel, every year we have had increasing numbers of bird-watchers from England or German executives wanting to wander in the forest, we have people from Madrid or Zaragoza interested in second homes to enjoy nature and escape the stresses of modern life.'

'It's certainly a beautiful village. I can see its tourism potential. So why in that case is the new property development halted?'

'Were you thinking of buying a house?' the Mayor asked.

'I wouldn't rule it out,' Julia said and, saying it, realised perhaps she wouldn't. 'But what's happened to the new houses? The project seems to have stopped.'

'My husband stopped them.' Julia's surprise was real. 'He did?' She had assumed the PP Mayor would be fully in favour of such a development, with the land reclassified for residential rather than agricultural use. And just a couple of hours before, Brigitte had said as much.

'It surprises you, doesn't it? I suppose, like most of you city liberals, you think all PP mayors are in favour of building development.'

'That is usually the case.'

'Not here. We are conservatives, *señora*. We like to conserve. We want new inhabitants in the village, but there's a number of old and abandoned houses that can be done up. My husband was working with people to renovate houses. That was his main priority. If we want to develop tourism here, we have to conserve our environment. A new housing estate is not the best way to go about it.'

'So why was permission given to start the project in the first place?'

'It wasn't. A group from Zaragoza was advised by a local resident that there would be no obstacle and that if they bought the land and went ahead, as a *fait accompli* they would overcome any objections.'

It was a reasonable assumption, Julia thought. This was not a country where building projects met much opposition. Most people seemed to think that the best way to deal with mud and bugs was to cover the earth with cement. Most councils were perfectly happy to benefit from the increased taxes that accompanied more housing and many a Mayor thought it was quite reasonable to accept a gift for easing along the reclassification of unprofitable agricultural land to productive building plots.

'The consortium from Zaragoza must have had a shock.'

The Mayor's head and shoulders moved slightly, which Julia presumed was agreement.

'But how's tourism going to help the people who've

always lived here? Aren't new, wealthier people just going to exacerbate divisions?'

'I firmly believe that the old rancour and conflict engendered by our fratricidal war have to be finally overcome. All this business of the Law on Historical Memory is irresponsibly stirring up conflicts that were dying away naturally. Time is a great healer, as long as we don't have demagogues forcing us to live in the past. If things go on like they are, I can well see us going through a new Civil War.'

'As you say, though, the town is divided. But take my colleague in this application, señor Jaime, he doesn't seem to me to be someone harbouring a grudge. He just wants to see his aunt buried with a proper tombstone and then he'll be satisfied.'

At the mention of Jaime el Moreno, the Mayor's elbows took up a symmetrical position on the leather-covered writing table and her fingers again pressed together in the form of a church steeple. Her finger-tips turned white and two red dots burned on her cheeks.

'Let me tell you something I don't think you understand. It's not your fault. How could you understand?' she replied. 'You may well imagine like Jaime that the people buried in the forest were paragons of virtue. Don't get me wrong, I regret their violent and extra-judicial deaths, but these were people with blood on their hands. When the anarchists came up from Barcelona and attacked this village in July 1936, they rounded up everyone, and there were five times as many inhabitants then as now, and declared all property cooperative, all land was to be worked together. The priest and the Mayor and two Civil Guards were taken down to the bridge by the river and brutally murdered. And don't think the Mayor was a big feudal estate owner, he was living here and working his own land.

He himself took his cows up to the high pastures in the spring. He was in favour of order not anarchy, so he was fingered by the poorer, more resentful villagers and killed. It's easy in this country to stir up envy and resentment. Envy's our national vice, isn't it? One of those outsiders who came up here from Barcelona, stirring up trouble, bringing conflict and blood, was your great-uncle, someone who had nothing at all to do with this village. When the Nationalists recaptured the village a few weeks later, they took revenge. It wasn't the best way to do things, but you should be able to grasp the bitterness caused by the anarchist murders and it was understandable that in time of war a few hotheads took things into their own hands. Now you're suggesting that a funeral procession be organised, that all the press will be here, that people come up from Barcelona with their long, wavy white hair and red and black flags and organise the reburial of these murderers as if they were saintly victims.'

'I haven't suggested that at all.'

'But that's the reality of what will happen and it will set back any hope of reconciliation for another generation.'

Julia had not expected to be on the defensive in this dialogue. Not only was the Mayor pleading the practical line of letting sleeping dogs lie; she was taking the high moral ground over history. Julia raised her hand. She assumed her most teacherly tone.

'I can assure you, *señora* Carmela, we have no intention of making any public demonstration with anarchists or flags. For our part, at the most it would be a dozen members of my family, led by my mother, who is 82 years old and always votes for your political party and knew Rogelio when she was a girl. I just cannot understand how you expect there to be reconciliation if people cannot bury their dead.'

'That's because you are an outsider, *señora*, and reduce events to simple formulas. You don't understand the terrible damage done to this village.'

'But you're an outsider, too. You came with your husband ten years ago.'

'Me? Oh no, you are totally misinformed.' Carmela laughed for the first time in the interview. Perhaps, thought Julia, it was for the first time since her husband had been killed. 'No, no, my dear, you've got it completely wrong. I'm not an outsider. My husband was, he came from Zaragoza, where I met him and where we lived when we were first married. My family's been here for generations. My grandfather was the Mayor of this village for seventeen years. He was one of the people murdered by the reds in July 1936. May he rest in peace.' She crossed herself automatically, her lips mumbling silently before she kissed her thumb, as she stood to terminate the interview.

Chapter Ten

The river was flowing fiercely, now that the first spring days were beginning to thaw the mountain snow. Julia leaned on the stone parapet and watched the water bouncing, ferocious and transparent, like people should be but weren't, off the rounded, smooth boulders. The Mayor was not a force they were going to be able to move. Jaime had told her that by phone: 'By all means go and see her, but I can tell you now, you won't get anywhere. She'll listen to you, though.' Carmela had listened, she'd even talked. Julia played over in her mind the conversation, the exact words already slipping away, memory so recent but already entering that imprecision where the sharp reality of the original began to blur like a breathed-over glass. Nor was it a neutral imprecision. As you told a memory to yourself or to others, it became moulded to your own words and preconceptions. Just imagine what happened to a memory after seventy years.

Julia heard a rustle and looked down at the gravel and coarse grass beside the water. She caught the flash of a small mammal darting away into reeds. She wondered just where the four people had been shot. The Mayor, the priest and two Civil Guards. She looked back up the path at the village houses, dark square bulks against the darkening sky. They of course were not buried here, but safely in the cemetery, the white-walled cemetery with its cypresses on a bare hill across the river. Not like Rogelio. And the injustice struck her again, with the same force as it had several times in these recent weeks since she first visited Valeria, making her gasp.

She rang Xavi on her mobile. 'Listen, no joy with the Mayor, but I think I've found something out.'

'Tell me.'

'The Mayor wasn't in on the property development. Quite the contrary. They started it without permission and he stopped it.'

'You sure?'

'It needs checking, because I met the lawyer's wife too today and she told me that he was in favour, but Carmela the new Mayor told me that her husband was against the development and it's still halted because she's following the same line.'

'So, if it's true, it means the people behind the property development have a motive for murder.'

'They've got a motive, but don't jump to conclusions. Murder's not just committed for money.'

Xavi laughed. 'If it's not for money, it's for sex...'

'Or envy. Or,' Julia paused and here she wasn't just repeating their previous conversation in Barcelona, in the comfort of talking to a close friend. Now she realised what hating someone in a village for years and years could do to you. 'Or being worn down. Drops of water drip-drip-dripping on your forearm year after year. All quite tolerable until one day h-w-oof, there's an explosion, because hate accumulates drop by drop until it finally reaches breaking point.'

'Quite a speech, Julia! But it's still more likely to be money and property.'

'I know. The Mayoress said it was a construction group in Zaragoza working with someone here.'

'I'll see if I can find out anything. How are things otherwise?' Xavi asked.

'I'm not sure. I'm OK. I'll call you later.'

'Be careful.'

She rang off because she'd seen a man in a straw hat walking down the dirt path from the houses towards her.

She shivered, in the cold and in awareness of the deaths that embraced the village. The presence of another person made her perceive her solitude, a stranger standing by the rushing river. The man had a blanket wrapped round his waist, with the end resting over one shoulder. He leaned beside her on the bridge's stone parapet.

'*Buenas tardes.*'

'*Buenas tardes.*'

She recognised him: it was the man who had tried to calm the row in the bar on the last morning of her first visit to Valeria. His white hair was neatly combed back. His face was long and lean. He cleaned his glasses on a piece of tissue that he chucked into the water.

'Chilly,' he said.

'I'll say.'

'We only get three months of summer up here. And even in August you get cold nights.'

'Have you always lived here?' The man took his time to answer, as if he was repeating the question to himself.

'No, I went to Barcelona like most of the village. There was nothing here for us when we were young. I drove a taxi for 40 years. Not a bad life, you get to meet all sorts. If you need a bit more cash, you work a few extra hours; and if you need time off for the family, you can always take a few hours. I sold my licence for 5 million pesetas and retired back here. Mid-winter, though, we usually go back to the city. It's tough here in winter. The wind drives the snow up to here against the north-facing walls.' He raised his arm above his head. Then they looked together at the tumbling water. The man lit a cigarette and threw the match into the stream. He offered one to Julia, but she shook her head.

'You know why I'm here?'

'You've made no secret of it, *señora.*'

'And what do you think?' The man continued to look at

the water. He wasn't in any rush. He even drew slowly on his cigarette. You wouldn't want to jump into his taxi if you were late for a meeting.

'About what?' he said at last, while the air seemed to chill by the second and the dark to roll down the mountain. There were houses and electric light with wood stoves just a hundred yards away, but Julia felt they were alone in a mountain wilderness. The killer must have felt that on the night of the Mayor's murder. She felt cold, but knew enough not to reply. He'd tell her what he'd come to say in his own good time.

'Most of us are related here, you know. I'm 72 years old and was born just before the start of the war, but of course my mother knew everyone involved. No-one talked about it afterwards. You know, after the war we had a big detachment of the *Guardia Civil* stationed up here. They were here because of the *maquis* who came across the border from France. No-one talked about anything that had happened, people just got on with living. Times were hard and we kept our mouths shut because we didn't want any more problems than those we had already. The Dúrcal brothers would strut around the village with their shiny boots and pistols. They were worse than the *Guardia Civil*. You tried to steer clear of the Dúrcals at all costs, but if you came across them, you did what they told you to do. We all knew they'd done bad things in the war, but no-one ever told kids like me the details of what had happened, you just picked it up. My mother had the communal oven, where the women brought their dough to be baked into bread. There were always women chatting, joking while they gave the bread a second kneading on the long table. It was warm in there and smelled of fresh bread and the pine and furze branches we used to heat the oven. I remember one day, there were half a dozen women waiting for the oven to get up to the right heat, when one of the Dúrcals came in, Atilano the younger brother. He was the one with more lip, though after his stroke, he didn't have much lip, he dragged himself round dribbling and people enjoyed ignoring him. Even so, he never received what he really deserved.'

The man spat in the water and was silent again while they both thought what Atilano's just desserts might have been. 'Anyway, one of the women, really just a girl, was complaining about the price of beans. You know, back then, as well as the communal oven, the village had a grocer's shop, which sold everything—or nothing, because there was little to buy and even less to buy it with. Of course, if you had money or connections, like them, the Dúrcals, you could buy on the black market in Zaragoza. This Atilano liked to mock the women, he'd show them nylon stockings he'd bought in the city for his wife, bananas or a chicken, which were all luxuries in those days. The truth is, if it weren't for hunting, and that was mostly illegal, most families would have died of hunger. Even so, people had a rough time.

"Hey, you," this evil bastard spat out at the girl, "you're insulting the Caudillo."

"Who me? No, not at all, *señor* Dúrcal. I'd be the last person to insult anyone and even less our *señor* Caudillo." And she crossed herself nervously.

Atilano, the wicked beast, went up to her. I was still a kid aged about eight and was standing in the entrance with a basket of firewood loaded on my shoulders, and the women scurried apart. He stopped in front of the girl and said with this tone of scorn that he used: "There are a lot of ungrateful people in this village, aren't there, girl? Our Caudillo works day and night to protect us from the atheist anarchists and communists, and there are scum who can't think of anything better to do than complain about the price of beans."

I didn't know who the anarchists, communists or atheists were, I only knew they were bad people who wanted to kill us all. You can't imagine, *señora*, the ignorance there was then. One of the women said: "Leave her be, Don Atilano, she didn't mean anything."

"And you keep your lip buttoned. We have to learn to think a little and be respectful when we open our big mouths, don't we?"

And he grabbed the girl by the arm and squeezed. You could see he was hurting her, but she didn't cry out, though she bit her lip and tears started forming in her eyes. He twisted her arm suddenly so she fell to her knees and cried out. I was standing like an idiot in the doorway wondering what was going to happen, my mouth open, the basket of fire-wood still on my shoulder, when Atilano turns to me and he says: "'We're going to teach this little bitch a lesson, so all the rest of you remember it." He has his eyes fixed on me while he talks and like a fool I nod. "Boy, don't stand there gawking like a halfwit, go and get some soap and scissors. Dance!"

I threw down the firewood and ran into the house to get what he wanted. He had the woman face down, while he sat on her back and wrenched her hair back. He grabbed the soap from me and shoved it in her mouth. He was completely out of his mind, shouting and swearing: "Think yourself lucky, you ungrateful whore, I'm being charitable. You insulted the Caudillo and you're going to have your mouth washed out. And the rest of you can stay and watch, so you remember." And he pulled her head back, with tears racing down her cheeks and sobs stifled by the soap in her mouth, and hacked off great chunks of hair. The scissors jabbed into her scalp and neck and dotted her skin with blood. When he left her lying there, moaning and not daring to raise her head, he flung the scissors across the room and they hit one of the women on her leg, it was only chance it was the handle and not the sharp end and he strutted away, the arrogant son of a bitch: "Don't forget, ladies. Gratitude, gratitude." '

The man fell silent. Julia was freezing, but she hadn't wanted to interrupt the story.

'My God,' she muttered. 'What a bastard!'

'Yes, but the worst is there were five or six of us there and we did nothing. He ordered me to bring the soap and scissors and I did what he ordered.'

'You can't blame yourself. You were only a child. No-one could have done anything under the circumstances.'

'Maybe not. But it made us ashamed.'

'What's your name?'

'Anacleto. They call me Cleto the Oven, because there's another man called Cleto *el Tomás*, because his mother was called Tomasa.'

'Anyway,' Julia said, 'the Dúrcals are dead. No-one can treat people like that now.'

'Of course not, but all of us here in this village carry these things in our hearts, however hard we've tried to forget.'

Julia said: 'I'm frozen.' They walked together back up the slope. And Cleto said the rest of what he had to say. Maybe it was easier to say personal things when you were walking along and not looking at someone.

'However hard we've tried to forget, we can't. It drags up base passions, even among the mildest of us. I think you should be careful going round asking people about the past. It's true the Dúrcals are dead, but their sympathisers and families aren't.'

'Someone must know who killed the Mayor, though.

And once that's cleared up, maybe now we can finally get the three in the glade buried.' She heard shrillness in her own voice and recalled Pilar the café owner's comment earlier: *you're the clever-clogs who's going to solve it, are you?* But Cleto remained calm.

'*Señora*, you're thrusting your hand into a wasps' nest.'

'You're not politely threatening me, Cleto?'

'You're quite wrong. I'm on your side. I'm warning you what some of these people are capable of.'

'You mean Folches?'

'Folches, perhaps. Not just him.'

In the square, he stopped and said: 'I live down there, the new metal door painted red. If you need anything, you know where to find me.' And they shook hands.

Later, she lay in bed in the *posada* in the same room she had occupied two months before. A dog barked and was answered by another. For a few minutes they seemed to pass messages to each other across the village night. Then the barking petered out, as if the answers were unsatisfactory or there was nothing more to say. In the background, you could hear what sounded like waves crashing onto a pebble beach, but she knew it was the sound of the wind whipping the high leaves of the poplars that stood like sentinels along the stream.

She had not been the only guest at the inn this time, but Toni had greeted her as if she were an old friend, with a hug and two kisses. 'I saw your bag and hoped it might be you.'

'I saw you too, playing cards in the bar.'

'I must have been winning or I might have been more aware of my surroundings, especially of the return of one of my favourite guests.' He was looking at her intently and Julia looked back, then smiled. It was the first time in years she had felt any interest in a man. She paused, not knowing

157

what to say. Then she smiled back at him and said without thinking: 'I'll think about it,' answering his unsaid question.

Seven people sat at Toni's supper table; a middle-aged couple who Toni introduced as neighbours, two teachers hiking a Pyrenean trail and a single man, serious, ill-at-ease with himself. Julia wondered if she came across like that, someone who wasn't quite sure what to do or say, someone a bit awkward, not at home in their own skin. The couple explained where they'd come from that day on the long-distance route round the side of the snowy peak, and the twenty kilometres to the west they hoped to cover tomorrow. The woman enthused: 'It was wonderful, on some stretches we walked in short sleeves in the hot sun with our feet in the snow. I love that feeling. Hot on top and cold below.' Their thick wool socks were drying on the back of a chair in front of the stove. Everyone was smiling, even Julia, even the ill-at-ease man, at her enthusiasm and commenting on the pleasure of snow on a hot day. It was relaxing to be out, away from home, out with other people who knew nothing about her.

Toni had made a rabbit stew with peppers, accompanied by rice. The meat was strong and dark.

'Did you hunt it yourself?' the woman teacher asked.

'Ah, that you're not allowed to ask, as it's not the hunting season,' Toni replied.

'It's wild, though, isn't it? I mean, from the taste you can tell, it's so rich.'

'I can only tell you that I don't hunt and have no shotgun,' Toni replied lightly.

Then the single man said: 'That means you must be a prime suspect in the murder investigation.'

'Come again,' said Toni, suddenly thrown, in midmouthful.

'I mean, everyone in the mountains has a shotgun and, if you haven't got one, the police must think you got rid of it. It would make you a suspect.'

'That's one way of looking at it, though I'd have had to have had one before and everyone knows I've never gone in for hunting.'

'What a dreadful thing to happen!' the woman teacher interrupted. 'The murder of your Mayor, I mean. It makes your hair stand on end.'

Everyone nodded in agreement. It was Julia who broke the silence: 'There were other murders here in the war, 70 years ago, and I've been wondering if there's any connection,' Julia said. It was as if someone had farted ostentatiously. The only noise was the clang of spoons on the plates. People who didn't know each other still didn't talk about the Civil War.

It was the single man who coughed and asked: 'Why do you think that?'

'I don't know if I do think that, but I came up to see the Mayoress today about a relative of mine, a great-uncle, who was murdered in the Civil War. He's buried in an unmarked grave in the woods along with two people from the village. Everyone talks about the Mayor's death, but when I try and ask about what happened 70 years ago, no-one wants to know. Don't you think we need more clarity about the past in this country?'

'A killing in the war can't have anything to do with the murder now,' the single man said. 'Unfortunately, people are killed in wars. It's a bit over the top, if you don't mind my saying so, to call a war death "murder".'

'He was executed without trial. That's murder.'

'You have to remember it was a terrible war, with right and wrong on both sides.'

'I used to think that,' said Julia, 'but what I've realised

since coming up to Valeria is that *wrong things* were done on both sides, but *wrong* was solely on the Franco side.'

Toni was saying over her, '...the deaths in the war do cast a shadow in this village right down to today.'

'But we can't live in the past,' the single man said.

'That's just it, we can't. And till we can bury the dead, we can't leave the past behind and live in the present,' Julia replied with passion.

The other couple at the table, Toni's neighbours, had kept quiet during this exchange. The man had a squarish, inexpressive face and broad shoulders. Now the woman, Julia's age she thought, wearing a thick multi-coloured jumper, said:

'This murder is an absolute nightmare.' She laughed sardonically. 'Imagine, we came up here from the Basque country looking for peace and quiet.'

'How long have you been here?'

'We moved from Eibar five years ago. The atmosphere was unbreathable there, between the cops and the *abertzales*. A cousin of mine was seriously injured. And now, well it's another nightmare. You change your life from the town where you've always lived, where you grew up, all your friends, your whole life. We find this dream village in the mountains, restore a great house, then other friends come and restore other houses. All perfect, then the Mayor doesn't let us register to vote, rumours start flying around that we're terrorists, fleeing the police in Euskadi, then this horrible, violent death.' Julia thought the woman might start crying as her voice cracked with emotion. 'Then these damned interrogations, where were we on the night of the murder? What do you think of the Mayor? Why did you come here? Making us feel guilty all the time.' The man put his hand on hers and she gulped down half a glass of red wine. 'It's a damned nightmare.'

'It is,' her partner said. 'We've fled right into what we were fleeing from. Murders. I don't know what we'll do now.'

Later, when the three other guests had gone to bed and the Basque couple had walked home in the starless night, she and Toni had sat by the stove.

'I was surprised to see you playing cards in the bar this afternoon,' she said.

'Why?'

'I didn't think you were the card-playing type, that's all.' She felt relaxed. She hardly knew the guy, who was now cleaning his glasses on the tail of the red-striped shirt he had pulled out of his trousers. She liked his easy-going nature, how he ran his inn. She realised how little she had gone out in the past few years. Since Anna died, she had closed down her world, but here she was in a new place with new people who knew nothing about her and she felt she'd found a friend.

'You can't sit here reading books all winter. Those of us left here in the coldest months visit each other, chat, sometimes make food for each other and we play cards. Or the men do.'

She nodded. It sounded nice. Maybe she could live here, as the Mayoress had mentioned. Then she remembered the murders. You wouldn't choose to live in a place where people tried to sort out their problems by killing each other. Whether it was 70 years ago or today.

'And are you going to stay?'

'Why not? I'll always be an outsider, a familiar oddity to the villagers, but I come from a society where people move around. Not like Spain where it seems if a son or daughter moves more than five blocks from the parental home it causes a major crisis in family relations.'

She laughed out loud. 'That's just what happened to

me! When I moved to another part of the city my mother cried, "you're abandoning us!"' '

'In England, though, people always abandon their parents. They go and live at opposite ends of the country. I always thought it was to avoid sorting out real generational problems, but apparently not. Here everybody lives in their families' pockets and problems are still not debated or discussed out.'

'But this village is even further than the other end of the country, Toni.'

'I danced right off the map of the known world.' He leaned back in the broken-springed armchair, took a sip of wine and swilled it round his mouth while he looked at the ceiling. He swallowed and grinned at Julia.

'So just why are you here, Toni, if you don't mind my asking? Why are you sitting here, letting out rooms and feeding hens and rabbits through freezing winters?'

'You know when you're young, well I don't know if you ever felt this, but I did and lots of people do, I think, when you're young and first go to a bar or a club, it seems so glamorous, people talking or dancing, drinking, having a good time and I fantasised about running a bar. So I'm living out something of a youthful dream, running a *pensión*. It's not a bar, but you get a mix, a random mix of people coming through. Look at tonight. So I like it here.' It wasn't a proper answer, but she let it pass.

'I'm sorry about tonight at supper. I guess I shouldn't speak out of turn.'

'It wasn't out of turn. It was alright.'

'You're kind,' she said, 'but I was a bit obnoxious. Tell you the truth, I'm a bit worked up about all this. And then the poor Basque couple.'

'It does her good to get the problem off her chest.'

'OK, but in your case you could run a *pensión*

elsewhere. Why did you leave England?'

'You're persistent, aren't you? You really want to know?'

'Of course.'

'I mean, usually people ask questions, but they don't really want to know.'

'Tell me.' She didn't share Toni's fantasy of running a bar, but here in front of the fire in a comfortable armchair sipping wine and listening to the attractive voice with that light touch of a foreign accent, like a new spice in a familiar meal, she didn't have to fantasise. Or worry. She smiled to herself. For once, she could live in the moment.

So Toni the inn-keeper explained why he'd come to Spain, how he'd ended up in a remote village. He was right, she didn't really want to know, she was too involved in her own concerns, too selfish, but she liked hearing him talk. 'I was one of Thatcher's orphans, people driven out of their own country in that dreadful decade, when she wrecked the lives of millions of people and told us there's no such thing as society, there's only individuals. She unleashed a stampede of egotism and greed—'

'Did she really say that?' *Am I a secret Thatcherite, living on my own, back turned on society*? But probably that wasn't quite what the Iron Lady had meant.

Then her mind drifted away to the glow of fire round the wood in the stove, remembering snatches of what Carmela and Cleto had said, watching blue and orange flames jump in shapes out of the charred wood. She inhaled the smell of warmth in the pine, while Toni's voice sang on...

'That guy,' Julia interrupted him, and the interruption didn't seem to matter, 'when I first came up here and again today, in the village, muttering about Pinochet. What's that about?'

'Oh, Ambrosio. That's Ambrosio. Some say he was in the Foreign Legion. He certainly knows how to iron his trousers and shirt with razor-sharp creases, which makes you think he could have been. What I do know is that he was married to someone in Huesca who kicked him out some years ago and since then he's been living back in the village in a hovel on some minimum pension. You can live on almost nothing in the villages. You just have to get through the winter. In the summer, people will always give you vegetables. It's true too that some years ago, after I came here, he was involved in an affray with a knife in some roadside bar or brothel outside Alcañiz. His sister had to come up from Barcelona and probably paid some money so they didn't press charges. Now he's just a harmless drunk, pickling the little brain he ever had in alcohol, but when he was younger he would hang out sometimes with the Dúrcal brothers and there's quite a few in the village who won't even say 'Hello' to him. Ever since he heard that Pinochet was arrested in a London hospital, he's got it into his head that he's going to end his days alone and under arrest. There's probably an Ambrosio in every village in Spain, followers of Franco.' Toni paused and caressed the crease down his face. 'And victims of Franco.'

'Victims?'

'Yes, because they identified with the dictatorship but were still losers. Unlike those who opposed it, who were losers for a good reason, it means they've never even understood why they're so poor. Double losers. He's just a poor devil, though that doesn't mean he wasn't dangerous.'

All this conversation, Julia was remembering while she lay in bed after the dogs had stopped barking. Now she heard the clear, tinkling bells of the three or four goats leading a flock of sheep. The dead Mayor's ban on sheep crossing the village was not being enforced. Julia jumped out of bed and watched the flock bleat as it flowed along the street in the moonlight. Flowing was the only word, as the hundreds of pale, fluffy animals all rippled as one, packed together, the flock flowing round her car, their heads bobbing. The shepherd walked behind, a millennia-old figure, with his blanket wrapped round his shoulders, his straw hat and his long crook. Sharp cries and whistles kept his dogs busy, snapping with little stifled barks behind the heels of stragglers, which then put on short spurts to rejoin the flock.

As she watched them through the window, she saw herself as a ten-year old. She was crouching in a long white night-dress, clinging to the cold bars of the balcony and watching the sheep come home on a summer night in her mother's village.

Watching the sheep flow, her bare feet cold on the floor, remembering that other village, she could feel she was part of an eternal rhythm, unchanged for centuries, of sheep, of pasture, of isolated villages surrounded by forest and rock, with cold fresh air in her lungs. Standing there in wonder, she could feel like a child again that the world was an agreeable place, tailored to human dreams and desires. At peace she lay down again in the bed under the piled blankets, then remembered, away from the flowing sheep transporting her back 40 years, that history was real. There was no unchanging, benevolent eternity; only the decisions of humans making it impossible to live together without troubles. And murders.

Chapter Eleven

Julia awoke in sudden full wakefulness, to the sound of tapping on her door. She rolled over, her shoulders tensed, head cocked to listen, shouted 'Come in' and it was Toni, smiling in the smell of coffee. 'This hotel's getting better and better. Breakfast in bed.'

'Don't count on it.' He placed her tray on the table and sat down on the edge of the bed, smiling at her as if his face would burst. He took her hand. 'You're a special guest for me.'

'Toni,' she said, turning to look at her watch on the bedside table. 'You're very sweet, but I'm late, I said I'd see Jaime first thing.' If she hadn't liked him, she'd have told him to back off. Easy. But she did like him. As he stood up again, his radiant smile faded to his placid look of benevolence. She took his hand and said: 'I'm sorry, Toni. I'm not ready right now.'

He bent down and kissed her cheek: 'Never you worry, Julia. Whatever you want or need, remember I'm here.'

He knew nothing about her, she told herself as she showered after he had gone. He'd only talked about himself. He hadn't deigned to ask her anything about herself. Who the hell did he think he was? Then, as she dressed while sipping the coffee he had brought, she thought the opposite: perhaps he'd asked her nothing to give her the space to have a fling without commitment and to explain herself when and as much as she wanted. Kind, not selfish.

Twenty minutes later she shouted 'Jaime', as she banged on his door. She expected no answer. She expected to pick her way over the heaps of broken tiles, stacks of bricks, the prickly pear in battered green petrol cans, engine parts and a rusted vehicle chassis at the side of the house, as she had done on her first visit. She was surprised by the door flying open. It was, Julia knew at once, Jaime's wife, the *golondrina*. Unlike the fleet, whirling swallow she had imagined, Aurelia was short and round. She exchanged two kisses with Julia before she bustled her into the back room. She wore a pink housecoat and black lace-up shoes. She grinned at Julia through thick-lensed black-rimmed glasses and sat her down beside the stove. Julia picked up a pine log from the basket and ran her finger across the bark while Aurelia fetched Jaime.

'Maybe I've got a bee in my bonnet,' Julia started, 'but why does everyone leave their doors open when there's a murderer on the loose? Who the hell killed the Mayor? I've found out that he opposed the new property development, so whoever owns it has to be a prime suspect.'

'Whoa, whoa,' said Jaime, 'slow down.'

'Why should I, though? I mean, everyone's telling me to slow down and take care, warning me off investigating anything for my own good.'

'So it's not easy,' he shrugged. 'Did you think you could just walk in and solve everything?'

'No,' she said. 'Or perhaps I did.'

He was standing in front of her. Aurelia the *golondrina*, her head no higher than Jaime's shoulder, looked at Julia steadily through her thick lenses and said: 'Never you mind now. Sit down and tell Jaime everything.'

'So you saw Carmela, our new Mayor?'

'Yes. You're right, I thought it would be simpler. Carmela upset me. I'm sorry.'

'What for?'

'For barging in here and sounding off. I had no right.'

Jaime walked away to his left, looked out the window and walked back to Julia. He blew his nose on a greyish handkerchief. He sat opposite Julia and leaned his round, reddish face towards her, legs apart and hands on his thighs. Nearly fifty years old, she felt like a little girl who'd done something silly.

'The police quizzed Folches at length, probably more than any of us. He had no reliable alibi for the night of the killing and a serious dispute with Enrique. They quizzed me too, on more than one occasion. Like Folches, I was alone at home that night, and I had a motive for disliking Enrique. Or like Toni the inn-keeper. Or Pilar, who runs the bar and gets charged a fortune for putting her tables in the square. Or the Basques from Eibar who Folches says are ETA sympathisers, though to my mind they're trying to escape the conflict there, not bring it here. A woman could have done it.'

'I know. I met the doctor today and he thought the person he met on the road was a man, but he also said that it could have been a woman who disguised her voice.'

'There you are. Then it could have been the doctor himself or the Zaragoza lawyer, Fernando, and his Dutch wife. In mid-winter, there's a dozen people in this village whom no-one sees from sundown to sunrise and any one of them could have walked across the mountains, intercepted Enrique's car and shot him.'

'How far is it, though? Ten kilometres. I can't see Pilar walking ten kilometres there and ten back. Anyway, who do you think did it?'

Jaime shrugged, opening his hands.

'So, if no-one knows, why do people leave their doors open all the time?'

'Because there's not some psychopath running around. Someone killed the Mayor because he wanted him out of the way. I'll tell you, even when the Dúrcal brothers terrorised the village in the 1940s, no-one locked their doors. If those bastards wanted to get in, they did, locks or no locks. So what happened with Carmela?'

She sighed. 'You were right, of course. No chance. She went on about how people had been killed by the anarchists, including her grandfather. I hadn't known about that.'

'I hadn't reached that part of Rogelio's story.'

'She made clear she'll oppose any initiative. We'll just have to pursue it through the courts.'

Jaime wiped his mouth with the back of his right hand.

'In this *comarca*, no judge will rule in our favour,' he said. He glanced at Julia. She was looking at him with stubborn calm. 'Did you hear me?' She nodded. 'And another thing. Here, the police are not an independent body. They probably aren't in Barcelona, either. But I know for a fact that here the police do what their political bosses tell them.'

'That reminds me, who's Teodoro Pérez?'

Jaime glanced up sharply. 'You have found out a lot. Pérez's a man you don't want to get on the wrong side of. For decades, he was the Mayor and then he sponsored Enrique for the post. But I tell you, if he thinks it more convenient that the police don't find out who killed the Mayor, then they won't.'

'But Jaime, that's not realistic, not in a case like this with a national spotlight.'

'The spotlight shines where the television cameras are pointed and someone tells the cameras where to point.'

She shook her head. Someone was killed and the police didn't investigate properly? Teodoro Pérez, who was Enrique's patron, wanted to cover it up? It didn't add up. That was just paranoid. She looked up at him.

'Yes,' he said, as if reading her doubts. 'I know I spend a lot of time on my own with my thoughts racing round my head, like a hamster on the wheel in its cage. But if they didn't investigate things in the 1930s when there was rape and murder, why should they now, when the descendants of the same people are in power?'

'But it's no longer the 1930s and from what you say Enrique Jurado was one of them, not an enemy.'

'No, but the same people as before are in power,' Jaime repeated. 'They've just changed their jackets. And who knows? Maybe Enrique fell out with Teodoro Pérez.'

'So, how come this Pérez's so powerful? From what I heard, he's just a local guy with a bit of land and a flock of sheep.'

Jaime looked at her with a crinkle of laughter in his eyes.

'It's not like the big city here. I'll give you an example. I've got a neighbour, Rosita, who's about 70 now. Her father fought with the Republican army in the war. He wasn't in any political party, but when he got back to the village, the Dúrcal brothers had him arrested. The mayor put in by Franco immediately after the war was Martín, the guy I told you about who cut Rogelio's arm.'

'I remember.'

'He'd been a caretaker in Barcelona before the war. Well, Martín went down to Zaragoza where Rosita's father was being held and gave him a clean bill of health. Said he'd never caused any trouble in the village, a man of impeccable decency who'd been forced at gunpoint to join the reds. It was a life or death question, as you can imagine. If Martín had given Rosita's father the thumbs down, he'd have been executed or at best given a thirty-year sentence. In fact, if Martín had told the truth, that Rosita's father Alberto was a lazy drunk who had gone off to Barcelona quite happily to join in the disorder, he'd have been shot. As it was, he came back to the village and died a natural death only a few years ago. Now Rosita, nearly seventy years later, goes in every day to see Martín's daughter, who's a querulous, complaining old woman she can't stand. But she does it to pay a debt. People's loyalties and fears go back several generations. That's why Teodoro Pérez's word is listened to.'

'So, which is it with him? Fear or loyalty?'

'Both. Pérez controlled the excesses of the Dúrcals, but he was a tough nut himself. Once he gave a physical and very public beating in the square to a guy who'd let his sheep stray onto Pérez's land. The goats that accompanied the flock had got up on their hind-legs and stripped the low-hanging fruit off some of his pear-trees.'

'Jesus, the place is like walking through a mine-field.'

'Shall I go on with your great-uncle's story?'

'Back in his home village, Rogelio worked through the spring on the ploughing and sowing. At first he enjoyed the repetitive physical work in the mountain air, pressing down on the iron blade in the wooden plough as he followed the two mules yoked together. He would try out the arguments he'd learned with the anarchists in the city.

"So why are we so poor, working from sun-up to sun-down, while in Barcelona I've seen grown men sitting at café tables doing nothing except sipping their coffee and having their shoes shined by old men kneeling in front of them?"

"Oh, Rogelio, some are born there. Others are born here. You don't want to get ideas, these ideas will bring you trouble."

The man he was talking to was short and dark, with a straw hat pulled down over his eyes. He was lying on a soft piece of grass under a walnut tree. He wore, as Rogelio did, *albarcas* of cord threaded over soles of old rubber tyres, cotton trousers tied lightly at mid-calf and a striped cotton shirt. Wound round his waist, the black sash that both held his trousers up and protected his lower back and kidneys from all the bending and pushing, which now he'd loosened as he stretched out.

They had been working together on one of the fields belonging to Rogelio's family and were waiting to go back to work. A mule, head bowed, stood beside them. They had stopped for lunch, *gachas* brought out by Rogelio's 12-year old niece in a basket covered by a starched white cloth. Rogelio rubbed his finger over the long scar on his forearm.

"I tell you, Pepe, things are changing. It may be how things have always been, but they don't have to be like this. Things are changing. The rich depend on our work and what I've seen in Barcelona is that when we workers band together and strike, we can win. Man, that's what's changing, people are banding together in unions."

"That may be so in the cities, but here we're all smallholders."

"Yes, but look, we still sell what we produce to the cities. If they cease to exploit us and pay us a decent price, then we'll all be better off."

"It's all very well, but you're forgetting human nature. If you get rid of the middle-men, the new buyers will end up just the same."

"But think man, that's what the priests say, that men are basically bad and sinners. So they have to be controlled by fear of hellfire and the *Guardia Civil*. The CNT doesn't believe that: men are not bad—look at us here in the village, we've always helped each other to plough, to build each others' houses, to sow and harvest crops—why can't all of society be organised like that? Men can be good and men can be bad. It depends how things are organised."

172

Pepe shook his head, shut his eyes and lay back on the grass. This was the day's moment of peace. The mule too shut its eyes, though it didn't lie down. Rogelio pulled his hat over his face.

"I can't see any good coming of it," Pepe muttered.

After a couple of months, Rogelio became restless. Fragments of news reached him from the salesmen who visited the village, men on horseback or with carts selling pots, cloth, trinkets, leather goods, anything at all. There were always travelling salesmen at the village inn, sleeping upstairs in the straw loft while their animals were tied up at the feeding troughs in the stable below. There were the *braceros*, too, landless labourers looking for work, who walked cross-country along the hill-top tracks, as he himself had done when he was 14 and had first set off to Barcelona, a journey he covered in seven days. At first he ate the ham rolls his mother had made. He slept in the shepherds' refuges. One night he stole apples from an orchard. A dog started barking and he raced away downhill while a man with a shotgun shouted. Another day, a farmer invited him to eat and he slept in the warmth of the hay-loft above the mules and horses snorting gently through the night.

The *braceros* told him that there were still demonstrations in the big cities and that some workers had been killed on May Day in Madrid, but none of them could make sense of what was going on. Nor could he. He missed the explanations of Sánchez, Germinal and the rest of the anarchists in Barceloneta, the glasses of yellow beer with foam in the Ateneu, his economics teacher with the long white beard, the conviction that a new world was coming. He hadn't lost his conviction, but it was hard to keep up your faith in the future of mankind talking to people like Pepe, who was a good sort, but did not believe anything could change. And if no-one believes, he felt, no-one will make a move, so nothing will change. Then one day, in mid-May, a group of actors arrived in the village. Rogelio took his teenage nieces to the play.'

'That would be my mother and aunts', Julia exclaimed.

'This was one of the political theatre groups that sprang up in the 1930s. There'd always been groups of players touring for little more than meals and a bed in the hay. The villagers might have nothing to pay for their entrance but an egg or some tomatoes. My mother told me they even got up to this remote spot before the war. Anyway, this was one of the political plays trying to explain what was going on. They would be students from Valencia or Barcelona, young actors inspired to bring culture to the backward parts of the country. They'd have sketches, some juggling, comedy that enthralled the villagers with the magic of the theatre. They set up on a Saturday evening on one of the threshing-floors, the men standing at the back and smoking, the kids cross-legged and open-mouthed at the front on the ground. The rest sat on long planks on blocks of wood and some brought chairs from their houses. The actors wore crude stripes of make-up and exaggerated their gestures. Dogs barked in the background and, as the evening began to turn to night, groups of swallows swooped over the threshing-floor, the last sun catching the silver in their wings as they turned. Among the knock-about and the jokes, there'd be poetry and sketches explaining what was happening in the country and why people needed to unite and improve their position.

Rogelio felt justified in his views that night and cuffed Pepe at the end, "It's not just me, thickhead, see." Afterwards he talked to the players. He found one of them who'd been in Barcelona just a week before, a tall thin man with a wispy beard, who'd recited a poem by Lorca on stage. Things were very tense, he told Rogelio. The Government was wavering, while the military was openly organising a coup. The CNT was preparing itself. This time it wouldn't make the same mistake as in 1934. This time it would have weapons.

I don't believe there was anything specific the man had said, but Rogelio had heard in his voice the tone of the Barcelona anarchism that had changed his life, that made him feel he was not just someone born to labour from dawn to dusk, but someone who thought, who could do things, *someone*. It was then that he decided to go back, even though no word had come from Germinal. With his usual self-doubt—you'll have realised by now that Rogelio was a big guy, loyal and impulsive, but he wasn't too sure of himself and, while he yearned for the magic world of Barcelona's anarchists, he wasn't confident of himself with them, he felt out of his depth. He didn't know if they *would* send word. He feared his behaviour might have made him a liability to the action squad. Probably what decided him was he wanted to see Juanita.'

'But how can you be sure of all this?' Julia interrupted. She had been impatient to get on with the story. All these bucolic passages in Rogelio's village just seemed so much embroidery. She wanted to get to the climax, the killings, their deaths, to understand what had happened.

'My mother told me.'

'No, I know,' said Julia. 'But so much detail?'

She let the doubt hang in the air, like the dust rising slowly through the morning sun that slanted through Jaime's back window.

'You have to remember, my mother knew Rogelio for four weeks. He was her sister Juanita's boyfriend. The sisters were close, though Juanita was seven years older. In those four weeks, they talked about everything. She heard

Rogelio's story from Juanita and she heard it from Rogelio. Then you have to remember that they died. The revolutionary month they'd lived together was etched in her mind, a special unrepeatable time. Etched by their deaths afterwards, which fixed that whole happy, intense summer month in her memory. It was a brief flash of freedom. For the rest of her life nothing comparable happened.'

Jaime took up his narrative again, his hands placed on his knees, his shirt tight over his stomach.

'The first time Rogelio saw Valeria he had little time to look at the village. He was in a group of a dozen people who were moving rapidly in single file down a path through the forest, led by Juanita who knew the terrain. Germinal, the leader of the group, followed Juanita. Marçal, Paco and Ramón, who had been with Rogelio in the strike action squad, were in the group too. They were five days now out of Barcelona and had met little resistance. The Revolution was spreading from Barcelona like a red and black tide and the fascists were fleeing before it. The village assemblies acclaimed the anarchists and were happy to collectivise the hated bosses' land.

The night before, Germinal had called the group together before they bedded down in the village's school room. "Don't think the whole war's going to be like this, comrades. The bourgeois have run away before we appear, but we haven't destroyed them. They'll always try and come back. Till we destroy them, we're not free. Another thing, everyone here says they're on our side, but that's not real. No-one becomes a revolutionary overnight. There's some keep their mouths shut now, but when we move on, they won't be so silent."

Then he'd explained that the next village was up in the hills, Valeria, Juanita's village. They had good reason to believe that the fascists were still there. It wasn't a case of just driving into the main square, shouting slogans and waving flags. They'd stop the lorry a few kilometres out of town and Juanita would take them on a short cut through the woods.

That night, while they sat out in the square under the stars, Rogelio asked Juanita why they thought the fascists were still in Valeria.

"There's some evil bastards in my village and they won't give up easy. But what's more important is that Germinal's fed up that we're missing the fascists and their local lackeys, they're disappearing before we get there. So for the last couple of days, he's let it drop in the villages that we'll miss out Valeria because it's too high and we haven't time, we've got to push on toward Zaragoza."

He put his arm round her, but she didn't lean into him. He squeezed her shoulder.

"Roge, I'll see my family tomorrow and we may have a battle with some of the people I've known all my life."

"We'll smash them."

"I know, we're winning, but it makes me nervous. There's no going back."

The wood came right up to the backs of a row of houses. Germinal waved Rogelio, Paco and Jordi, a young student with a long nose and open mouth, up towards one street. Another group ran further on round the backs of the houses. Germinal, Juanita and the others went into a yard and through the back door of a house. A dog started barking fiercely and then it seemed every dog in Valeria started barking. Even the chickens in the wood-and-wire hen-houses clucked louder.

Rogelio felt the sweat run down his back, like a sardine

sliding between his stiff, cotton shirt and skin. His hands were clammy on the rifle butt. But no-one jumped out to challenge them. They turned into the street from the house-backs and they themselves jumped, as an old woman with a head-scarf and a stick as curved as her back nearly bumped into them. Paco brought his finger to his pursed lips and hissed at her to keep quiet and she hobbled on without even a hitch in her uneven walk. Perhaps she hadn't even seen them, sidling as they were along the wall. They reached the square and screwed their eyes up against the unshaded expanse of bright stone and compacted earth. They recognised the town hall on one side by the Spanish flag that hung limply from its staff. Opposite, under an arcade with weather-eroded pillars, dogs lay immobile, exhausted by their bout of barking, in the only shade.

"It's funny, there's no-one around," Jordi hissed in Rogelio's ear in his strong Catalan accent.

"It's normal," he replied. "It's midday, the men are in the fields, the women are cooking dinner."

Despite his reply, Rogelio felt uneasy. It was strange there were no old men enjoying the shade beside the dogs. While Paco watched their rear, Rogelio lay flat on the street and watched the Town Hall. He thought he saw movement behind a window, then he was sure of it. The window slowly opened. When metal glinted, he jerked his head back and rolled into a sitting position behind the wall as a bullet pinged onto the dust beside him.

"They're in the Town Hall."

"We should get round the back," Jordi said.

There was no secret about their presence now, they'd have to take the Town Hall. At the noise of the bullet fired at Rogelio, Germinal's group opened fire. Paco, Jordi and Rogelio heard glass breaking and an exchange of shots, as

178

they ran back behind the houses, down a slope of scrub, then up to the trees beside the Town Hall. Rogelio ran forward, pulled the pin on a grenade and hurled it at the front of the official building. It bounced back and exploded in the road. *That'll make the bastards shit themselves*, he thought as he scrambled up the slope to the back of the building. Now there was steady firing from the front of the Town Hall, returned by Germinal's group from the other side of the square. There were no ground floor windows at the back and they would be protected from above as long as they kept close against the wall. After signalling to Jordi and Paco, Rogelio took a deep breath, stepped out of cover and charged the back door with his shoulder. He heard the wood crack under his weight as he tripped, staggered and fell on the ground. Feet came racing overhead and on the stairs, then stopped. Paco signalled him back and tossed a grenade onto the bottom stair. Back outside, flush against the wall, they felt the whole building shake in outrage at the explosion. A cloud of smoke, dust and noise blew out of the door.

Rogelio jerked his head at Paco, who gestured in agreement, then groaned as he slid down against the wall.

"Paco?" Rogelio said and bent down after him as blood spilled out of his mouth. A bullet smacked into the wall where his own head had been.

"There," Jordi shouted and fired towards the forest fifty yards away. A figure darted for a moment between trees, then disappeared. Rogelio grabbed Jordi's arm and pulled him inside. The first few stairs were smashed and the twisted body of a Civil Guard lay smashed with them. The firing had stopped upstairs. The dust and acrid gunpowder made him sneeze. Rogelio unbolted and dragged open the front door.

"Watch the back," he shouted at Jordi. "We're inside,"

he screamed at Germinal, then leapt up the stairs, unable to avoid treading on the dead Civil Guard's shoulder. *That'll teach you*, he thought. He was sweating and shaking with rage.

Their mood was sober. Paco was dead, laid out on a table downstairs. It was the column's first death. Two dead Civil Guards lay on the floor in the same room. Upstairs, the militia sat around, drinking water. Germinal had placed a guard in the back room with the Mayor and the priest, captured by Rogelio and Jordi. They denied they had been shooting at all, it was the *Guardia Civil*. But rifles with their barrels still hot lay by the window. Germinal tore open their shirts, bursting buttons, and the red bruising on their fleshy shoulders from the rifle recoil betrayed their lies.

"Shits," the militiamen around them muttered. "Bourgeois scum." Another militiaman was on guard at the other back window, the Mayor's office by the looks of the metal filing-cabinet lurking in the corner and the ink-stained oak table, in case the man or men who had fired from the woods were still prowling about.

"Not worth chasing them, they know the terrain better than we do," Germinal thought aloud.

Juanita went with a militiaman to see her family—no-one was to walk about on their own, because of the danger of fascists lurking—and to get them to organise a midday meal. The men and women of the village were gathering by the bar under the arcades. Germinal went down unarmed to tell them they had nothing to worry about and summon them to an assembly that afternoon at 6 o'clock when it was cooler. Rogelio took down the Government standard and hauled up the red and black flag in its place. Two militiamen had gone back for the lorry.

"Watch out for those bastards loose in the woods." Forest, oaks and pines, covered the mountains all round the village. It would not be an easy place to defend. Out in the square, Rogelio turned right round to take in the whole of Juanita's home village, the first they'd had to take by force. He felt pleased with his leading part in the battle.

The Mayor, a mild-mannered, silver-haired man with a monocle on a silvery chain, his hands behind him against the wall, had announced bravely: "I am the elected Mayor, under the legally constituted Government of the Republic."

It was then that Germinal had torn his ironed shirt to look at his shoulder and then squeezed his throat till his face went red and his mouth opened and closed like a drowning fish. After this indignity, it didn't take the Mayor long to try and pass the blame onto two brothers, associated with extremists, members of the Falange, who'd forced them to take up arms. He himself was a man of peace. The two fascist extremists had slipped away, smarter birds than they: it would have been one of them who had killed Paco. Then Juanita came in and the Mayor's face went white: "You!"

"Did you think I'd never dare come back?" Juanita said and her face was as pale as his.

"Shall we take them on their last walk?" asked Rogelio, his hand on the gun in his sash. He thought of Paco, dark, alive and laughing who he'd shared a room with in Barceloneta before the war and he spat towards the priest in his grease-spotted chasuble.

The priest crouched in the corner, head bowed, fingers telling his beads at frantic speed and muttering the rosary.

"We will have a trial at six this afternoon," Germinal replied, his hand firm on Rogelio's shoulder. "The whole village is invited."

The militia stood outside the Town Hall. The accused sat on chairs in front of the villagers filling the square. Germinal climbed onto the back of the lorry.

"Brothers and sisters, welcome to this first assembly of the free village of Valeria. As you know, we are waging a war against the military who rose up in arms and were defeated in Barcelona, Valencia and Madrid by the workers and peasants, arms in hand. We are fighting against the fascists and also against the bosses who have oppressed us for centuries. Ours is a revolution where we are tearing down the old order and bringing freedom and equality for all the oppressed. From now on, the factories and the land will be held cooperatively, in common, there will be no more working from dawn to dusk only so that others can get rich and fat. In this village, we captured two men who were firing on us from the Town Hall." He pointed to the Mayor and the priest. "And we killed two Civil Guards in the fighting. One of our dear comrades was shot dead, too. Today we want to know what you, the people of Valeria, want to do with your oppressors."

Germinal was a man with a sense of theatre. His eyes, narrowed against the sun, looked from right to left across the hundred or so villagers who stood and sat, on the ground or on wood and reed chairs they'd brought from their houses. Then he looked back slowly again across the crowd from left to right. His black hair was uncombed and trailed over his ears, his face was weatherbeaten and brown, like the faces of the people of the village looking up at him, and his unshaven chin stuck out forward from the rest of his face. A pistol was shoved into his belt.

"Things have changed. Now you decide," he said. He sat down on the edge of the lorry and there was silence in the village square. No-one spoke. No-one moved. It was the silence of the end of normal life and the start of what few dared to imagine.

Rogelio saw a woman step up from the shade on one side of the square and walk round the edge of the crowd. She wore a shawl over her head, a white blouse and long skirt, like many of the village women. Her clogs thudded dully on the beaten earth. She strode with confidence and looked straight ahead. She walked like a proud and free woman. With a sudden shock, he saw the young woman was Juanita, *his* Juanita, without her militia trousers, rifle and red and black scarf, now stepping forward as a woman of the village.

"Until I went to Barcelona three years ago, I lived in this village all my life. Everyone here knows the story I am about to tell, but no-one has ever told it in public before. Because of shame and because of fear. It's my story, but there are other girls and other families who have suffered the same. If you don't talk about it, then it didn't happen, did it? We can get on with our lives, get married, be decent girls and our suffering's kept under wraps, inside the thick walls that keep us cool in the summer and warm in winter, the stone walls that tell no tales. What I'm telling you is that, if we talk about it, as I'm talking now, then it will end. It won't happen again. We can be free.

That day I took lunch up to my father and two others in one of the upper fields and was coming back through the forest when this disgusting pig stepped out in front of me. If we'd known he was in the village, my parents would never have let me go out on my own, but he'd been away, I imagine in the casinos and brothels of Zaragoza or Madrid. It wasn't festival time or even a weekend, just an ordinary working day. Well, I fought him, I scratched him and bit him, but he was stronger and half-knocked me out with a piece of wood. Of course, if I'd just acquiesced to my destiny in silence, then no-one would have known, like so many others, but I got home with my blouse torn and blood on my face and people had seen me and tried to help me in the street, so my mother and grandmother washed me and bathed me and mended my clothes to no avail, because the story was already all round the village.

All of you here knew my father, Domingo, a man who worked hard all his life and gave us a decent home. He had a failing, though. He believed in law and order. He'd heard the Republic had come—this was before the Two Dark Years—and the old order was changing. So he went to see the Mayor, but the Mayor advised him nothing could be done on the basis of unsubstantiated suspicions, it was best just to forget about it. My father was a stubborn man. I haven't inherited his belief in law and order, but I've inherited his stubbornness. So he got up before dawn, as usual, one day, but instead of picking up his mattock, he got on the mule and rode down to Villa Baja."

Rogelio stared at the Mayor, but the man sat with his head in his hands, looking at the ground. Juanita continued to talk calmly, firmly, as if she was explaining ordinary details and not revealing the secrets of her life to him. To the villagers, she was not revealing secrets, but making them unavoidable by stating them out loud.

"The duty magistrate took down his statement and read it out and my father signed it and the judge countersigned it. Then he bought some nails and some oil and rode back up to Valeria. I watched him for some weeks, though he said nothing to me, but I could see he was expectant. I don't know what he expected, maybe that news would come that the *Guardia Civil* had gone to the rapist's flat on *calle del Coso* in Zaragoza and arrested him. Perhaps he thought that when the rapist appeared in the village again, he'd be carted away in Republican handcuffs. At last, my father received a message from the Mayor, asking if he could pass by at his convenience. The Mayor told him that the complaint he'd lodged had been dismissed with prejudice. My father replied that he didn't know what the phrase meant. My father had no false pride. If he didn't know something, he asked. He didn't pretend he was better educated than he was, yet to my mind he was the most civilised man I have ever known. The complaint was thrown out. There were no witnesses, no medical evidence, the alleged assailant had denied the accusation. The Mayor was sitting behind that oak table that's still in there."

And here Juanita pointed in two directions, first back at the Town Hall, now in shadow behind her, the incongruous anarchist flag hanging limply in the windless evening from the pole, and then across the eight or ten metres that separated her from the Mayor and the priest.

"My father stood before him. The Mayor had offered him a seat, but my father refused. 'If you want a bit of friendly advice,' said the Mayor, '*déjalo correr*, let it go. As a father myself, I sympathise with you, but there's nothing to be done. No evidence, you see.'

That night my father was pale and didn't touch his food. I said 'Papa', ignoring my mother who tried to restrain me with her hand on my arm. I left her hand there, as my mouth was doing the talking. 'Papa, you've done what you can. For your own good, try and forget it. Me, I'm leaving, I'm going to go and work in Barcelona.'

'He has dishonoured you, Juana, he's dishonoured us. We can't accept this.'

'Papa, he's abused me, but it's only dishonour if we live it as dishonour. And this I'm not going to do. I am going to live my life and this ugly shit's not going to stop me.'

Then he gave me a slap across the face that shook the roots of my teeth. 'Bad language,' he said. You'll remember the rest of the story. This was the last time I saw my father until he was in his coffin, as I got up and left the next morning as soon as he had gone out to the fields. My father, who'd always been so discreet and respectful before, began to tell everyone of the injustice. He said there was evidence, a dozen people had seen his daughter bleeding and with her clothes torn and it was the *Guardia Civil's* job to investigate the case, to find out who'd done it. One winter day, when I had already changed my field-work skirts for a maid's cap and the white apron that crackled with starch and was serving in a house in the Ensanche in Barcelona, my father tackled Atilano himself in the café."

Juanita pointed across the square to the village bar and half the people in the assembly turned their heads and followed her finger with their eyes, though they knew very well where the café was.

"It was perhaps the next time that Atilano showed his face in the village. When my father accused him, the rapist shouted out in front of everybody, 'Are you crazy, you old fool?' and pushed him so hard that my father lost his balance and fell. But Atilano's voice trembled, since he knew that although they said nothing, everybody there knew that my father was right because the same thing had happened to too many other girls. On each occasion, it was a family secret, but Atilano knew that they knew.

One day when neither Atilano nor his brother were in the village, towards nightfall, when my mother was putting the pot on the fire and the men were returning from the fields, a lad came running into the house, sobbing. '*Señora* Ataülfa, *señora* Ataülfa, there's been an accident,' he said. My mother only had time to take off her house-coat and step outside when she saw four companions, heads down, carrying my father's corpse home on a stretcher."

The sobbing of a young woman could be heard.

Rogelio, standing behind the mass of villagers who were listening in the assembly to Juanita, searched for the source of the crying and it was the first time that he saw Juanita's younger sister, my mother Amparo.

"The four men explained that they had found my father at the bottom of the ravine that opens up below the bridge. It wouldn't have been the first time that someone had tripped and killed himself in the ravine. My father's clothes were torn and his body had bruises consistent with having fallen, bouncing from rock to rock. What was strange was that the men who brought him home had heard shouting and a shot, making them run towards the noise and once they had climbed down the ravine, they saw a bullet hole in my father's chest.

Atilano is not here today, although the neighbours have told us that he and his brother Antonio slept in the village last night. They think they're smart. They were able to slip away before our attack and it is very likely that it was a bullet from one of them that killed our beloved comrade, Paco. Don't have any doubts, we'll catch them and they will have to respond to the people's justice, as bourgeois justice did not want to act. Meanwhile, what have these two done, Father Vesga and our Mayor? For years they have covered up the rapes committed by the *señoritos* and the systematic exploitation of the *señoritos'* employees. They have been the authority here and they have accepted these outrages. The good priest hasn't killed anyone but he does confess and cleanse the sins of the exploiters and all of them, happy as newly-dressed babies, dine together, drink *coñac* and play cards in the Dúrcals' parlour. What does our ever so elegant and erudite mayor do? Knowing there are murderers and rapists running loose like mad dogs in the village, he doesn't lift a finger to stop them, but on the contrary invites them to sample his vintage wines and his stews, or rather the stew cooked by his cook. He's happy for the village to live in fear. That way it's easier to control, isn't it?"

Suddenly, Juanita jumped down from the makeshift platform, the back of the old lorry confiscated from a transport company in L'Hospitalet and still showing off through the dust the glow of the new anarchist slogans in red paint. The one visible read *Unite to Smash Greed, Militarism, War* with, above it, the letters CNT and a red and black flag. Juanita walked with the same simplicity and bounce as when she had stepped out to denounce the prisoners. The total silence in the square was broken only by the clack of her clogs and the swishing of her skirts. Rogelio followed her with eyes and mouth wide open. It was the first time he had heard her story. He felt confused: he swore to himself that he would protect Juanita, taking vengeance on this unholy son of a great bitch Atilano, and at the same time he felt isolated and distant from her life. While everyone in the village assembly knew this story, he was just a simpleton, ignorant of it. And of her. And then he felt proud of her. She had done nothing to be ashamed of. On the contrary. He knew he could never have spoken with such clarity and honesty.

While the assembly was still watching Juanita's route to where her sister was sitting, a man of about 70, his skin browned and wrinkled by the sun and snow, stood up and spoke: "If everything's going to change, let it change at once is what I say. What Juanita says is the truth. We all know it. There's nothing invented. Domingo didn't fall off the cliff, they shot him dead. I was there. I myself saw the damage to his chest. There's been no justice in this village. I'm old now and have little to give, but I'll die happy if I see that we've got rid of these exploiters."

The man had nothing else to say, but his words broke the spell cast by Juanita's speech and the people began to shout that the rapists and the people who covered for them should be punished and *Long live the Revolution*... The two prisoners turned even paler, seeing how at any moment the scum was going to jump on them and break their bodies bone by bone. Germinal, his hands rising and falling like slow bellows, gradually restored calm.

"Our comrade Juanita has accused the priest and the mayor of covering up the rapes committed by this Atilano and his brother, Antonio, and of obstructing the legal investigation into these crimes and the murder of her father. I see from your reaction that the vast majority of those present believe this accusation is just. We the revolutionaries are not barbarians, despite what the fascist propaganda says. Here we are conducting a popular trial and this means that the *gentlemen* have the right of reply."

With a certain dignity that Rogelio had not anticipated, the Mayor asked Germinal if he could be untied from the chair, so that he could stand. He brushed down his trousers, dusty from the floor of the room where they had been held. Then he coughed with one coiled hand before his mouth, as if he were about to move a resolution in a council meeting, and spoke: "Fellow-citizens, I am your elected Mayor."

There was a low hissing or collective intake of breath.

"Yes, you voted for me as your Mayor."

Again there was a noise from the public and someone shouted: "Fascist pig."

Germinal said: "There is no hurry. Let the man say what he wants to say."

"Under the laws of the Republic, I am your Mayor. Everyone, of course, may make mistakes, but I am innocent of these accusations. I have never obstructed any legal investigation."

His voice was light, not heavy with unnuanced truths like Germinal's. Rogelio stared at the ground, unwilling to be seduced by the soft voice's rhythms.

"How could I? I am not a judge. I merely told Domingo, the father of *señorita* Juanita, what the judge had told me. It's not right to condemn me just because I'm the messenger of bad news. As for the fact that I have covered up crimes, of rape, even of murder, this is hearsay. No man can be condemned in a proper court of law on the basis of hearsay. I repeat, I am the elected mayor and if you kill me because of the speech of our fellow villager, Juanita, how will you all feel later?"

Then the priest shouted and at the same time threw himself forward in an effort to stand, forgetting that, while his hands were free to keep telling the beads of his rosary, his feet were still tied to the chair. He fell headlong and from the ground, with a strong voice that belied his lamentable appearance of filth and of blood encrusted on his cheek, shouted: "I am a man of God. It is a mortal sin to kill a man of God."

Beside Rogelio, Marçal spat at the priest and shouted over him in Catalan: "God doesn't exist. And if he did, he wouldn't help a shit like you."

The crowd was on its feet, moving toward the priest and Mayor. Rogelio ran forward. Brandishing his pistol in one hand, he grabbed the Mayor by one arm. Marçal was gripping his other arm. They were surrounded by shouting villagers. A woman, with beads of sweat like pimples on her forehead, tried to slap the Mayor's face, but Rogelio put out his arm and pushed her aside. The children were running round their legs and once Rogelio tripped and almost fell, making the Mayor stumble with him, while they rushed down the uneven path that led to the bridge. The Mayor's feet and legs ceased to move and the two militiamen dragged him along by his arms.

"Back, back," Germinal shouted when they reached the bridge. "No kids."

Death wasn't something that children should see. They'd see enough in time. Rogelio then raised his pistol and, before he could think, shot the Mayor in the back of the neck. The Mayor shouted something, but Rogelio didn't catch it because of the noise. A villager, trembling with passion and screaming swear-words against religion and the church, hit the priest on the head with the handle of a mattock. The priest shouted, staggered and fell to the ground. Germinal pushed the villager aside and shot the priest twice in the chest. Each time his body jerked as if he was trying to get up.

Rogelio flung himself full length onto the grass, splashed his face with the ice-cold water of the river and drank deeply from his cupped hands. He threw water over his head and slowly his breathing returned to normal. He emptied his mind into the fast-running water that cleansed the sweat from his hair and face. He rubbed out a line of blood specks splashed across his forearm. When he raised his eyes, he saw a group of children staring at him from the other side of the stream. They'd had the perfect view of the Mayor being killed. He'd died in mid-scream, before he even hit the ground. There was a boy in shorts tied at the waist with cord; he had bare feet and brown legs with a scab on his knee. He reminded Rogelio of himself. Rogelio smiled at the boy and without getting up raised a clenched fist above his head.

"Two fascists less," he shouted across the tumbling water, excited by an audience. The children did not answer him. They stood and lay on the dried grass on the other side of the stone bridge and stared at Rogelio, taking in every detail. Then Marçal caught Rogelio roughly by the arm and pulled him up.

"What?"

"Come on, man," Marçal insisted. And Rogelio started to tremble. He shook himself free of Marçal's hand on his arm. "It's cold," he muttered. But it wasn't. The wound where the caretaker had cut his arm throbbed, though it was long healed. Rogelio tramped up toward the village houses, not daring to look at the two bodies. He heard Marçal chasing the children off, until no-one was left at the place of execution. Gradually his teeth stopped chattering.

The crowd had returned to the village. On the way down towards the river everyone had run as if it were a carnival procession, dancing and shouting in fright and excitement. Now they walked slowly back up the same track, in small groups and talking quietly, if at all. Death separated the crowd that had been as one into each person's individual thoughts. To kill two people was a serious matter. There was no return.

As the anarchists climbed the slope, tired now, their weapons in their hands, a woman in a long dress appeared in front of them: "You are murderers! Scum! God will condemn you all for what you have done today. I want a priest!"

It was the Mayor's wife. Germinal answered calmly, "There are no priests here and there will never be any again. You better get used to the dawn of the new world." He ordered two villagers to escort her back to her house. She was led away shouting and insulting everyone around her, with a fearlessness that impressed the anarchists.

Later, at dusk, a mixed group of the militia and villagers took the corpses of the two Civil Guards down the slope from the Town Hall in two wheelbarrows and buried all four bodies in the soft earth of the riverbank beside the bridge.

Chapter Twelve

Julia still had time before lunch for her next call. As she crossed the square, she stopped to look at the Town Hall, with its Spanish and European flags. She could not help reliving the day of the battle, Germinal and Juanita advancing across the open space, the policemen, the mayor and the priest firing from the upstairs windows, Rogelio her great-uncle running with his comrades round behind the building, Paco shot dead and Rogelio's own head narrowly avoiding one of the Dúrcals' bullets. The story of the past that Jaime was telling her took place right here, in this square. And everyone's descendants from the 1936 story were still alive—Jaime himself, the Mayoress, Martín's daughter and Julia herself, Rogelio's family member. Valeria, little changed except for Pilar's brash red plastic tables and the blue European flag with its circle of yellow stars, embraced her in just the same place where her great-uncle had heard Juanita's speech 71 years before.

She was surprised not to have noticed Brigitte's street before and wondered how much more was hidden in the apparently simple village. The cul-de-sac was paved with cobbles and curled up the hill off one of the three streets that ran out of the square. The house had a Virginia creeper twisting up the drainpipe, spreading its leaves across the wall of slabs of dark stone. The red bud of a rose in a blue ceramic pot swelled beside the heavy front door, which was panelled with thick opaque glass. The first-floor balcony was made of wrought iron worked into soft curves of metal. Red geraniums and their dark-green leaves pushed between the bars. No geranium moths burrowing through the stalks up here, thought Julia. Too cold. This was a house that had been completely renovated. A sign hung beside the door. *Nuestra Casa*. Julia grimaced and rang the bell.

The woman who opened the door was dressed in a knee-length leather skirt, a pale pink blouse and a simple, gold necklace. Her hair was washed and styled by a hair-dresser, unlike Julia's, which was cut only every six months and curled over her ears and across her shoulders. Brigitte didn't come to the village to work or be rustic, but to live in her peaceful house as if it were a city flat. While Brigitte was fetching coffee, Julia caressed the polished fossils on the shelf beside the hearth in the downstairs drawing-room. There were oysters shaped like ears, small pointy black sea-urchins and a series of large flat ammonites, fossils of cuttlefish and squid, round stones with raised ridged lines. Brigitte came back with a tray, biscuits and two cups of coffee, Julia's third that day. 'Are these local?'

'Aren't they lovely! No, I found them in a shop near the basilica in Zaragoza.' Brigitte wasn't the sort, it seemed, who went out walking and looking. They must do their birdwatching from a telescope at the bedroom window.

'I came by because I wanted to ask you—'

'Ask away.'

'I wondered why you told me Enrique Jurado had reclassified the land for the new estate.'

'Why I told you? Well, it's true, isn't it? They built on what was agricultural land. You can see for yourself. All these towns are mad about getting more income by building. Councils encourage building to get more residents and thus more allocation of funds. Of course, by doing so, they ruin the landscape. You know the whole Spanish economy would collapse if people stopped building. The other day, *El País* said that there was the same amount of building in Spain last year as in England, Germany and France combined. Can you imagine? No wonder the coast has been wrecked, and now there's no room left by the sea, they're cementing over the mountains, too. And every new house built means not just profits for the property companies and the *paletas* who all call themselves constructors nowadays, but more income for the councils, given the system of local government financing that operates in this country.' Julia was surprised at her passion: she *did* care about something other than her clothes and house.

'You feel strongly about it.'

'But don't you? It's such a shame that these beautiful villages are being ruined.'

'I do think that, but I think the situation here may be more complex.'

'Oh, it is very complicated, I know it's complicated.' And Brigitte's voice drifted away, her wave of passion, it seemed, spent.

'You see, I want to get my great-uncle reburied, but it seems nothing's going to move unless the murder of the Mayor is solved. Who do you think did it?' Julia took a sip of her coffee, feeling simultaneously a bit guilty and thrilled at enticing this woman to talk. Though she didn't seem to need much encouragement. Brigitte had a rather puffy white face and blonde hair which arched above her forehead. She sat with her legs, in the knee-length skirt, crossed and shoes with heels that wouldn't find it easy to manage the cobbles outside. Brigitte laughed nervously at Julia's question.

'God, I don't know. I wish I did. It's caused so much unpleasantness, I wish it were all over and we could just get on with our lives. I really do.'

'Yesterday, though, you told me you hoped it wouldn't be solved, because solving it would aggravate all the conflicts here.'

'That too, that too,' she said, not overly worried by the contradiction and vague as she hadn't been when she talked of the mountains becoming covered in cement.

'But you've thought about it, you must have, you were there on the mountain that night.'

'Don't remind me!' Brigitte did a stage shudder.

'You suggested I come and see you yesterday. I thought you might want to tell me something.'

'You sound just like the police questioning us. They make you feel guilty because you don't have an answer. You know, they didn't believe we didn't have a hunting gun and searched the whole house and our flat in Zaragoza too. Evidently everyone but us has a gun here, licence or not, and if we didn't have a gun, then it must have been because we'd got rid of it, which made us prime suspects. It was horrible!'

'But what did they ask you, to make you feel guilty?'

'It's just like in the TV series, they make you go over your story again and again, on different days, with different people, to see if they can trip you up. I'll tell you, they asked Fernando, that's my husband, what clothes I was wearing, and one day he told them I was wearing a blue sweater and another day a beige one, well the silly fools acted as if we'd been making up lies, but I can tell you, as I told them, if I walked down the Gran Vía in Madrid wearing my knickers outside my skirt, he wouldn't notice.' Julia laughed, as Brigitte seemed to want her to.

'You can laugh, my dear, and I can too, now it's all over, though who knows, as they haven't solved anything, any day now they might decide to have another round. Then another thing, they were always trying to catch us out by interviewing us separately. They were fascinated we don't own a shotgun. What they thought, you see, was we'd met the Mayor there on the road, we'd stopped, there'd been some sort of altercation and Fernando had shot him. These Spanish cops are conventional and sexist enough to always assume it was him, not me. On one occasion they thought they were being ever so clever and asked me casually, and where does your husband buy his cartridges, was it that hunting shop on the *calle* Bordeta? Trying to trap me into admitting we had a gun. My husband was asked so many times, "what did you do with the gun afterwards?" that in a fit of sarcasm, he's like that you know, he said finally, "oh, OK, I'll confess, I threw it into the back of a lorry with French number-plates at a roadside restaurant." It took him ages to get it across to those thickheads he was joking. "It's not a laughing matter," they said. "You could be prosecuted for wasting police time." What a cheek, the amount of our time they wasted without even an apology. We're probably still under covert surveillance, still on the list of the Top Ten suspects.'

'So who's top of the list?'

'God, it could be anyone. For a long time, my bet was it might well be the only other foreigner here, that English inn owner.'

'Toni?'

'Toni yes, because he'd fallen out badly with Jurado, and he doesn't have a gun either, but several other people had fallen out with him too and the prime suspect of course has to be Arturo Folches, the forest ranger. Jurado had turned down his application to open a rural bed-and-breakfast, you see, but of course it wasn't an honest refusal, because Jurado himself owned the other hotel. Folches appealed right up the ladder, but through his friends on the county council, the regional council, the *Diputación*, Jurado always won. The forest ranger couldn't get anywhere. The PP have got this place sewn up, you know. If you don't have the right contacts, you can't open your mouth without the risk of a fine.' She laughed a little recklessly. Julia wondered if Brigitte was a morning drinker.

'So what was Toni's dispute with the Mayor?'

'Like with Folches, some stuff about threatening him with closure because he'd done renovations to the place without Council permission, and of course without paying a fee for that permission. But I mean, no-one here's ever gone through all these procedures just to do up their house. Nothing would ever get done—you'd have to get an architect in and that costs a small fortune. We renovated this house from top to bottom and even though the Mayor himself used to drop by and chat to us during the building work, no-one ever asked us to go through the rigmarole of getting formal planning permission or paying anything.'

People might hate outsiders meddling, but then they liked to talk to an outsider, Julia thought, especially once they find out you're not press or police. 'How do you know I'm not from the press or the police?' Julia had asked her.

'You don't look it, dear—too old for press, they send out twenty-something-year-old amoral bloodhounds on stories like this and too soft for a cop.' The comment irritated Julia. She didn't think she was soft, though she had no vanity about not being young.

'As far as I'm concerned, but I don't have any say in the matter, I'm all in favour of reburying your uncle and Jaime's aunt. I'm Dutch, you see, and we remember what happened in the war, I've got no liking for Nazis. You know, the only man ever to stand up to the Nazis in Spanish football grounds was Gus Hiddink, a Dutchman, when he was Valencia's manager. He said, unless the police removed the Nazi flags from the terraces, he wouldn't let the match start. And he stuck to it.'

'What happened?'

'They removed the flags.'

'You know,' Julia said. 'I really did think you wanted to tell me something.'

'What?'

'Yesterday on the square, when we met at lunch. I thought you had something that could help me.'

'But why would you think that?'

'You more or less invited me to come and see you.'

'I don't remember.'

The Dutch woman, torrential when she ran with a subject, now looked into the distance beyond Julia's shoulder and rubbed an ear-lobe with a finger. Julia wasn't surprised the police had kept interviewing her.

As she walked away from the prettiest house in Valeria, if you liked city flats that is, she heard footsteps clip-clopping over the cobbles behind her. Brigitte caught hold of her arm.

'You know, I do know who did it,' she said softly.

'You do? You saw who it was, that night?'

'Not exactly, but I know. It was Arturo Folches, the forest guard. Folches knew the mountain trails by night and had the strength to walk there and back to the spot where the Mayor was killed. But everyone knows that. There's another thing, you see, that only I know. Well, me and my husband.' She looked round and leaned forward. Julia could smell the scent of coffee and sugar on her breath as she whispered: 'When we were up on the mountain that night, I smelt him.'

'Smelt him?'

'I've got a very keen sense of smell and people have their particular smells.'

'So what did you smell?' *Maybe she's not a morning drinker, but just plain nuts.*

'I smelt a person. Arturo Folches.'

'Did you tell the police?'

'Of course I didn't. Do you think a smell can stand up in a court of law? I'd be a laughing-stock.'

'But what was the smell?'

'It was his particular smell, you understand. You can't put it into words, you just smell it. It has leather and oil, his horse, a mix of things.'

'But everyone here must smell like that.'

'No, everyone's different. And then there was his cologne. He wears a particular cologne or after-shave that lies on top of his other smells.'

As Julia crossed the square, she suddenly saw the man himself. Arturo Folches in dark glasses lounged against a pillar under the arches by the café. Old-fashioned name, she thought, no-one's called Arturo nowadays. She tossed her bag into the car and turned to cross the square towards him. She had an impulse to run towards him, sniffing to see if she could inhale his smell. But he was gone and where he had been, a dog lay as if it had been there for several hours. She wondered if the tension of getting nowhere was causing her eyes to play tricks. She looked all round the square. She went into the café and he wasn't there either. Relief mingled with her irritation. Though she wanted to confront him, she was happy not to be able to through no fault of her own. There was no-one she knew in the café: an old man she might or might not have seen before, drinking a beer, a younger one reading yesterday's paper. She asked for a bottle of water, which she zipped into her small rucksack. The girl who served her dragged her feet to the cash register in flip-flops and tight green shorts. There was no sign of Pilar.

'Have you seen *señor* Folches?' she asked. The girl

looked up and stared.

'The forest whatsit?' the girl mumbled and shook her head.

Julia was shaken by Jaime *el Moreno's* story. So Rogelio had killed someone. Her feelings were confused: however justified, her great-uncle had killed someone. And she knew enough about the Civil War—she remembered her arguments with Ferran—to understand that even those on the right side could be thugs, like Rogelio and his mates, too fond of too quick a vengeance. Could she rely on Jaime's story, a story dwelt on, repeated to himself and polished over the years to a shine, like Brigitte's fossils?

She set off back across the square and a dog followed her. She stopped and the dog stopped a couple of yards behind her. She shooed it away, but it looked at her without moving or blinking and when she set off again, off the square onto the rutted track behind the Town Hall that led up into the forest, it followed her a few yards behind. There was nothing to be done. It looked as if the dog, a smallish brown mongrel with a piece bitten out of one of its ears, was going where it wanted to go and for some reason that was with her. She passed an old *corral*, now roofless, filled with rubbish: not consumable daily rubbish, but old washing-machines, one-legged chairs, twisted bed-frames, a smashed television, shattered glass and broken crockery—the village dump. Better than throwing it into the ravine, she supposed. In a few minutes she was out of the sun and out of sight of the village, walking uphill through a wood of low, twisted oaks, draped with moss and lianas that gave them a phantasmagorical look. Green lichens spotting the trunks and boulders cushioned by moss told her how unpolluted the air was. She was not unhappy that the dog continued to follow her. While she walked, she reflected on the strange Dutch woman. So she had had a purpose in inviting her round: to tell her the killer was Folches. Or maybe this was just something Brigitte had made up on the spot. Smelling a killer? She'd never heard that one before. Julia wondered what she herself smelt of. Sugar and spice and all things nice. She doubted it. Sadness, disappointment, middle age. Could you smell that? And overlying it, like Folches' after-shave, a new bright purpose in her life. To bury a murderer.

Beside the track she came across a small cairn or monument. She didn't know what to call it. It was just a pile of stones holding up a stick. A tattered red and yellow flag with an imperial eagle in the middle hung from the stick. She recognised it as the old flag, the Spanish flag from Franco's time. A board was tied precariously to the base of this improvised flagstaff, with the words *¡VIVA GENERAL PINOCHET!* scrawled in black paint. As she straightened up from studying the board, she looked round with a shudder. The dog stood behind her, patiently or indifferently. She thought of Brigitte's acted shudder just an hour before, but her own now was involuntary, fruit of the dark wood and the shrine to Pinochet. The only head of state to attend Franco's funeral. *What the hell's going on in this village, where in the 21st century the powerful images of murderous fascism are revived?* she thought.

'It's stupid,' she told the dog, 'it's just that village drunk with his fantasies.' The dog neither agreed or disagreed. She took off her small rucksack, unscrewed the bottle of water and drank. Then she found her mobile and took a picture of the only monument to General Pinochet in the whole of Spain. Then she turned round and took a picture of her new dog.

Several minutes later, the path emerged from the forest and entered a treeless plateau, which she didn't recall from her previous journey. She wondered if she had taken a wrong turning, but remembered no fork in the track. At first glance, the plateau looked barren, but soon among the occasional bushes bent double by the mountain gales, the red earth and the boulders cracked and splintered by the sun and ice, she found a multitude of life. She knew where to look and what to look for. Often with Anna she had traipsed across the countryside and shown her the land's hidden treasures. Now alone, but with memory accompanying her, she scanned her immediate surroundings. She knelt and poked a twig into several round holes in the earth, until from one a small tarantula jumped up in the air to chase off the twig before falling back into its lair. She smiled, remembering the startled pleasure of her daughter when a spider had jumped and they'd both jerked back in surprise. She looked down into the hole again and the lidless eyes of the spider staring up at her glistened in the dark like precious stones.

She watched the pile of debris beside an ants' nest. The ants carried out the dark husks of seeds from the hole in the centre to deposit on the pile. A new butterfly stretched its perfect wings, pale with black lines like Chinese calligraphy, to dry. All the while, chaffinches, nightingales, tiny warblers and sparrows screeched and twittered in the flattened bushes. Above the background music, soared the sharp tune and indignant cries of what she thought was a golden oriole. She peered into the dark trees, but could see no flash of yellow. When she looked up into the light, an eagle was wheeling above the trees, dark-bellied against the cloudless sky, a guardian of the mountain or the avenging angel.

She walked on across the moor. The path twisted, dipped, then climbed again. Different smells assailed her: tough bushes of thyme with their twisted branches, the herb savory with its little white flowers, juniper, smelling of gin. The juniper's stiff, prickly leaves grazed her arm as she reached in for a smooth round black berry to suck. Each of these coarse, harsh bushes, flourishing in this adverse climate, released its pungent fragrance as your arm brushed it. As she trod, dozens of stone-brown grasshoppers leaped aside and turned blue as they opened their wings. She saw a short snake on the path, a viper she thought, which slid away through the stones. She was not religious or superstitious and followed the snake, sliding fast in its silent zig-zags, till it disappeared under a rock. Before it vanished, she was thrilled to see it stop for an instant. It raised its head and its thin mouth, no more than a line in the wrinkled, grey head, opened and its thin, forked tongue flashed out and in. To see animals, to feel she was just another animal in the landscape, fully alive in the present and unburdened by time, calmed her.

Then she, and the path, re-entered the forest. The trees had changed. Instead of holm oak, they were pines, only just a bit taller than her, planted in straight lines. Brown needles softened the track. Cones lay in piles round the jumbled undergrowth. Twenty minutes later, climbing steadily, she reached the glade. The grass was green under the trees. Wild mountain flowers covered the clearing: little orchids, coloured dirty yellow to imitate a bee's belly, blue gentian, purple violets like tiny elves' velvet robes. It was a beautiful place, if it wasn't for what had happened here.

Once she had been with Ricard on holiday in the Highlands of Scotland. They raved to each other about the lochs, the isolated stone houses, the mountain crags. Yours is one of the most beautiful countrysides in the world, they told an old man they met on a hill-path. The man replied: 'Oh yes, but there's only sheep left, no people any more. The people who lived here, they were slaughtered or deported.' It was beautiful only if you came with no history to the place. The man's stark information changed their feelings. Thereafter, they found the windswept Highlands as mournful and lonely as the old man.

She sat on a stone in one corner of the glade, from where she could see the highest peaks of the range, snow still stuck like cement to the most shaded flanks and hollows. After drinking and resting her eyes with the long gaze on the mountains, she took out her phone and took pictures of the glade. Tired, she lay down, at peace, on the grass in the midday Spring sun. The dog lay down too, maintaining its polite two-metre distance from her. She laughed, don't be soft. She'd never cared for dogs, but she thought if she lived in a place like this she might get one.

She was woken from her light doze by her phone ringing.

'Hey. Everything OK?' Xavi's voice.

'Yes. I'm in the forest, in the clearing where they killed and buried Uncle Rogelio.'

'You went on your own?'

'I wanted to clear my head, get a bit of fresh air.'

'Take care.'

'There are no bears or wolves any more.'

'I was thinking of wild animals of our own species.'

'A dog's accompanied me.'

'A dog! You?'

'Yes, me and a dog. And why not?'

'You don't like dogs.'

'I don't like dogs who smell bad in city flats and shit on the pavements. They're OK in the countryside. Have you found out anything?'

'I have. It was easy. Too easy, really. I'm in Zaragoza now. I've been in the registry and the land where they're building the estate belongs to the forest ranger, Arturo Folches.'

'Belonged or belongs?'

'It looks like he still owns it. He will have gone into partnership with the building company which puts up the capital, but he maintains ownership of the site.'

Xavi thought the Mayor's refusal to allow the company to build was the strongest motive any villager had to kill the Mayor. Near conclusive, he said. It was only circumstantial, Julia said, and anyway the police investigation would have uncovered all this and decided not to proceed. Any press reporter would have uncovered it. You only had to look up the property registry.

'We're playing at cops and robbers,' she told Xavi. 'I can't see how we're likely to turn up anything the police have missed.'

'You have more confidence in the police than I do,' her nephew replied. 'In a *comarca* like this one, the police will investigate more or less thoroughly, depending how the political bosses direct the investigation.' This was what Jaime had said.

'Even in a murder case that reached the national press? If you can find this out in one morning on a visit to the provincial capital, any reporter could do the same and, even if the police were corrupt, they'd be careful not to be exposed like that.'

'Maybe,' he said, 'maybe you're right. But if you want a job on a national paper nowadays, forget about investigative, independent reporting. Journalists are just transmission belts for the editorial line and the editorial line of course comes from the political and business bosses.'

'I do know that, Xavi. You don't have to lecture me. Even so, something as obvious as this...'

She put her phone away in the rucksack, drank from her bottle of water and splashed water into her eyes. She put her rucksack on again and walked across to look at the improvised monument to the anarchists.

31/8/1936
Here three victims of fascism were vilely murdered.

Below, a stiff piece of cardboard had been nailed to the main stake. She was touched to think that Jaime had acted on her suggestion to include the names of the victims.

Juanita xxx, aged 23
Rogelio xxx, aged 27
Evaristo xxx, aged 70

She said the names out loud. She wondered if Evaristo was an anarchist or just someone who spoke out of turn. Someone who stood up in the village assembly and spoke the truth. An old man fed up with a life of keeping his mouth shut. Then she heard a branch crack and whirled round. She felt as if she'd conjured up the devil with her mind. Folches himself, leading his black horse by the reins, stepped out of the pines. He looked perfectly ordinary, even small, on the other side of the glade. She controlled an impulse to disappear into the trees. She had wanted to talk to him, but in the village, under the arcades or at a table in the bar. Not here, not alone in the beautiful glade. Not here in this lonely glade loaded with history.

'*Buenas tardes*,' he said, tying the reins of the horse to the trunk of a pine. It snuffled and chewed at the grass. 'I heard you were looking for me.'

'Where?' Her mouth felt dry.

'They told me in the bar.' He stopped a few yards from her. He wore wide trousers, with leather sewn into the seat and inside of the thighs, like cowboys'. His cap shaded his eyes, the skin round them wrinkled by the sun and outdoor life. There was no sign of the dark glasses he'd worn in the village. He bent down and broke off a piece of long grass. He peeled back the outer layer and put the green shoot into his mouth to chew. He tilted his head and waited for her to speak. The thought that he seemed to be enjoying her discomfort prompted her to reply.

'I wanted to ask you why you didn't mention the development of 30 houses on your land when you gave your interview to *El Mundo*.'

Folches stayed in the same position and then he let out a soft, studied laugh. 'I thought you wanted to bury your relative.' He waved his hand towards the monument. 'Now, I realise you're just another vulture sticking your beak into our problems. What are you doing, writing a book about Jurado's death, making money out of murder and other people's suffering?'

Folches' outburst made it easier for her than his politeness. 'The development, stopped by the Mayor, gives you an even stronger motive than the bed-and-breakfast licence he refused to give you.'

'Yes and I could add a whole host of other disputes Enrique and I had. It may be difficult for someone like you to understand, but we actually got on quite well. We'd known each other for a long time, we had interests in common. In fact, only two weeks before he died I was dining in his house with him and his wife. That's what makes me angry, that small-time journalists like you come up from Barcelona and Madrid and think you know what makes our village tick. You charge in here with your cameras, notebooks and preconceptions and you only hear what you want to hear. My interview with *El Mundo* was an attempt to defend my neighbours who are fundamentally defenceless. As I'm someone who's lived here much of my life and have a certain level of education, I wanted to use my abilities to put all this rumour-mongering to rest.'

'Until the case is solved,' Julia said, 'there's bound to be rumours. Who do you think did it then?'

'I have my own view, but I've got no wish to be quoted by you in some scandal sheet—'

'I'm not a bloody journalist,' she shouted.

After his rant, Arturo Folches was now the cool guy. 'No? So what are you then?'

'I'm a biology teacher and I'm only interested in burying my great-uncle. But it seems we can't do that until this murder's sorted out.'

'And not afterwards either, I can tell you now.'

'Maybe not. We'll see.'

There was silence. They'd each got angry then calmed down. They could both hear the animals, repetitive like their thoughts: birds that chirped in the bushes or the cracking of dry twigs as a shrew scurried away. There was never silence in the countryside. She breathed in deeply, trying to inhale Folches, but all she could identify were the pines. She could not catch the smell that Brigitte had distinguished as Folches' own.

'He's already buried,' the forest ranger said, jerking a thumb towards the monument. 'Why don't you leave him and us in peace?'

'Would you leave a member of your family in an unmarked, shallow grave like this?'

'Just forget it, that's all I'm saying.'

'What I don't understand, *señor* Folches, is why you were so hostile when we met before and why you're so aggressive today.'

And then he was shouting. He jabbed toward her with his finger to underline his words. 'If you don't understand, then go back to your pretty little flat and students in

Barcelona and think about it. It's clear enough to anyone with a grain of sense that you're sticking your nose into an affair that's none of your business.'

Though she'd controlled her fear till now, Julia responded to his gestures and step toward her with a physical surge of pain in her kidneys. The dog, which had been standing placidly behind her, growled and ran past her toward Folches. Afterwards, she did not know if the pain had hit her before the dog moved; or if the dog was driven to action by the same rage in Folches' voice that had affected her. She liked to think later that the dog had reacted to the chemistry of her fear, in order to defend her, though that seemed unlikely. It growled and jumped towards Folches. 'Son-of-a-bitch,' he shouted, stumbling back off-balance and kicking out with his boot at the same time. Without really intending to, he caught the dog a blow on its skull with the boot's reinforced sole that resounded through the glade like a hammer on steel. The dog dropped to the ground and let out a shrill grunt. It moaned and shook its head as it tried to stand up. 'Damned dog,' said Folches calmly and walked away towards his horse.

Julia started forward. 'Don't touch it,' Folches said without turning round. She caressed the head of the dog, which was panting, its eyes wide open and its wet tongue dribbling saliva from its open mouth. He rode up on his horse. 'Stand back,' he said. 'A lot of these half-wild mongrels are sick and dangerous.' Without getting out of the saddle, he leaned down and with one hand shot the dog. The shotgun barrel jumped in the air after he pulled the trigger. The horse threw its head back and whinnied. Julia covered her ears and gritted her teeth. The dog coughed and, by the time she had lowered her clenched fists to her sides, it had stopped moaning.

When she opened her eyes, loosened her hands and

looked up, she saw the bushes just beginning to close round the wide swaying bottom of the black horse, as the forest ranger rode into the trees. In front of her, in the peaceful and beautiful mountain clearing, her dog lay dead.

Chapter Thirteen

At 7 o'clock on a May evening, the streets were packed with kids roaring and running and groups of idle adults who blocked the pavements as they chattered. She was lucky and grabbed a table outside the *Quimet*, where a couple were just leaving their empty beer glasses and a saucer of olive pits. She liked this café, with its elegant beige awnings wound down against the sun. It had been recently refurbished, restored to how it was in the 1930s, with a design of a parrot carved into each piece of plate glass in the doors and windows. They used to have a live parrot inside, a blue-headed red-winged *guacamayo* or *papagallo*, she wasn't sure which. This was when parrots were exotic, long before the gangs of wild parakeets had established themselves in Barcelona and their yellow, green and red feathers flashed low over the streets, cawing coarsely and hoarsely and stealing bread from the bedraggled pigeons. Health regulations meant that now a wooden green and red bird swung on the parrot's former perch. She wondered if Rogelio had ever been here. Probably not, as this was no workers' café and was in the outskirts of the city, nestling under the Collserola hills.

'Hey,' she said as Ricard appeared through the crowd on the pavements and she got up to kiss him on both cheeks. A familiar smell that threw her back to when they had shared their lives. Smells were on her mind.

'Sorry I'm late. I'm not too late, am I?'

'No, you're not at all. I'm early. Sit down and stop fussing.'

'Just like you.'

'What?'

'To be early.'

'Listen, Ricard,' and she lowered her voice while she pulled him towards her. She was not one of those who broadcast private affections at full throttle. 'That comment belongs to an intimate relationship.'

'What?'

'*Just like you.* That comment belongs to an intimate relationship. But we're not living together now. We can't treat each other the same as before. You have no right to make comments about what I'm like, any more, in fact less, than you would with some student of yours. You have to treat me differently.'

'Ah, yes, well OK,' he said, holding up his hands to appease her. This annoyed her, this assumption she was angry, but she could not afford to fight him at every turn.

'I thought I ought to tell you about the dig I visited, seeing as you gave me the initial contact with Ferran, and what was happening with the reburial.' It came out more rushed than she had wanted.

'Oh, you don't have to.'

'I know I don't have to, but I want to. It was going up there, to Valeria, this mountain village in Aragon, you see, that made me decide in the first place to get my mother's uncle reburied. I don't know if you ever heard the story about my great-uncle Rogelio who was supposed to be living in exile in France, but then Jaime, this guy in Valeria, while he was investigating his aunt's murder when the village was taken by the fascists in the Civil War, discovered in some old document at the Town Hall that Rogelio had been killed at the same time. He got in touch with my cousin Charo—it seems she'd registered Rogelio as missing on the Registry that the Associations for Historical Memory had built up.'

'The one with 114,000 people that was presented to Garzón?'

'I guess, but it's got complicated, because Valeria's Mayor was murdered in February and it's going to be difficult to get Rogelio and Jaime's aunt reburied.'

'So, sorry for being a bit slow, but what's your part in all this?'

'Charo couldn't go, so I went up there and Jaime told me Rogelio's story—or a lot of it, we haven't reached the end yet.' She paused. 'I've got involved. I want to see Rogelio reburied properly. There were three of them and they were dumped in this clearing in the forest. It's a beautiful place, but we can't just leave them there.'

'But why not? I mean, if it's a beautiful place,'

'We want them recognised. That's the point of recovering Historical Memory. The powers that be, the new Mayoress, who's the grand-daughter of the Mayor who was killed by the anarchists, won't countenance their reburial. Jaime sees it as a political fight, to recognise the victims of the war, not just the victors. And I think he's right.'

'You've got your dynamism back,' Ricard said slowly, picking his main word with care. What he meant, she thought, was *Thank God, that's a relief, at last you've got over my leaving you and I won't have to feel bad thinking you're unable to get on with your life because of me.*

She smiled at him, both ignoring his comment and answering him indirectly: 'The whole business in this village has brought home to me the hundreds of thousands of people in this country who have suffered the death of a loved one. And they spent a lifetime buttoning it up and getting on with their lives as best they could.' She stopped. It had been years since she had talked to him so much. She signalled to the waiter, Guillem, a witty and sarcastic young man with shiny black hair, white sideburns and an ironic goatee, to bring her another *tallat*, a coffee with a splash of milk.

215

'Under Franco, that was the only way they could live,' he said.

'Yes, but you pay a huge price.'

Guillem brought the coffee and Ricard's glass of red wine. She handed him back the sachet of sugar, with a parrot drawn on it. She stirred the coffee, even though she took no sugar, and watched it circling round the glass.

'Do you think much about Anna?' she asked.

'I do. All the time.'

She didn't know whether she believed him or not.

'I've read that there's no word for a parent who loses a child. *Vice versa* and the surviving child's called an orphan. If your husband dies, you're a widow; if your wife dies, you're a widower. But if your child dies, there's no word to describe it. You and me were meant to die first, we gave her life so she could go on. I feel I let her down, I didn't protect her.'

'Of course you didn't let her down, Julia. It was an accident. There was nothing you could do.'

'I know that,' she snapped, 'but the feelings that invade us can't always be controlled by what we know, can they? It was my job to look after her, Ricard, and I failed.'

'Our job.' She nodded.

'You know, now it's years ago and my life has changed, people see me as withdrawn from the world, isolated, too serious. They tell me, you'll get over it in time, but I'll never get over it. In fact, I don't want to get over it, because if I get over it, I'll have forgotten her and I don't want to forget her. Does this make sense?'

It was Ricard who now nodded and had nothing to say.

'I don't want the pain of remembering, but I don't want the pain to stop. If I lose the pain, I lose the memory of her.'

She started to cry and Ricard put his hand over hers.

She shook her head in annoyance at herself for crying. Out of the corner of an eye she saw Guillem glance at her, checking on his customers, then look away. He was a nice man. The thought of his discretion made her want to cry even more.

'I'm being stupid,' she said and laughed, wiping her face with a handkerchief. 'I'm sorry. It's not your fault.'

'No, it is partly, Julia. I was never attentive enough.'

'No, probably you weren't, but you know it's not about being attentive, it's about feeling.'

'I feel things too, Julia. Perhaps I just didn't know how to express it so much or empathise with you.'

Then Julia felt it was a mistake to have met. His gentle words were soothing. But she didn't want to be soothed. She'd never wanted sympathy or the hand that stroked her arm in kindness. She preferred the hard light of true feeling.

As she strolled back home down the narrow alleys of her urban village, she realised that if Ricard hadn't left her, she'd have left him. She had withdrawn after Anna's death and that had been the start of their drift apart. And why was that? Because he didn't feel the same grief? He just wanted to get on with his life. Not that it was his fault. It was sensible of him.

As she walked in the door, her mobile rang. 'Turn on the news. I'm on my way up to see you.'

'But what's up, Xavi?' She hated peremptory orders, sudden intrusions into her thoughts.

'I'll be there in half an hour.'

She found a news channel and was in time to see a man in a village street in handcuffs being bundled into a car. His head was covered with a blanket, but before they said his name she recognised the wooden plank on two stones that served as a bench in front of his house and his muddy boots and trousers covered with chicken shit. It was Jaime *el Moreno*. Her friend. But what had he done? Had he finally snapped? Killed someone? Hopping channels, she found no further coverage.

She was on her second whisky when Xavi arrived.

'You've seen it?'

'It's Jaime, isn't it?'

'He's been arrested for killing the Mayor.'

'For killing the Mayor! They've suddenly decided he killed the Mayor. What evidence have they got?'

'The shotgun, is all they said on the news flash.'

'The shotgun that killed the Mayor? But that's absurd. They'd already searched the houses of every single person in the village and run tests on all the shotguns.'

'They must have searched again.'

'I can't believe it. I know him. He's a cuddly, kind man. He wouldn't hurt a fly.'

'Julia, you may well be right, but tread carefully, for that's what Hitler's beloved dogs felt about Adolf.'

Chapter Fourteen

The Modelo prison for men occupied a strange position in the centre of Barcelona, an entire city block near the main railway station, Sants. Convenient for out-of-town relatives, thought Julia, who had come on the metro. It was the stop before Sants, on the blue line. She had always known the prison was there, but had never needed to visit it. She was lucky, it occurred to her now she thought about it for the first time: in over 40 years she had never had to go there.

The Modelo was a disordered-looking complex of buildings behind the standard windowless red-brick high walls. Above but behind the walls were windows you could easily see from the other side of the street. The third and fourth floors of the middle-class flats in the block opposite the prison looked right into these windows and the prisoners could stare out at the flats. It didn't seem fair on the prisoners to be given such views of freer, wealthier lives; at the most, flowers, or a tree or a patch of blue sky, or birds like those Saddam Hussein fed, she had read, in a small patio while he awaited death. Prisoners deserved to dream in long lonely hours, but not to have their routines disturbed by visions of an outside life. The prison had a huge mediaeval door with metal studs and iron bars criss-crossing the wood, but she went in beside it, where a notice said *Visitors*, as if it were a hospital, up two steps and through a normal human-size door.

The prison was not what she had feared: the glass partition with a grid for speaking through that you saw in the films, with stern-faced warders ordering you out as soon as your ten minutes were up. The warders were young. Nowadays you had to pass exams to work in a jail.

The warder who took her along a passage after a cursory search, less thorough than you get in airports, had longish hair and glasses like a student. He showed her into a room, an old room because the prison was old, but otherwise painted cream and with a pot of plastic flowers on the table. The room had a window that gave onto an inner patio. And then, before she had time to get nervous, Jaime came in. As a prisoner on remand, he wore his own clothes. They were clean, she noticed: Aurelia the *golondrina* would have visited him. He was familiar to her now and she was grateful he was as friendly as ever. He kissed her on both cheeks, held her hands and said: 'Thank you for coming.' She resisted the impulse to hug him, for grateful as she was for his friendliness, she didn't like having to come here.

They sat down. The hard-backed chairs had red plastic over foam cushions to soften the seats.

'I'm sorry, Julia, about all this.' He gestured at the room.

'I'm sure you don't want to be here,' Julia said primly. Xavi had cast doubt in her mind. She had wondered during a night with little sleep whether Jaime was guilty. Why else would they arrest him? So she did not smile at him, nor ask just what had happened, nor tell him she'd fight to clear his name, because she was shy of being deceived and did not want to behave like one of Hitler's stupid dogs, fawning on the monster and too easily swayed by smiles and biscuits. She said simply: 'I wanted to hear the end of Rogelio's story.' He lit a cigar.

'They let you smoke here?'

'Oh yes, soon it'll be the only place left in Spain where you're free to smoke.' He laughed. 'What do they care if the inmates kill themselves?' Then he continued with the story.

Rogelio was sleeping on a chair in the Town Hall. The sleep of the exhausted, those who can disappear from the world twisted in any position or even standing like a horse. You might think his sleep was fitful, as he had killed a man that day. He did dream, but more than a dream it was a memory in half-sleep. It was dream-like because he saw himself, an unshaven, big man spattered with blood, his pale-blue shirt stiff with sweat, and the intense eyes of the village kids staring at him as he wiped his pistol across the grass. He saw every detail of what the kids saw; and at the same time he saw the kids' ragged shirts and great brown eyes that stared from the other side of the stream, mouths open in wonder and concentration because they would always remember this moment of death that he was responsible for. They soaked up every detail.

Then he was awake, sitting up straight and at once wide awake, though his breath was furry and his eyes sticky and it was his Juanita looking gravely at him.

"Come on," she said, "come and meet my sister and mother. You can wash and change your clothes."

He remembered when he had carried water in the long-necked white jug from the street-pump to his room in Barceloneta and she had washed off the smell of fish from the market stall in the white basin. Now she brought in a similar jug and watched him as he stripped off his shirt and bathed. She took his blood-splashed shirt to soak. He dressed in his one spare change of clothes. Her mother and sister were in the front room and, when Juanita brought him in, they both kissed him seriously on both cheeks. "This is your house," her mother said. "We are glad to have Juanita back. If she's chosen you, you're welcome." Rogelio didn't know what to say. He tilted his head and grinned, suddenly clumsy, pushing a hand back through his hair.

That night, the anarchist militia slept in the church, exhausted by the events of the day, except for Rogelio and Juanita, who slept in Juanita's mother's house.'

'I wonder what she really thought of her unmarried daughter with this strange man,' Julia said.

'By this time, my grandmother didn't care a fig for conventional morality. You've got to remember what she'd been through, the rape of her daughter and murder of her husband. Obviously she didn't become an anarchist overnight, but she was quite happy to see the old order overthrown. Those women were tough. Don't forget, under the Republic things were much freer than at any time since. And if her daughter who'd been abused so savagely came back with a man she loved and who loved her and she was taking revenge on her abusers, my grandmother was pleased. When she was old, my grandmother told me once, just as my mother did when she too was old, that the 1936 summer of freedom was the happiest she'd ever known. That August the sun was high, she said, there were no shadows, the future was bright. It was only looking back afterwards that the shadow of the future was cast over the summer. But at the time...'

'It's hard to believe,' Julia murmured, not because she didn't believe Jaime, but because they were all so used to thinking that the rural past was all oppression and obscurantism. Like her own family's in another remote part of Aragon. No-one ever explained the liberating joy of that revolution.

Jaime continued. 'The push towards Huesca and Zaragoza was still on, though little did they know how soon it was going to stall and they would be spending the winter in mud-, louse-, rat- and shit-filled trenches on freezing hill-tops 30 or 40 kilometres from the city. Valeria was a little off the main column of the march, up a side road into the mountains. The anarchist group decided they would leave a couple of *milicianos* in the village, as they had in several of the villages they'd taken, and the rest of them would go back down the mountain road before pushing forward again to join the main column. Four young men, including the nervous man who had struck the priest, and two young women from the village volunteered to go with the militia. The anarchists left in the village would have the tasks of overseeing the collectivisation of the land, supervising political education and keeping a keen eye open for fascist activities. Germinal was worried about the Dúrcal brothers loose in the hills, though he assumed they'd crossed the mountains by now and were back in the bars and brothels of Zaragoza. Finally, he decided they could only afford to leave two people behind. With the loss of Paco, only nine of the original group were left. Rogelio and Juanita were the obvious choices. Though Rogelio told my mother he thought he ought to be in the front line, his attachment to Juanita overcame any doubts. They felt lucky, they were safer here. He too seemed to relax, confident of Juanita's love now that she had shown her family and her village that they were together.

After the assembly that decided on collectivisation, everything changed in the village, though nothing changed. It was harvest time and Rogelio and Juanita took up scythes with everyone else and worked their way across the fields of corn under the burning sun, as had happened every summer for hundreds of years. Then the mule pulled the *trillo*, the heavy board with hundreds of sharp quartz stones set into it, round and round the threshing-floor of beaten earth to crush the ears of wheat, barley and rye and separate the grain. Women then threw the corn in the air to separate the chaff from the grain. Heaps of grain lay in piles while the chaff floated away on the breeze. The dust and chaff made Rogelio's eyes sore and red.

What was different was that they harvested the Dúrcal land and the Mayor's land without any supervisor breathing down their necks and they collected all the grain together, to keep for the village bread and sell the surplus to the city. It wasn't easy. People were resistant to losing control over the corn from their own fields, though there was no controversy about harvesting the rich people's lands.

It was during this time that my mother talked with Rogelio. He would sit in his work clothes in the cool of the evening and chat to her about his village and his life in Barcelona. You've seen the bench, a plank on two stones, in front of my house, that's where he and Juanita would sit. The plank's changed a couple of times over these seventy years, but my mother remembered sitting on the step while Rogelio drank a glass of wine or whittled away at a stick with his knife. He had a scar running along the flesh of his arm where he'd been cut by Martín's knife and he carried a clasp-knife in his sash. At first, he took his pistol everywhere, but as the weeks passed, he left the pistol in the house. It wasn't comfortable if you were scything in the fields. They heard on the radio that more villages had been taken in the advance on Zaragoza. They began to feel they were safe in the rearguard. Every few days they had a General Assembly, where practical questions were thrashed out. In the evenings, there was a political meeting, where anyone who wanted could come and discuss the revolution. It was Juanita who led these debates, but sometimes Rogelio felt proud because he could explain:

'It's not just here, comrades, but all over Spain, in every village not taken by the fascists, that we've got rid of the landlords and priests. They lived without working and they got fat from the produce of our labour. All that's finished now.' He told them about Don Lucas, the priest in his own village. And he explained the new economy: 'The landlords have fled to Burgos, so now they can't cream off their surplus. The middlemen who pocketed their share from buying cheap from us and selling dear to the markets in Barcelona and Zaragoza have gone, too. Now we can sell direct.' As if to prove his point, two representatives of the Barcelona City Bakeries Committee arrived one day on a battered, dusty motorbike. They were touring the villages fixing dates and terms for buying grain.

'As you know by now, Julia, after four weeks, the fascists returned. Do you really want to hear this?'

'I have to hear it all.'

'They came in the early morning before light, even before anyone was up to prepare for work. My mother was awake because the dogs were barking. Later, she said, "the dogs could smell death in the air, they were just a day early." The doors were smashed open, front and back. Before she could jump fully out of bed, a man in dark glasses and a black beret was dragging her out of the room. "Shut the fuck up!" he shouted as she screamed. She heard Juanita shout upstairs. A chair toppled over. Then, as she huddled against the front wall of the house, trying to become as small as possible, thinking she would be shot there and then, she watched Juanita in her night clothes being dragged out of the house by her hair and Rogelio in just his underwear, barely able to walk. His feet dragged along the ground, blood dripped from his face and he was held up by two soldiers in uniform. Behind them, Atilano Dúrcal, his eyes bright-red with excitement, pistol in his right hand, dark glasses in his left.

"Leave my sister alone, she's only a child, she's got

nothing to do with this," Juanita shouted, twisting round.

"Shut up, bitch, you don't give orders now and you never will again," said Atilano, jerking an outstretched finger at her on each of the final four words and hardly raising his voice, which made his power still more fearsome. He looked at my mother and pointed his pistol at her. At such a moment, she told me, you're not especially frightened, you just freeze. He stared at her and she stared back at the little, round black hole at the tip of the barrel. Then he smiled, not at her, but in pleasure at himself.

"The bastard had won and he was content," my mother told me. "He was happy on that summer morning that ruined our lives."

"Leave this one here with her mother, she can't get far,' Atilano said, lowering his pistol. She watched her sister and Rogelio being dragged away along the street. He was trying to walk, but one of his bare feet, she remembered, kept turning sideways. She had not exactly frozen in her moment of facing death, but had stopped, melted. Everything had stopped working, body and mind, for she found she had wet herself for the first time since she was a baby. When the prisoners were out of sight, she went in to change. Then she comforted her mother. ' "That's the day I became a woman," ' my mother told me. "The day I was so scared I wet my knickers."

That was not the last time she saw her sister. She saw her twice more. Later that morning, when it was light, my grandmother and mother went out. The village was silent. No-one was going to work or bustling in and out of houses on their daily chores. Doors and shutters were closed. The chairs under the vines and creepers by the front doors were empty: the old people were not sitting outside today, either. The village was silent, but the two women walked in their clogs down the middle of the street, hand in hand. My grandmother carried a basket covered with a white cloth. When they reached the beaten earth of the square, they walked steadily across the middle, not fast and not slow, while the soldiers sitting or slumped under the arcades watched them. At the door of the Town Hall, the man on guard refused them entry, but went to fetch the corporal.

"Hey, Amparico," the corporal said to my mother, "you don't remember me, do you?"

"She was too young when you went away, Martín, and you look different with that broken nose," my grandmother said.

"I remember you. You told me you'd look after Juanita in Barcelona and look where we are now. My girl dragged out of bed, beaten and imprisoned in the Town Hall and you in the rebel army, it appears."

The man did not reply at first. My mother looked up at him and it was true his nose was bent. "Your darling Juanita's boyfriend," he said with scorn, "was the thug who broke my nose and I never had from Juanita a single word of sympathy. Now, *señora* Ataülfa, they've got involved in a very serious matter—it's one thing to be an anarchist or break your benefactor's nose, you can even be forgiven for this, but they've killed innocent people. It's really serious." He nodded once, then again, to affirm what he had said.

Now it was my grandmother's turn to say nothing. She looked at Martín, the corporal. He turned his face away, then looked back and shouted: "They wanted revolution, death and destruction, can't you see, and it's led to this." There was a mixture of scorn and entreaty in Martín's words. It was as if he was pleading forgiveness for what had not yet happened, knowing he was going to have to spend the rest of his life living with the silence of Juanita's mother. A silence more crippling to a weak man than fierce words, which could be replied to with the anger they engendered.

My grandmother, who was not a tall or big woman, just continued to look at Martín. Then she said: "I'm not concerned with any of this. I've brought breakfast for my daughter and her husband."

"Husband. A violent ruffian of the worst sort!" he said out of the side of his mouth and spat theatrically on the beaten earth. One of the dogs staggered to its feet and sniffed the spittle. "I'm not authorised," he said, "to let anyone see the prisoners."

My mother looked up at my grandmother, but my grandmother said nothing, did not move and continued to look at Martín. She would have stayed there all day, I'm sure of it, my mother told me. Then Atilano appeared in the doorway. He had a cup of coffee in his hand. "*Buenos días, señora*, once more. Hello, pretty little girl." He bent down and tickled my mother under the chin. "We're not barbarians, unlike the anarchists who rape nuns and burn churches. Let the girl take the young tart her breakfast. Even a red's entitled to a last breakfast." My grandmother kept hold of my mother's hand and stepped forward to go in with her. Atilano caught my grandmother's wrist. "Just the girl. You wait here."

So my mother took the basket up the steep stairs and to a room—presumably one of the rooms where the priest and the mayor had been held on that dramatic day just over a month before—where a soldier unlocked the door and she found Juanita, blood and flies on her face and white lime from the wall and dust on her clothes, slumped in a corner. No sign of Rogelio. There was a table against the wall with chairs stacked on top. Underneath the table, papers were heaped up in disorder, as if someone had swept them there with one angry stroke of a broom. The room was dirty with dust and brown leaves from the vine that twisted up the back of the Town Hall and half covered the window. When Juanita saw my mother, she pulled herself to her feet and they hugged, both crying.

"I've brought you something to eat." She put the basket down on the floor.

"Listen, my darling," Juanita told her, "you've got to be grown-up and brave. We've been fools and they've caught us. You don't have to be a fool, you're my smart little sister, get away from this village with mama, always be on your guard, don't let this scum, Atilano, Antonio or Martín near you. Not one of them." She was speaking in a whisper. "You've got to promise me, look after mama whatever happens." My mother clung to her, breathing in her familiar smell. Juanita had only come back so recently and now she was talking as if she were saying good-bye again.

"You, you—" she mumbled.

"I won't be here any more, Amparico. Promise me, look after mama, you're the big girl now." My mother gripped her sister's waist. Juanita squeezed her and kissed her. Then she pushed her away.

Very early the next morning, my mother slipped out of the house and set off up the path across the river into the woods. News travels fast in a village, even when all the shutters and doors are closed tight. No-one told her where her sister would be taken, but she knew. It was easy to hear the truck climbing the track behind her and know without any feeling that she had guessed right. It was easy too to step into the undergrowth and watch its headlights bounce past. The back of the lorry was closed, canvas drawn together by cords through metal-rimmed holes. After it had disappeared out of sight, she started running after it. Once she fell, tripping on a rut, because it was still dark, but she was young and ran on, unhurt. When she reached the clearing, she threw herself down behind a bank of earth and was in time to watch the three prisoners pushed out of the truck. First light was coming fast now and she saw across the glade Rogelio tumble out, his tied hands not allowing him to steady himself. Then her sister jumped down and stood with her head up, looking around and sniffing the air. My mother said she thought Juanita sensed her presence there. In the years to come, she was comforted to think that Juanita had known that her sister accompanied her in her last moments.

There were two soldiers carrying rifles, the driver, also in uniform but unarmed, and Atilano, who wore no uniform. The driver propped a spade and a mattock against the side of the truck. At first, she couldn't make out what was happening. Atilano grabbed Juanita by the hair and was saying stuff to her my mother couldn't hear. She heard Juanita shout, "Pig," and kick Atilano on the shin. He lurched back and swore. Then he stepped forward and cracked his fist against her jaw.

Rogelio screamed: "You piece of shit, act like a man. This is a war, treat her right."

"It's a war and you lost," Atilano shouted back. "I'll show you what a man is."

A soldier rammed the butt of his rifle into Rogelio's stomach and he lay groaning and gasping for air. Then it was unclear what was happening. Atilano was fighting with Juanita. It was an unequal battle as he was stronger and she had been beaten and her hands were tied behind her back. Her skirt was torn and Atilano was on top of her. "You red whore," he shouted. "Now, you'll find out once again what a real man is like." While he raped her, he slapped her face. My mother thought Juanita had passed out, but she hadn't because afterwards she tried to stagger to her feet, but only managed to get to her knees. The soldiers stood several metres away with their rifles at the ready. Evaristo sat leaning against the lorry wheel with his eyes shut.

Rogelio lay on the ground, trying to crawl, but the cord on his ankles and wrists prevented him. "You bastard," he said again. "You'll rot in hell for this."

"I thought you anarchists weren't religious," Atilano said.

"Your life will be hell on earth when they catch you," Rogelio said.

My mother wanted to run, but was gripped by the scene as if she were tied to the bushes around her, just as her sister's hands were tied behind her back. Like Evaristo, she wanted to shut her eyes, but she held them open with her fingers. Whatever happened, she had to stay with her Juanita.

Without realising, she must have cried out, because Juanita's head turned towards her and Atilano, buttoning his clothes with one hand, the other gripping his pistol, waved at the soldiers and they ran across the glade towards her hiding place. The spell broke and the girl, now a young woman, was racing for her life, and my life in her future, through the woods. She heard the soldiers close behind her. She knew the terrain and, being smaller, glided like a fox through the bushes, while they crashed into branches and their clumsy rifles caught on lianas and their big boots on roots. Soon they gave up the pursuit: the woods were alive and conspired against them. My mother stopped when she heard no more pursuit.

Then Rogelio shouted, far away now, "bastards." He shouted again, a sort of wordless scream. There were other screams. She raced away down the hill. She was running so she could not cover her ears. A few seconds or minutes later, she heard shots, how many she did not know, but more than three.

Jaime's head was bowed. 'That's the secret knowledge my mother carried with her all her life. That's one of the reasons I want the makeshift grave in the glade opened—to find out what actually happened. You see, they weren't killed cleanly, Julia.'

'I can't tell this to my mother.' Julia got up, pulled her white hair back from her face, walked round the small, badly painted room. Of course, she'd known how Jaime's story ended. Yet the telling shook her.

'Not cleanly,' she muttered.

Jaime went on as if he hadn't heard her: 'That's why people often went to their deaths quietly. You know, I've often heard people criticise the Jews for being too passive. But if you've been stripped of all your clothes, possessions, identity and dignity and you're being herded, weak, frozen and ill, into the gas chamber, then there's a good reason for just getting it over with. If you turn round and attack the nearest guard, or even if you're just defiant like Juanita, then imagine the further pain you suffer before the forgetfulness of death. Or that your loved ones suffer.'

But if you are defiant to the end with the guts that Juanita had, thought Julia, then you keep the human spirit alive for future generations.

Chapter Fifteen

'It's not bloody well right,' Julia's mother was saying. 'It's not right these idiots won't let us bury my uncle Rogelio. What did he ever do to anyone? I remember him playing with us when he came back to the village. He was always joking.'

'Well, he may not be as innocent as you think.'

'What do you know? You never knew him.'

'All I'm saying, mama, is that the situation is complicated. After the murder of the Mayor in this village, it's very difficult to get anything done. We have to be patient.'

'Patience! It's all very well for you. You can wait. I've waited all my life. Now I'm over 80 years old and I have to be patient.' Her mother was in dramatic mode. 'What would my own poor mother think, to know that her brother Rogelio was still unburied?' Her voice broke in a sob, which dissolved into a sigh.

Julia was sitting on the bench in the patio, the phone jammed between her shoulder and ear while she shook the compost through the big silvery sieve that left behind the roots, avocado stones, mussel shells and other pieces that had not yet decomposed. The rotted vegetable and fruit leftovers now exuded the rich smell of damp soil. It was a smell that comforted her, satisfying something basic. She converted rubbish to food. Shit to gold.

The day before, after Jaime had finished the history of Rogelio and Juanita, they had sat in silence in the prison visiting room. She stared at the wall, following uselessly the whorls of paint or the scuff-mark of a chair. Julia looked down at the floor. If she looked at Jaime, she would cry in misery at the situation. The past and the present.

Her first impulse was to comfort him, but the thought that he had killed the Mayor held her back. She could remember him serving her coffee in his house or leaving her in the glade, with unwonted delicacy for such a rough man, to be alone with her thoughts beside Rogelio's shallow grave. He had treated her kindly. And that was rare enough. She hadn't been generous to him in return. She hadn't even brought him a cigar.

It was Jaime who broke the silence.

'I suppose you won't come again.'

'I understand the feelings that could make you do this.'

'Do this? You mean, kill the Mayor? Julia, Julia, I'm not guilty.'

'Of course not,' popped out from her. Then she did look at him. He was watching her. But his look was not cunning. 'Oh,' she said, flustered, opening her hands. 'You didn't do it, then? I mean, they say they found your shotgun.'

'Julia, listen. The shotgun they removed from my house was a shotgun I had never seen before.'

'What do you mean?'

'Just that. It wasn't my shotgun.'

'Whose was it then?'

'That's what I'd like to know.'

'So you didn't do it?'

'No. Of course, I could have. But I didn't. I hope I would have killed the Dúrcal brothers, if I'd had the chance, but why would I kill the Mayor?'

'You're saying not only that you didn't do it, but that the police have framed you. I don't know what to think,' Julia said.

'The police may have framed me, or someone else might have placed that shotgun in my cupboard and informed the police.'

Julia did not know what to think. She wanted Jaime

not to be guilty, but how could she know?

The door-bell rang. She left the sieve on the big, brown flower pot and raced up the metal stairs. A young man and woman were at the door. They wore jeans and casual jackets or she'd have taken them for mobile phone sales reps, but reps always wore boring uniforms of dark suits, ties and brilliantine or heels, black stockings and eye-liner, according to gender.

'National Police,' the woman said and held up a card. They were both young, early 30s, and if she'd met them in the street she certainly wouldn't have taken them for cops. If nowadays millionaire businessmen looked like long-haired drop-outs, why couldn't cops look different too? Looks, appearance, clothes, haircuts, everything was more open and democratised, while real economic power was increasingly undemocratised and concentrated. Her mother thought that she herself, in her old blue cardigan with a hole in the elbow, white hair and soil under her nails, didn't look like a proper schoolteacher.

Once they were sitting down at the kitchen table, the man put on glasses, pulled out a red notebook and prepared to take notes. It was the woman who did the talking: 'We're investigating a complaint.'

'Ah good,' said Julia in the Catalan she normally used in her work and in public. 'I'm surprised that you've come to see me. We'd thought you'd just write.'

'I'm afraid we don't understand Catalan, *señora*. We are from Aragon.'

'From Aragon? You came all this way? What I said was I'm surprised you didn't just write.'

The policewoman looked as surprised as Julia had. 'Write?'

'To call us to a hearing.'

'*Señora*, there may not be a hearing. We wanted to

hear your response to the allegation. This is a preliminary visit to try and establish the situation. We are not seeking any formal, signed statement at this stage. Nevertheless, my colleague's notes of our conversation, I have to advise you, may be used in a court hearing, should there be one.'

'What allegation?' Julia asked. The two women stared at each other in mutual incomprehension. The policewoman had the trained, neutral expression of a state functionary, with just the lightest hint of impatience at the fools she had to deal with.

'The forest ranger of Valeria, Arturo Folches, has lodged a complaint that you threatened him.'

'Me? That I threatened him? But he shot my dog!' Julia laughed. Even as she did, she knew it was a histrionic laugh. She stopped, putting a hand to her mouth.

'According to *señor* Folches, you told him—' the policewoman nodded at her colleague and he held his little book up in front of him and read: '—that he had killed the Mayor of Valeria and you would stop at nothing to see him ruined and that you set your dog on him.'

'That's outrageous,' Julia said, aware as she spoke how hackneyed the word was. She laughed again, humourlessly. 'Really though, it is outrageous. I said nothing of the sort. He threatened me, shouting at me, and then he shot my dog. Well, it wasn't actually my dog.'

'What do you mean, *señora*? Was it your dog or was it not your dog that you allege *señor* Folches shot?'

'It was a village dog that was accompanying me.'

'A village dog that was accompanying you,' repeated the woman in a flat voice.

'Yes,' Julia said. 'It was with me, so it was my dog in that respect, but it did not belong to me.'

'To whom did it belong, *señora*?'

'I've no idea, it was just a village dog that decided to

accompany me on my walk. When Folches shouted at me, it reacted by jumping at him.'

'You agree then that the dog attacked *señor* Folches?'

'In a manner of speaking, I suppose it did, but his reaction was totally disproportionate. He kicked it in the head, knocking it to the ground. Then he fetched his shotgun and killed it. It was an act of aggression against me.'

'Even though it wasn't your dog, *señora*?'

'His attitude was aggressive, I'm telling you, he had been shouting at me. His shouting made the dog react. Then he wielded a gun in front of me. I thought for a moment he was going to shoot me.' She was nearly shouting herself.

'Perhaps your reaction was a little exaggerated. It is *señor* Folches' job to patrol the forest. If a stray dog, with no owner, attacks him, he is perfectly justified in defending himself.'

Julia stood up. The policeman went on writing and the policewoman looked at her, expectantly. Julia started to speak slowly and as precisely as she could.

'My nephew and I lodged a complaint about the refusal of the Mayor of Valeria to allow us to rebury our relative. When this incident with Folches occurred, I was in the forest glade where my relative was murdered and summarily buried.'

The young man turned the pages of his notebook. '*Señor* Folches stated that you were extremely upset about this.'

'I am upset, yes.'

'He explained that you had been in Valeria on several occasions, inquiring about this relative of yours.'

'And?'

'Nothing else,' said the man.

'A word of advice, if I may be so bold,' the woman said. 'The village has been under enormous stress in recent months due to the murder of the Mayor. I'm sure you can understand it's not the best time to be asking questions and pushing for this reburial. There are due channels to pursue, *señora*.'

'Are you telling me I can't go up there?'

'Of course not, *señora*. Please don't take my remarks that way. You have the right to freedom of movement, just as any citizen does, but your actions may be easily misconstrued. Indeed, your previous activity, running round with probing questions as if you were a private detective, was dangerously close to interference with an ongoing police investigation. Everyone hopes that now the probable culprit has been detained, normal life can return to the village. Meanwhile, I advise you to apply to the appropriate courts for permission to rebury your relative.'

'But we have done. That's what I told you at the start, when you arrived. I thought you'd come about that.'

'Doubtless you will receive notification by certified mail in due course.'

'What do you mean, that my actions may be easily misconstrued?' Julia felt like a dog with her teeth worrying away at someone's trouser leg. And liked the taste.

'*Señora*,' the policewoman said, rising now to her feet. The man closed his notebook and placed it and his pen inside his jacket pocket. 'You have had a close relationship with the alleged murderer, now detained, with conclusive material evidence against him.'

'Conclusive, a shotgun that suddenly turns up out of nowhere! What does that mean, 'close relationship'? Am I a suspect too?'

The policewoman sighed. 'Under the rule of law, *señora*, everyone is innocent till proved guilty. And of course, everyone in a murder investigation is a suspect.'

'Why don't you arrest the real criminal, not Jaime?'

'And who is that?'

'Folches.'

'Have you evidence to present to the police, *señora*?'

She didn't. She felt stupid at having got into this exchange. 'Not yet, but we will. He is a violent man. He's aggressive and his shooting my dog was designed to intimidate me.'

The policewoman sighed again to express her extreme patience with an ignorant citizen. 'You should be careful, *señora*, about what you say. As I'm sure you can see, there is no relationship between *señor* Folches committing murder and his shooting a stray, possibly rabid dog, which enters into his duties as a forest ranger. However, I appreciate you are in a stressful situation and we are quite prepared to overlook your allegation.'

Patronised by this woman twenty years younger than her, Julia bit back her retort. She had said too much, anyway. She was unaccustomed to seeing the police as her enemy. The three stood around her kitchen table without saying anything.

'Is that all?' said the policewoman. 'Is there anything further you wish to say?'

'Nothing at all,' said Julia, moving to open the door. 'You've made your position quite clear.'

Chapter Sixteen

Everything now seemed clear to Julia. And clarity brought a plan, which at first light seemed a bright, pure plan.

On Friday evening, she went up to Valeria for a third time. The cool was welcome as she drove into the mountains, leaving behind a Barcelona sweltering in its car fumes and air-conditioning units that threw extra heat onto the cement streets in the first humid days of summer. When she drove across the village square, she saw the tables in front of the café were full of summer residents and visitors. It was dark and she could pick out their heads profiled against the light from inside the bar and from the single lamp on the corner. A red dot suddenly glowing showed a smoker inhaling and a breeze of laughter drifted to her ear. She did not stop to sit and sip a beer in the fresh, summer night of a mountain village, though that would have been perfect after the long drive. She wanted to be discreet on this visit, though she hoped discretion would not mean she would draw attention to herself by being secretive.

She parked the car in a deserted *corral* behind the *Posada del inglés*. Toni embraced her, kissing her on both cheeks. He hugged her and she wished he hadn't, just as she wished now she had hugged Jaime when she saw him in the Modelo.

'It's so good to see you again, Julia,' he said, leading her by the hand across the yard full of pots, stacked tiles, a pile of logs and weeds, or plants, sprouting from the packed earth. A weed was just an unwanted plant. Village junk. There was no shortage of space in villages, so everything just piled up anyhow.

'We're all shocked,' Toni shook his head. 'I can hardly believe it, Jaime *el Moreno* being arrested.'

'Well, don't believe it, Toni. I mean, he is under arrest, but he didn't do it,' Julia told him.

'But the evidence, the gun?'

'Work it out, Toni. It must have been planted. The police searched the house before and never found it. Now they find it in a cupboard they'd already searched due to an anonymous tip-off. His lawyer thinks the case is as flimsy as a coracle in a hurricane and won't stand up in court. But apart from that, I know he was framed.'

'How can you *know*, Julia?'

'I'm sure, but I'd rather not tell you now.' Her doubt when she had visited Jaime had been transformed into this certainty not just by Jaime himself, but by the visit of the two Aragonese police who had come to warn her off.

'Have a glass of wine.'

'Later.' She saw the hurt in his eyes at her brusqueness and lack of openness, his disappointment that she had stepped back from the easy, flowing conversations of her previous visits. 'I'm a bit tense, Toni. We'll talk later, I've got to go and see someone first.' She touched his arm and smiled tightly.

Her visit took her out the back, treading with slow care past the *corrales* and across the open land, its bushes and grass cropped by sheep. From a *corral*, locked for the night, several bleated as she passed. Looking at the houses from the back, she was unsure which one was Jaime's and after all had to come round the front into the street. She saw no-one, though that did not mean no-one saw her. His house was in darkness. She banged on the door, but there was no reply. She shook the handle, but it was locked. That meant no-one was there, she supposed. She went round the back again. The hens were gone, which definitely meant the *golondrina* was not there. She would be staying with her sister in Barcelona, a summer rather than an autumn flight, after the arrest of her husband. She wondered what you did with your hens if you had to leave the village suddenly. She let herself back into the *pensión* and went straight to her room. She had wanted to make sure the *golondrina* was not in the village and she wanted to avoid Toni. Now she could fully focus on her plan of action.

First thing in the morning, before Toni could think of bringing her breakfast in bed, she showered, dressed and slipped out. There was no-one about in the street or the main square, which lay still as a picture in the clear light of the fresh morning, awaiting the heat. The rose that climbed the front of Brigitte's house was loaded with yellow, scented flowers. Their car—the same car that had passed along the mountain road the night that Enrique Jurado was murdered—was parked in front of the house. Julia paused, but it was no time for indecision, and she tugged the cord of the bell and the clanger sounded a shrill call all along the street. So much for discretion.

Brigitte opened the door, her eyes puffy, wearing a blue, silky dressing-gown.

'Come on up, dear. The coffee's on.'

By the time Brigitte had dressed, Julia had poured the coffee, was sitting on the couch and was leafing through a glossy magazine about country living.

'I took the liberty—'

'Of course.' Brigitte waved her hand to stop Julia getting up and sat down opposite. 'Now tell me what you wanted to tell me that you couldn't on the phone.' The Dutch woman wore brown trousers, a white t-shirt and no make-up and looked ten years younger than she had a few weeks before.

'OK, look. I've been thinking about this. You told me it

242

was Folches on the mountain that night. I believe you're right that going to the police is not going to help. Like you said, they won't take you seriously and a court of law is not going to accept your saying you recognised his smell as evidence. I want to ask you to do two things. One is to make a sworn affidavit as to your identification of Folches and the other to come with me this afternoon to see Folches himself.'

'I can't do that,' she said at once and brought her finger-nails to her mouth, then lowered her hand again.

'Circumstances have changed, Brigitte. We're not at the stage any more of letting the police investigation die suffocated under its own paperwork and lack of progress. Now, a man has been falsely arrested and we have to help him.'

Brigitte stood up, shook her head and fetched a cigarette from a silver box.

'I don't usually. Listen, Fernando and I are looking for a quiet place to get away from Valeria for a few weeks. We're not heroes. If I confront Folches, what good can it do? He'll just laugh in my face and my position here will become impossible. Four months after the event, I come forward and say I smelt a man on a mountain. The police, the press, the village will laugh me out of Spain.' And Brigitte laughed nervously, in anticipation of that public mockery.

'If the police thought the doctor hearing the killer would be admissible in evidence or at least useful in identifying him, I don't see why smelling the killer shouldn't be.'

'It's not the same. I shouldn't have told you.' Julia thought too that smelling and hearing weren't the same, but couldn't quite see why. They were both senses.

'But, Brigitte, you did tell me. Why did you unless

you're prepared to stand up for the truth?' Now Brigitte did begin to bite a nail. She glanced at Julia with a look almost of hatred, then looked away.

'Shit,' she said and Julia chose to take that as not entirely a refusal.

'Anyway, people won't necessarily laugh at you, if that clinches the case. I think they will admire you. Remember Gus Hiddink, who stood up to the Nazis, who did what was right.'

'Oh no, don't try that one. This is completely different. Hiddink was a man of influence, of power. Me? I'm nobody.'

Her husband, the lawyer from Zaragoza, appeared in the doorway to the kitchen. Julia stood up and greeted him. She had hoped she could get to Brigitte without having to tackle him. Fernando was a tall man, with a roundish face and small eyes behind round glasses. His large face and lanky legs seemed at odds with each other. When Julia had seen him before in the square, he had seemed distant, wary of her. Now, leaning on the door jamb, he swallowed his coffee and said:

'Brigitte, she may be right, you know. Perhaps we do have to act now.'

'But it was you who never wanted to. We talked about it.' Brigitte's voice was shrill. She had been comfortable accepting his opinion. 'Now you've gone and changed your mind.'

'Circumstances have changed, as Julia says. The arrest of an innocent man means we have a responsibility. We can sign the affidavit without any problem.'

'They'll say it was too long ago,' said Brigitte.

The lawyer turned to Julia. 'But maybe we should go to the police. I understand you don't have much confidence in them and I don't blame you. But if you don't go to them, you put yourself in a weak position.'

'If we do, Folches may be forewarned.'

'Forewarned?' Brigitte echoed.

'But look,' the lawyer went on, 'you're not going to get Folches to suddenly admit he committed a murder just by confronting him.'

'I tried that, in the forest, and he shot my dog.'

'He shot your dog? You had a dog?' She could see in the way Fernando leaned toward her and could hear in his voice that it sounded outlandish and unprovable. The lawyer was even now shifting his view of her.

'Well, not mine, but the dog accompanying me. But look, that's another story. Listen, if he thinks Brigitte actually *saw* him... I intend to have someone record the interview. I know it's weak, but I've thought it through. He's a man with a short leash on his temper and maybe we can fluster him into saying something rash.'

There was quiet in the room. Brigitte blew out a long column of smoke and Julia stared through the window at the pine forest climbing the mountain and thought she'd blown it talking about the stupid dog. The poor dog, she was the stupid one.

'Folches may not even be guilty,' the lawyer mused. 'We're just making assumptions.'

Now it was Brigitte who clinched it. She crushed an imaginary doubt in her fist and said, glaring at her husband for doubting her:

'It was definitely him on that mountain.'

'Then Julia's right.' The lawyer shrugged. 'We have to act.'

Julia rang Xavi in Barcelona. Her plan was in motion. Now she had nothing to do but wait. To avoid Toni and any awkward questions, she walked out of the village, past the abandoned development owned by Arturo Folches and along a path into the woods. It was a different direction from the glade where Rogelio was buried and the path began to wind downhill. Suddenly the forest ended. The country opened out and she was crossing a gentler landscape of undulating corn-fields, with slabs of stone set flat in the uncultivated ground between the fields, like graves in the floor of a cathedral cloister. 'Sheep tombs,' she had joked to Anna on a country walk when they had come across a similar sea of stone.

Again, she remembered walking with Anna by the hand, pointing out to her the small concealed flowers, the holes in the ground where spiders waited, a tree blistered black by lightning, only half of it in green leaf, the rest shattered like a person who'd had a stroke, birds that flew up from the fields. If they were lucky, they might see rabbits, a shrew, a snake or a deer that raised its nostrils then wheeled and cantered away. Once they had seen a group of partridges, a red-legged plump parent with perfect, sleek feathers and five pale, scruffy chicks, scurry in single file across the path. In the country, walking on her own, was when she had felt closest to Anna. She could enjoy the memory, let her mind relive those days of pleasure, without the grief pouring from the sudden images that could assail her on a city street or at some random comment.

Now, while she waited for the meeting later, a walk in the country was the way she could avoid thinking about Folches and worrying about her stupid plan. She caught a whiff of animal and stopped. It was an unmistakeable smell, like a rotten cheese or seaweed piled in the sun on the beach after a storm. She did not find it disagreeable. And when she went on, round the next corner, an elderly man was standing on the track, his blanket folded over one shoulder under a grey rucksack, while his flock of sheep

246

grazed the coarse-stemmed rosemary and thyme bushes and two goats chewed on spiky, yellow-flowered gorse. The goats' long teats loaded with milk banged against their back legs as they moved. This looked uncomfortable, but they didn't seem to mind.

'*Buenas tardes*, where does this path lead?'

After staring at her for several seconds, the shepherd replied:

'Across the ridge to the lower fields, then round the mountain.' He pointed with his stick, gesturing with it to describe the path dipping and rising. 'They say it goes to France, but I've never been so far.' She stared along the path that might wind its way across the flank of the mountain to France and then looked up to the clear sky.

'Look, vultures.' The shepherd turned and squinted. Fifteen or twenty large birds circled, rising on the thermals and dropping again, their wings outstretched and still, nearly overhead.

'That's where we leave the dead sheep. Someone's left an animal.'

Julia walked on to the place where the shepherds dumped the dead sheep, sheep that couldn't be sold for meat, because they were too old or ill. She thought, if she could smell goats, why the hell couldn't Brigitte smell a man?

She was crouching beside an oak, its trunk twisted and branches flattened by the wind, when her phone rang. She was watching a feast she had not seen before: a dozen vultures, their dirty-white necks like low-class prelates' ruffs, tore at a sheep's carcass. They jostled each other, wrenching their heads sideways as they gripped the corpse with a long-nailed claw and ripped off flesh with their beaks. Streaks of blood ran down their jaws. She could imagine what their breath smelt like. To one side, a bird was gorging itself on a chunk of meat pulled from a sheep's leg.

'It's on,' Xavi told her. 'Five o'clock.'

'Did he sound as if he suspected anything?'

'I don't think so.'

'We'll cross our fingers he doesn't check with the paper's office.'

'Fingers crossed.'

'See you later.'

Julia had conducted the conversation in a whisper, lest the vultures hear. Now she moved forward, with some apprehension, for they were big birds and suddenly she felt frail, out alone in this wild country. As she drew near, they began to rise into the air with slow, powerful wing movements. A vulture glanced at her briefly and dropped the chunk of flesh in its mouth. In some panic, the bird began to run, flapping its wings. It just managed to take off, but then came down again. It was so bloated with food it could not get off the ground. Finally, it got its breath back, waddled to a stretch of open ground and began to run as fast as it could, taking steps much tinier than its huge body would suggest, until it took off wobbling like a small, overloaded plane. The vulture wheeled just above the tree-tops and with slow flaps of its wings disappeared towards an undisturbed place to digest.

Julia walked forward to the spot where the vultures had been feeding and found she was in a sheep graveyard. Bones of every kind were scattered among the bushes: single vertebrae with the hole where the spinal cord had been, whole spines with the vertebrae still joined, leg bones, skulls with their teeth. She picked up some of the loose vertebrae that were completely clean. She would use them for key-rings.

She saw a couple of yellow-eyed dogs skulking at a safe

distance. Sheep remains at various stages of decomposition surrounded her. The whole process of decay was laid out like a classroom diagram. First came the vultures to feast on the meat. Then dogs and crows moved in for what was left. But there were still other scavengers, who arrived when the big players had taken their fill. These were the cleansers. On one carcass she saw wasps feeding off the remains that were stuck too close to the bone for other animals to tear them off. There were lines of ants, efficient armies that in a few hours, Julia knew, would strip away every last piece of flesh or cartilage. Then, in the final act, the most beautiful of insects, delicate fluttering yellow and white butterflies were sucking the last specks of decomposed meat.

Julia sat and watched them, *papallones* in Catalan, *mariposas* in Spanish, *pinpilinpanka* in Euskera, *papillons* in French, *farfalli* in Italian, *schmetterling* in German, the most beautifully named and beautiful insects, butterflies. It fascinated her to think of the perfect beauty of decomposition, how every last bit of flesh disappeared, to nourish these thin-winged, colourful creatures. This was how the bones became completely furless and fleshless, just dried white bones, which she could pick up and take home if she wanted. They were firm, dry and clean. No flesh, no blood, no smell. Nothing suggested that these hard, bright bones were the remains of soft, living mammals. *Like me, like Anna.*

In nature there was no need to worry about burial. If all humans were like the Parsees in Mumbai, who left their dead on high platforms for the vultures to devour, there would be no need to worry about burial or reburial. Though, she had read, the residents of the new estates near Parsee platforms complained that the funeral birds sometimes dropped pieces of meat as they flew away.

There was nothing clean, clear about death, a part of Nature and apart from Nature.

Later, when she was in the hospital, on the third evening, after all her visitors had gone, she got Xavi to tell her just what had happened. Till then, she had floated in a warm cloud of drugs. The dull, distant throbbing of her shoulder fastened her to the bed. Plastic tubes carried coloured liquids in and out of her. Slowly the sharp questions in her mind pierced the fuzziness of her head and Xavi explained what he had done that day.

After Julia called that Saturday morning to say that Brigitte had agreed to take part, Xavi sat for ten minutes staring out of his window across Barcelona's flat roofs towards the sea. He watched a gull peck at a limping pigeon, too feeble to defend itself. *She's crazy*, he thought.

('Please, don't make me laugh,' Julia gasped from her hospital bed and tugged on his hand. 'Laughing hurts.' He put on an ultra-serious face and caressed his beard. 'Oh don't,' she panted).

The gulls lacked food in the modern Mediterranean and were invading the city. The pigeon was not moving now and the white gull busily dug its beak into the pigeon's soft stomach.

Maybe she was crazy, but he couldn't stop her now. He breathed deeply, banged in the number he had looked up the evening before and asked Arturo Folches to do another in-depth interview, like the *El Mundo* one. He told the forest ranger he'd been looking through all the press files on the case. 'Yours was by far the most informative, señor Folches. That's why we thought you might have some interesting comments to make about the recent arrest of the presumed murderer.' Most people couldn't resist a press interview. In normal life, it was a struggle to get anyone at all to listen to you. Now, someone wants to hear your opinions and, what's more, will distribute them free to every corner of the country.

'What paper did you say it was for?' said Folches, his voice slow and clear.

'*El Periódico de Barcelona*. If you're free, I'd like to drive up today.'

'Well, I could arrange my business to give you an hour or so after lunch.'

Xavi parked in the main square of Valeria. Though it was the first time he'd been there, he recognised the café, the Town Hall, the cracked lines in the cement that covered the sun-baked square and the dogs, the malodorous dogs that lay with insolent, dribbling naturalness in the shade. 'I recognised everything from your accounts of the village,' he told Julia, 'rather as one recognises Manhattan from the movies.' An old man meandering across the square told him where Folches lived.

Xavi was dressed in light trousers, polished brown shoes and a dark-blue shirt. Over his shoulder he carried a small bag containing his wallet, a tape recorder, journalist's notebook and pencils. He had trimmed his beard and cleaned his glasses. He thought he looked quite the picture of a big-city journalist. Folches' house was built of large slabs of local stone like nearly all the other houses in the village, but it was set apart on its own plot of land. An iron fence ran round the house and some trees, a quince, he thought, and a cherry tree covered with red-streaked blossom, shaded the front yard. A polite few minutes after five o'clock, Xavi lifted the latch on the iron gate, pushed it open, strode up the path past the lush scent of cherry flowers and knocked on Folches' door.

'Good afternoon, *señor* Folches.' The man who opened

the door looked down at him for a long second before squeezing his hand without smiling. Folches said 'Come in' and looked over Xavi's shoulder. 'Just you?'

'Just me,' said Xavi brightly. Why the hell hadn't he come with someone? The house was dark and cool after the mid-afternoon heat. He took off his sun-glasses.

'That other fellow from *El Mundo* came with a photographer.' Folches led him up the stairs to a wide room that ran the whole width of the house. A spectacular plate-glass window framed the pine-covered mountain. Two glass cabinets held fossils. Two brown leather sofas were piled with papers and cushions. The floor's wooden planks were varnished to a sleek dark glaze.

'This is not really a photo feature,' Xavi explained. 'But I will certainly take a photo, with your permission of course. After the arrest of the murderer of *señor* Jurado, we thought you would be an authoritative voice to speak on behalf of the village. I was hoping you could also offer a perspective for your village's future after such a terrible tragedy.' He thought he was gabbling.

Folches nodded, waving Xavi to the sofa in front of a low table stacked with papers on one side and decorated with polished black stones inset with snail-like fossils. 'I could tell you a few things. We've been through some terrible months, that's for sure, and things can only improve now.' The forest ranger talked tentatively, quietly.

'Can I turn on the tape recorder? Ask a few questions?' Folches waved his arm in assent, but dismissively as if the question was unnecessary. But he did not sit down. On the wall behind him a locked glass case held two shotguns, with black, polished barrels. They hung from thcir trigger-guards, barrels resting on a nail. There was room for a third shotgun, but the position was empty. Xavi could not recall whether the *El Mundo* article had said that Folches had two shotguns or three.

'Shoot,' said Folches.

'Right,' Xavi said, pressing the Play button. '5.10 pm, July 16, 2007, Valeria. *Señor* Folches, can you tell me your reaction to the recent arrest of the suspected murderer of Enrique Jurado, Mayor of Valeria?'

'Well, far be it for me to judge anyone. I've known Jaime all my life. It was a great shock when he was arrested, but the police must have their reasons.'

'Was he someone you had suspected?'

'No, no, like I say, it was a great shock. We were all suspects, you understand, but I hadn't thought that he was the guilty party.'

'You said in an earlier interview that the police should look at the Basques who had moved to the village in the last few years. Do you agree now it was a mistake to say that ETA might be involved?'

'No, I didn't say that. What I suggested was that it was wrong to focus just on the village's internal problems. The problems might well have come from outside. All avenues of investigation should be kept open. Indeed, in some respects the problem has come from outside. We're talking about a crime committed by a man unhealthily obsessed with events over 70 years ago.' As Folches started to talk more freely, he began to walk up and down behind the second sofa.

'You did say it could be ETA, *señor.*'

'You can't take everything quoted in the press literally.'

'And of course what happened 70 years ago happened here. It wasn't imported by outsiders.'

The ranger stopped walking, turned and leaned his hands on the back of the sofa. He was about 50 years old and he had strong eyes, enhanced by the wrinkles and weathered brown skin of his face.

'Don't twist my words.' He stared at Xavi and Xavi nodded in acceptance and looked down at his notes. 'What I want on the record is that this village deserves to live. If I have any intelligence or influence at all, I want to use it to explain to your readers that we will get over this murder. That's why I said yes to this interview. This is a beautiful place where many different people have chosen to make their lives. The blight of this murder has meant that the sensationalist press and television channels have made out that this is a guilty, unhappy village. Nothing further from the truth. This village will not die like other mountain villages. We are not divided and I will make damned sure we all work together to get over this—'

'But if I can interrupt you, *señor* Folches, it's well known that there were deep divisions about the Mayor's actions. I understand that some people even celebrated his death in the bar.'

'That's a stupid lie, invented by the sensationalist press. You should be ashamed to repeat these ludicrous stories.'

'You misunderstand me, *señor* Folches. I'm repeating what's widely said in order to give you the opportunity to put the truth on record. I want to do you a service.'

Before Folches could reply—and Xavi never knew if he was about to be thrown out or not—they were interrupted by banging on the downstairs door. 'Who the hell's that?' muttered Folches. 'Come in,' he shouted. Xavi heard steps on the stairs. Then a woman rushed through the door. 'Brigitte!' Folches said. 'Look, I'm busy at the moment.'

'I won't keep you.' She stepped across the room and gave him a kiss on each cheek. Xavi believed she inhaled especially deeply, but could not have sworn she actually did. Knowing what was happening could make you imagine you had seen what you expected to see.'Then you appeared in the door,' he told Julia. 'You seemed supernaturally calm. You looked steadily at Folches as Brigitte, her eyes still on Folches, stepped backwards across the polished planks of the long room towards you.'

'I certainly didn't feel calm,' Julia muttered.

'You?' Folches shouted. 'What the hell's going on here?' He glanced at Xavi, who shrugged (*I'm just a journalist*), then back at Brigitte and Julia. 'Well?' Julia said. 'It was him,' said Brigitte. 'I smelt you and I saw you on the mountain.' Her voice was a sliver of sound. 'What?' shouted Folches.

'Say it again,' said Julia.

'I saw you on the mountain the night the Mayor was killed,' Brigitte said and her voice was suddenly loud until it cracked at the end of the sentence. 'You were there. I saw you.'

'You couldn't have! It was pitch dark.'

'I have excellent night vision, Arturo. When I was at school, they called me 'The Owl'.'

Then Folches laughed, but his change of humour was not comforting. ' 'The Owl!' Oh, I get it, this is a bloody set-up, isn't it? You, you interfering bitch,' he shouted, pointing his finger at Julia. 'Get out of my house and you, turn that bloody machine off.' He whirled towards Xavi.

'It was pitch dark, was it Folches? So you were there,' Julia said with a steady voice that Xavi could only admire. His own mouth was dry and he didn't think he could get a word out. 'You killed Jurado, didn't you? Because you couldn't stand his thwarting you in your building development.'

'I won't tell you again,' shouted Folches. 'Get out of my fucking house.' Folches bent down and when he stood up, he had a shotgun in his hand. Xavi didn't see where it had come from. The barrel, dull and scratched unlike the two hanging on the wall, pointed down toward the floor. Xavi saw the gun shaking as Folches' hand trembled with rage. 'I knew you were trouble from the moment I saw you, bloody communist, stirring it up where you're not wanted, poisoning our village.' Julia had waved Brigitte down the stairs behind her. Xavi jumped up, bundling the tape recorder back in the bag and holding out his hands.

'No need for the gun, *señor* Folches.'

'Keep out of it, you. Sit down.' Folches raised the shotgun and pointed it at Julia. 'Out!' he screamed. Julia stood her ground in the doorway, staring at the ranger as if she were in a trance.

'Don't be silly,' she said. 'You don't want—'

Xavi lunged forward and whirled his bag at Folches, screaming 'No'. Folches half-turned towards him. The bag thumped into Folches' arm. The shotgun went off in a roar and a pungent stench of powder. Julia spun sideways in the doorway. She screamed shrilly and clutched her right shoulder. She looked straight at Xavi, before she crumpled to the floor. Folches swore and turned towards Xavi. Xavi screamed 'Julia', picked up one of the painted stones from the table and hurled it at Folches. The speed of events, which gave no time for thought, created the reverse effect in memory, where everything occurred in slow motion. The stone seemed to hang dreamily in the air. Then it caught Folches with a crack on the forehead and the forest ranger fell straight down, his gun skittering across the floor and banging against the wall. It left a black mark where it scuffed the paint before bouncing back.

There was a second of silence. It was Brigitte who moved first. She rang 112 and then her husband. Xavi put a cushion under Julia's head. He could not stop his hand trembling. It was quickly covered in the blood that stained Julia's shirt and dripped onto the floor. She moaned.

'Julia,' he croaked and she moaned again. She seemed to be losing too much blood. Brigitte told him not to touch her, found a tea towel in the kitchen and bound it round Julia's shoulder. Then he found he could talk. 'Are you alright? Julia's pale. She's losing a lot of blood. Where's the ambulance?'

'Quiet,' said Brigitte, kneeling beside Julia and holding her pulse. 'Sit down. There's nothing we can do.' He looked round the room to clear his head. The noise of the gun reverberated in his ears still and the acrid smell of powder tickled the small hairs in his nose.

Both Julia and Folches were alive, but out cold. Xavi sat on the floor, holding Julia's hand. Brigitte's husband, a tall, gangly man, was the first to rush up the stairs. Then the police were there, talking urgently into phones, and a while later—he did not know how long it took: time was distorted—he heard the whirr of the air ambulance approaching up the valley. He looked out of the window in time to see dust and pieces of plastic swirl into the air, as the helicopter landed in Folches' backyard. He saw the black horse, tethered in the field behind, rear up on its hind legs. Before the rotor blades had stopped, two figures in red anoraks scampered across the yard, their heads bowed. He heard their feet running lightly up the stairs. They looked quickly round the room. They carried red and white bags. One muttered *Excuse me* and pushed him and Brigitte aside. He winced as the second person, a woman in a blue jump-suit, squatting over Julia, tore her blouse with a rapid tug and slammed a bandage on her shoulder. Julia's arm lay with her fingers splayed open on the pine-board floor. Then the other paramedic, a man, grabbed the arm, as if he were going to pull her to her feet. Instead he turned the arm over and pushed a needle into the back of her hand with slow, urgent delicacy. Xavi wondered how he could do this so firmly, without his hand shaking. Down a pale tube, life-giving serum flowed into Julia's right hand. As the woman in the blue jump-suit pressed, the blood stopped flowing out of her left shoulder.

Folches and Julia were strapped to stretchers, carried down the stairs and, enemies though they were, loaded like bed-mates side by side in the helicopter. Xavi watched the yellow and black machine turn down the valley in a rising shriek of noise and flurry of dust, which faded and settled as it crossed the trees and disappeared. Julia's blood lay shining on Folches' polished floor, with the plastic wrappings of the bandages and needles scattered in and around it. Xavi was left sitting on the same bulky, brown-leather sofa where he had started to conduct the interview. They hadn't let him accompany Julia. Now it was him who was being interviewed.

'Well, can you explain, sir, just what the hell's been going on here?', the unfriendly policewoman asked. Understandably, she was herself quite shaken up.

Chapter Seventeen

The county capital Villa Baja was a small market town in the valley, still high at some 700 metres but much lower than Valeria. Many of its two- or three-storey houses had elegant wrought-iron balconies. All of them had wooden shutters, mostly brown, though some had green slats and these, instead of being wound up and down on cords like the normal brown ones, opened outwards. There were shops here, a hair-dressing salon, a municipal internet centre, a supermarket, a bakery, two bars and a hotel, and of course the Town and County Hall. But though Villa Baja was the *comarca's* capital, it was little more than a village.

A river fertilised a narrow valley of fruit trees, apples, olives, almonds and peaches, she thought, though it was hard to tell peach and almond apart without a closer look. The green valley ran between stark cliffs of bare red rock. It was a gentle pastoral valley with the poplar-lined river running down the middle through the loam-rich fields, but when you looked up your eyes met the naked red cliffs, constant reminders that the land was harsh and the fertile strip by the river was the exception. Julia parked in front of the hotel-restaurant and walked up the steps and into the bar.

She had been told to sit at a table in the window, or nearby if that table was occupied, and someone would meet her. She asked for a *cortado*, sat down at the window and rotated her shoulder. It felt stiff after the drive from Barcelona. The physio had told her to move it as much as possible. The movement hurt, but would do it good. No-one was on the street: even at 11 am the digital thermometer on the wall of the pharmacy opposite, though still in shade, read 31º. Her mind was calm, though she wondered how she would feel if Folches himself were to walk into the bar. Not impossible, now she was back in his *comarca*.

Folches had been discharged from hospital after being kept in overnight for observation for possible concussion. On getting back home to Valeria, he did not even have time to call someone to come and clean Julia's blood off the floor before he was arrested. He was taken to Zaragoza in handcuffs and charged with shooting Julia. His lawyer argued that he was a person of good character, with a responsible job. It was pointed out that the two women had burst into his house and verbally abused him, making intolerable threats and accusations. Xavi had seen on the TV news a short round-faced man in a cap, identified as Teodoro Pérez, who appeared at the court. Apparently this Pérez said he'd known Folches all his life and vouched that Folches would not flee. Folches was released on the surety of one of Pérez's nieces. He was free to return to his job whilst awaiting trial (everyone knew that this could take several years) as long as he did not interfere with any witnesses. His lawyer filed a counter-suit against Xavi for impersonating a journalist and assaulting Folches.

Julia had been treated as a minor celebrity on the trauma ward at the *Vall d'Hebron* hospital. They didn't have many firearms cases and hers was in the papers. Her injury was not life-threatening despite the blood she had lost and the drama of the flight from the mountain village to the Barcelona hospital's helipad. She lived her days in the hospital bed in a strange feeling of exultation. She kissed everyone who came to see her, even Ricard. Her mother visited every day with her sister.

'Look at you,' her mother said. 'Getting involved in criminal proceedings.'

'I didn't shoot anyone, mama, I was shot.'

'There is no smoke without fire,' her mother said, not without reason, sitting down possessively at the foot of the bed.

Julia told Xavi late one night, when the visitors, colleagues from work, family, even cousins whose names she couldn't recall and whose grown-up children she didn't know existed, had all left, that her plan to entrap Folches had been little more than an impulse, which her own rashness and desperation on concluding that Jaime *el Moreno* had to be innocent had forced her to put together. She had had no idea what to do after appearing in the doorway with Brigitte except face Folches down.

'Well, you certainly did that,' Xavi said. 'He as good as admitted he was there.'

'But that's what I want to ask you. You think he did admit his guilt?'

'Absolutely. I don't know how it will stand up in a court of law, but it convinced me, the way he told Brigitte that it was too dark for her to have seen him. That was pretty definitive evidence he was there.'

'I don't know. He can easily argue he knew it was a dark night anyway.'

'Like I say, it may not stand up in court. There's all sorts of angles his lawyer can argue. But his reaction convinced me, his rage as well. And as you know, I wasn't convinced of your friend Jaime's innocence before.'

It was hard to focus clearly on just what had happened, exactly what was said. And she was scared by her wound, the feeling of physical vulnerability, how in that moment it was only a matter of a few millimetres difference in the line of fire and she would be dead. She could not remember exactly what was said and in what sequence. It scared her, too, that she might have been wrong about Folches.

'You really think he admitted it?'

'No doubt in my mind.'

'Bring me the tape.'

Then Xavi sighed and shook his head from side to side. 'I can't'.

The police had questioned Xavi as soon as the helicopter had taken off that afternoon. He had to explain the plot to pressure Folches. The police inspector took a dim view of his impersonation of a journalist. She impounded his tape recorder. Brigitte also had to make a statement. Xavi did not know whether she had told the police she had smelt Folches on the mountain-side or, even, that she had seen him. She and her husband returned to Zaragoza the next day. They did not want to stay in the village and risk bumping into the forest ranger. No restriction was placed on reporting and the press made hay with this new twist in the saga of Valeria.

When Xavi got his tape recorder back, the tape was gone. When he objected, a very polite young policeman told him: 'Perhaps you forgot to put a tape in, sir. Look, there's no listing of a tape on the receipt.' Together they read through the list of items in his bag that he had signed for when the policewoman had taken it away on the afternoon of the shooting. And indeed there was no mention of a tape. 'There was one in the recorder, though. I mean, I was doing an interview, for God's sake.'

'I'm sorry, lots of people, I've done it myself, sir, lots of people swear blind they've put a film in the camera or a tape in the recorder and they haven't. If it had been there, it would be on the list.'

'There's some mistake,' he muttered.

'This is why we always ask people to check through the list before signing for everything, sir,' the policeman said.

'But I *know* there was a tape in there. I was nervous and I remember that I checked it several times.'

The policeman pursed his lips and opened his arms in sympathy.

So there was no evidence Folches had betrayed his presence on the mountain in his exchange with Julia. There was no tape Xavi could play back to Julia to double-check her confused memory. Yet Xavi and Brigitte had been present too, so Julia knew she wasn't alone and mad in her conviction. While she lay at night in a half-waking, half-dozing haze, pain-killer for her throbbing, bandaged shoulder dripping down the line from the plastic bottle hung upside down on the IV pole into the thin needle taped to the back of her hand, her mind had time to think. Her body floated happily in the drug-filled haze while she explored what she could do. Folches was out of jail, though facing a serious charge of wounding her; but Jaime was still inside, accused of killing Enrique Jurado.

'*Buenos días. Señora* Julia?'

'Yes,' she said.

'Don't get up.' The young woman who sat down in front of her in the Villa Baja hotel bar had long black hair, tight trousers and a white blouse. She took off her dark glasses and smiled. She had long eyelashes, too.

'I'm Natalia.' They shook hands across the table. 'Glad you could come. Finish your coffee, there's no hurry.'

'Where are you taking me?' said Julia. She didn't want to go back to Valeria and have to give explanations to anyone she might meet.

'Don't worry. It's close by, we've got a *finca* just outside town. We'll go in my car, then I'll drop you back.'

'Why all this secrecy?'

'It's not secrecy, but my uncle's old, he needs to protect himself against visitors.'

The *finca* was only a few kilometres outside Villa Baja, but in another valley. They took an asphalted single-track road across the narrow, green plain with apples and plums almost ripe on the trees' bent branches, and crossed the fast-flowing, brown river, though here it was wider and calmer than at Valeria. Then they left the valley on a winding dirt road up over the cliffs. To their left, a ravine, its steep side scruffy with purple-headed thistles, bushes hunched low and loose boulders, then an expanse of green at the bottom. The dust from their car formed a cloud behind them. Over the top and the track curled down again into the next valley. Through the oaks and poplars Julia saw a big, modern house, surrounded by a high board fence. A few minutes later, Natalia drew up, spoke into an Intercom and the metal gates rolled back. She drove in and the gates shut again behind them. How would I get out? Julia thought momentarily. The yard had small trees with hanging branches heavy with little brown apples and then a verandah with a deck-chair and a cuddly spotted tiger.

'Excuse me', said Natalia, running her hands over Julia's body. 'It's just routine, in case anyone brings a weapon. Don Teodoro's had threats, you see. I hope you don't mind.' Then she looked through Julia's bag. Julia was carrying no weapon and she bore the search calmly. It confirmed to her that she just might be right. If Teodoro Pérez needed so much protection, then he still carried influence. At nights in the *Vall d'Hebron*, half-delirious on drugs, in that half-waking half-dozing state, she'd thought, or dreamed, of just taking a gun or a knife and shooting Folches or stabbing Teodoro Pérez. Later, sitting in her garden, doing her exercises to recover full use of her left arm, under the grape vine that gave her shade as it stretched across the frame, she knew that the fantasy of revenge was not going to get her what she wanted. Xavi had watered her plants while she was in hospital and had tied little white muslin bags over the bunches of grapes to protect them against the birds. When she first gingerly walked down the stairs—her arm was still in a sling and she was unaccustomed to walking—and sat alone on the bench against the wall of the block of flats, she had burst into tears for the first time since she was shot. For the first time, perhaps, since the day Anna was killed. The birds had risen, dozens of them, protesting at her invasion of their peaceful, cat-free patio. She had sobbed her heart out to see the patio so well cared for and so many little bags so neatly tied round the grapes. Anna and she had often sat on that same rickety bench, staying still for several minutes, and the birds that had fled in outrage when they came down the steps slowly returned. In whispers, they identified them. *Sparrow, wagtail, robin, greenfinch, turtle dove, blackbird...* The stroppy, beautiful, bold, loud-mouthed blackbird, their favourite.

During her recovery, the long hours sitting with the plants and birds, the brushing between the pots with one hand, she came to realise she could engineer no complete solution. Bury Rogelio, get Jaime out of prison and more she could not do. Burying Rogelio was what she had gone to Valeria to achieve. This is what she would focus on. This idea had brought her to this enclosed *finca* near Villa Baja.

The impact of Teodoro Pérez was all the greater because he was not a man you would normally notice. He wore a blue open-necked shirt, jeans with the bottoms rolled up, a pair of espadrilles on his feet and on his head a faded-red cap with *Repsol* written across the peak. He was not tall and his face would be hard to describe. If you met him a second time, you might not be fully sure it was the same person. He was holding the hands of a child who was taking uncertain steps.

'He's learning to walk,' Pérez said unnecessarily.

'Your grandson?'

'The second boy. There are two girls, too.'

Natalia brought Julia the orange juice she'd asked for and left them again. Julia did not know now how to start. She decided to wait for Pérez, but he was in no hurry. So she looked out of the window, across the yard to the high board fence, with the sheer, red cliff behind. There was a bird wheeling in front of the cliff, but she could not make out what it was.

'You see a lot of eagles from here?'

'Yes, several kinds of eagle, though there are more vultures. They nest in the cliffs.'

She turned. 'I came to see you, *señor* Pérez, because everyone says you are a man of great influence in this *comarca*.'

'People get funny ideas,' the old man said, tickling the child under the chin. 'I'm just an old man, retired. I still like to go out with a few sheep or goats and I have my grandchildren to keep me entertained.'

'I see you like children.'

'Children, animals and plants. All, God's work.'

'I'm very grateful to you for receiving me. I won't waste your time telling you what you already know. I need your help. I was a fool. I thought I could sort this out by myself. But I can't. I want to get Jaime *el Moreno* out of prison. He's a good man and I don't believe he did what he's accused of. And I believe you know he's innocent, too.'

Teodoro Pérez looked at her for the first time. She had thought he might have piercing blue eyes, but his eyes were an old man's, faded brown and mild. She wondered where the guy's charisma lay.

'And another thing, *señor* Pérez. The most important. What I came to Valeria for. I want to get the three bodies in the glade reburied in the cemetery.'

The old man looked down at the floor, patted the hand of his grandchild, then looked up at her again. She had no idea how he'd react to her crude statement of intent. Perhaps he'd call Natalia and have her thrown out. A tremor ran through her wound, like a ripple in a tensed muscle. The tremor was comfortable. She felt calm.

'How's your wound, where you were shot?' Pérez asked, as if he had perceived the ripple.

'Oh, it's fine now.' She touched her shoulder carefully. 'Getting better.'

'You shouldn't have done that.'

'What?'

'Put your life at risk.'

'I didn't know—'

'I think you didn't care what happened to you. That may make you bold, but it doesn't make you strong.'

She hadn't believed she didn't really care what happened to her, but she had had time to think there was some truth in Pérez's perception. After Anna's death, her own fate seemed less important.

'What does make you strong?' she asked.

'I like your white hair,' Teodoro Pérez said. 'My wife, may she rest in peace, had white hair. Most women dye it, but I like it to be natural. People should accept their age.'

She could handle this chit-chat: 'It's what I reckon, too. Otherwise you're just kicking against the inevitable. And that's stupid.'

He nodded.

'So will you help me?'

'Why should I, *señora*, even if I could?'

The child began to cry at this question, registering how Teodoro Pérez's attention moved from him to Julia or catching the edge of steel in his voice. On cue, Natalia came in and swept the child up in her arms. 'Let me take him, *tío* Teo.'

Teodoro Pérez let the boy go without a word, then tapped his thigh. 'I was shot once, too. Nothing very serious, in the leg, just a flesh wound, but it probably saved my life. I was with Muñoz Grande in Russia. Half my battalion was wiped out in the snow near St Petersburg. Leningrad, the reds called it. To my shame at the time, I was invalided out before the worst of the cold and slaughter. When I got back here, things were bad. Most people in this *comarca* were hungry. My mother's house was one of the few not to go hungry, because of my army pension. And there were abuses. There were men who did what they wanted in the name of the Caudillo. There was a girl in the village, Vicenta, a bit simple, her father was killed in the war and her mother was sick. There was probably nothing wrong with her that one good meal a day wouldn't have cured. They lived in a hovel, no better than a sheep *corral*. People are cruel, *señora*, we're all cruel, especially with those who are weaker. Vicenta would go begging from door to door. Imagine, so hungry you begged off starving people. She was filthy and she stank. One day the two Falangist *señoritos* decided to have some fun with her. They brought a bath-tub out into the square and dragged her out of her hut. A crowd of men appeared. There are always idlers when there's a spectacle.' To her surprise, Julia registered that Teodoro Pérez was a moralist, not a cynic.

'The crowd gathered round. The Falangists stripped her and shoved her in the bath and started to scrub her. She didn't scream. When I got there on my crutches, she was whimpering and shivering, the water was cold of course, and the men were laughing. Several of them were scrubbing her at once. She was just skin and bone, you

268

could see right through her she was so thin and as the dirt came off you saw her skin scrubbed red and she looked even thinner. I said to the two lads, you'll have heard of them, the Dúrcal brothers, I said: "That's no way for Falangists and Catholics to behave. You think my comrades gave their lives on the Russian front so you could mistreat this poor girl?"

You could hear a pin drop. "Hey, Teo, don't take it to heart, man, we're doing the poor little tart a favour, getting her cleaned up," one of the Dúrcals said. I let the silence hang for a few moments more.

"Hey", I said to one of the onlookers, "go to my house and ask my mother for a towel." Then I rolled a cigarette and everyone waited. People who are cruel to the weak are the same people who lick the boots of the strong. And being strong is taking a risk. And calculating the odds. Otherwise you're a fool.'

He looked up at Julia. She assumed he thought she hadn't calculated the odds right.

"Anyone got a light, boys?" I asked and several rushed forward.

"Well," said Antonio Dúrcal, "our Vicenta's good as new now, eh?," slapping her lightly on the cheek. He could see which way the wind was blowing. He hadn't dared have a go at me, with my war medals. He knew he'd be in hot water with the authorities, you see. And another thing, I left him and the others a way out. You've got to win, you know, but leave the others their dignity. If you back 'em up against a wall, they'll bite you, like cornered dogs. I saw the bloke approaching with the white towel. I said: "We'll get her dried, boys. You go on to the bar and have a drink on me, I'll be over later." Vicenta's still alive, 84 years old, same age as me. Never married. That scum put her off men for life.'

She didn't think Teodoro Pérez was expecting a reply. He was just painting a self-portrait.

'Don Teodoro, I'm not interested in court cases. I'm aware I acted in a headstrong, perhaps foolhardy manner. Folches' shooting me was entirely accidental. I am no longer concerned about the unknown person who killed the Mayor of Valeria.'

Pérez tried to stand, one hand pushing against the chair, but he flopped down again stiffly. Julia held out an arm and he leaned on her as he got up. They stood together at the window and he let go of her arm.

'I heard that Pilar, the woman who runs the bar, was thinking of standing as the new Mayor. She'll probably be unopposed. I think that Arturo Folches would be too controversial a figure after all this bother, don't you?' Teodoro Pérez said in a conversational style.

'You mean Carmela's not going to stand?'

'After the tragedy, she felt duty-bound to carry on, but I think she'll be happy to resign. The people of Valeria need a new face, someone who can reconcile the village. I believe Pilar will live and let live. The new estate would bring in business for her and I imagine she'd have no strong objection to the reburials.'

Teodoro Pérez called for Natalia. He turned toward Julia and shook her hand. He was so short he had to look up at her, but this did not diminish his stature. 'What we all want is that Valeria doesn't die. Let's hope it can recover from this terrible tragedy.' During her whole time in the house she had not sat down.

In the car Natalia said: 'So did you get what you wanted?'

'I don't know. He told me a story.'

'He tells everyone a story.'

Julia laughed. She didn't know if she'd been clever and

got what she wanted or had wasted her time. Maybe Teodoro Pérez had just been playing with her. Natalia changed gear to climb the hill and said:

'Don't laugh, *señora*. Don Teodoro is a man of his word. What he says he will do is what he does.'

'That's good to hear, Natalia. But I'm not sure exactly what he said he would do.'

Chapter Eighteen

It was not till the spring of the following year that they could finally organise the reburial in the cemetery of the remains of the people killed and scantly buried in the beautiful glade in the forest. Julia drove Xavi, her mother and Charo up to Valeria. They had decided not to stay overnight. What was the point of spending money sleeping in someone else's bed when your own was more comfortable and cheaper? her mother said. That suited Julia. She didn't want too many of Toni's attentions. He'd visited her in the hospital. He'd offered to come and shop and cook for her during her recuperation. She liked him well enough, but... Maybe, she thought, but not now.

Just as the press reports were dying down, they had flared up again: the case against Jaime *el Moreno* was dropped. The evidence rested entirely on the gun found at his house, which was indeed identified by ballistics experts as the murder weapon, but there were grave doubts, his lawyer argued, as to its provenance. This was the word the lawyer used, as if the shotgun were a forged painting, when interviewed on the steps of the Zaragoza law courts. The radio and TV microphones with their yellow and red foam nozzles jostled in front of him. In the previous, thorough searches of Jaime's house, no gun had been found. It was curious, the lawyer pressed this point, that in this third search they searched only Jaime's house. It emerged the police had received an anonymous tip-off. It was pointed out that any villager could walk in and out of houses, as no-one ever locked their doors. 'The whole situation stinks of a set-up,' the lawyer thundered with studied rage to the impromptu press conference. 'The sudden, suspicious appearance of this weapon amounts to the opposite of evidence. Evidence, in fact, of my client's innocence. In addition, anyone who knows the history and background of my client as an ardent fighter for social justice and the personal background of his family knows he cannot be guilty of such a violent crime.'

They parked in the square and sat at one of the red tables in front of Pilar's bar. Julia's mother wore black, as if it were a funeral, and of course it was. The small group of diggers from Santa Maria de Descorcoll had recovered the bones from the forest. The remains had been identified— Julia herself had given a DNA sample—and placed in black plastic bags and then coffins, which were now in the Town Hall. Julia had received a stark, one-page report. The investigators found evidence of mistreatment before death. Some of Rogelio's rib-bones, a cheek-bone and an ankle were broken, consistent with fierce blows. Jaime had been right: they had not died 'cleanly'.

All three, of course, died violently. Their skulls had a hole at the back of the head, a hole with rough edges of splintered bone. Rough edges that, when she studied them in the photos, made her wince in awareness of the extreme force of bullets.

Her mother sat in her dark glasses looking round at this unfamiliar village square. 'So this is where our poor Rogelio...' she muttered, dabbing her eyes. Julia feared she was going to cause a scene at the ceremony, but Xavi had said: 'Let her... Why not?'

'She just wants to be the star of the show.'

'OK, and why not? She is one of the stars.'

His calmness infuriated her. She wanted to challenge her mother, change her. 'Wisdom is accepting you can't change something that can't be changed,' Xavi would say pompously and did so again now, while he held up his hands in mock appeasement. At least he had undertaken to

273

look after her mother during the day. It was going to be hot, she thought, black's hardly the best clothing. Julia herself wore light trousers and a shirt she wore to school. Her only extravagance was that she had pinned to her shirt a little red and black pin she had found at a Saturday stall in the Plaça Orwell.

Then things moved rapidly. Jaime *el Moreno* and Aurelia the *golondrina* joined them at the café and Toni arrived almost at the same time. Both men looked strange, wearing clean, well-ironed clothes. Toni kissed her on both cheeks and she pressed his arm. He had been kind to her, though she did not want to sleep with him. She stood up and led him aside.

'I wanted to ask you something, Toni, you told me you were one of Thatcher's exiles, but I was thinking, why didn't you stay and fight her?' This was a day for straight talking.

'I'm not like you, Julia, I preferred to step sideways off the battlefield.' *Like me?* she thought. It was strange to glimpse how another person perceived her. She nodded. Then she did what she had wanted to do since she first met him. She ran her finger down the long crease in his face that led from his left eye to the edge of his mouth. 'Thank you for everything, Toni. Come and visit me in Barcelona.'

Jaime got into conversation with her mother, who was lamenting loudly their losses: 'Of course, you lost your aunt, may she rest in peace, poor woman, dying so young, and I lost Rogelio, my poor uncle, who used to play with me in the *pueblo* when I was just a little girl.' Jaime seemed happy to listen to her stories and to help them along with a comment or two. Julia needn't have worried. She got too angry with her mother, but here with people her mother didn't know, she fitted in fine. *Better than I do.* Then the church bell began to toll slowly. Solemnity replaced chit-chat. Everyone left their coffee cups and torn sugar sachets on the red tables and made their way across the square towards the Town Hall.

There was a hand-cart in front of the door. As the crowd assembled, Evaristo's coffin was brought out by two members of his family and loaded carefully onto the cart. Then the other two, with the remains of Juanita and Rogelio, were carried out. To Julia's shock, they were just wooden boxes, no bigger than children's coffins. Two young men from the Barcelona CNT spread black and red flags over the two anarchists' coffins. Simultaneously, Jaime *el Moreno* and Julia's mother stepped forward hand in hand, touched all three coffins and made the sign of the cross, bowing their heads as they kissed their thumbs.

Several of the archaeologists from the dig began to push the cart up the track towards the cemetery. One of them was the vehement young woman with one red ribbon braided round a lock of her otherwise short hair. She'd strode up to Julia earlier and said: 'Well done'.

'It was luck,' Julia shrugged.

'Bollocks,' said the young woman, tossing her red braid back over her head and taking a grip on Julia's forearm. 'Someone's got to fight these fascist bastards and that's what you did.' Julia, nearly 50 years old, felt extraordinarily proud to have won the respect of this twenty-one year-old.

The families walked behind, along with the priest from Villa Baja, a tall African of about 30 dressed in a brilliant-white surplice that hung magnificently from his shining, black neck. The population of Valeria was too small, or irreligious, to warrant its own priest. And once-Catholic Spain was too materialist to provide its own priests and had to import them. Julia looked round and the procession was large, several dozen people in the sun behind the cart with the three coffins. She hadn't expected many, but most of the village must have come.

The cemetery was enclosed by four whitewashed walls. No trees grew on this stony hilltop, but large boulders lay like silent sentinels around the walls. Inside, an area of rough earth with patches of grass was covered with crosses higgledy-piggledy. In former times, people had been buried in the earth without a gravestone, but in recent decades crosses and stones had been put in place and, when the ground was almost full with marked graves, a row of thirty niches, ten long and three high, had been built.

The three coffins lay on the cart. The priest said his words over them, spraying holy water. Then Jaime stepped forward, turned round to stand beside the priest, pulled a piece of paper from his pocket, put on his glasses, held the paper out at arm's length, coughed and began to read in a strong voice:

We are gathered here today to inter and to honour the memory of Evaristo, Juanita and Rogelio, who were vilely murdered on 31 August 1936. It is long ago and we are not interested today in any arguments about who killed them and the rights and wrongs of our Civil War. I will only say that they fought for justice and they didn't deserve to be tortured, shot at dawn and dumped in an unmarked grave. They lay there too long. For their families, those of us who are here today—

He stopped and coughed again. He looked up from the paper in his hand at the silent crowd, then glanced up at the tall black man beside him. The priest nodded in encouragement. Julia thought, irreverently and as Folches had said, the dead were probably better off in that beautiful mountain glade than on this barren hill. But their bones were in their coffins: funerals were for the benefit of the living. Then Jaime cleared his throat again, bent his head over the piece of paper and read his final words quickly.

What those of us gathered here today want is simply that our relatives, our fellow-villagers, fellow human beings lie in marked graves. Their families can at long last live in peace. Thank you.

Then the coffins were raised easily into the niches. She recalled what she had told Toni on one of his visits to the Vall d'Hebron hospital. 'You know what happens to bone?' She showed him a fish spine, sucked clean as a freshly boiled comb, on her dinner-plate. 'We all know the flesh decomposes and is eaten by animals, but then in a slower process the bone disintegrates too. That's what's started to happen to those corpses in the glade. It's not just our memories of them that fade with time. They fade away physically too. There'll not even be any bones left in a few more decades.' He had shaken his head:

'It's a morbid thought, Julia.'

'I find it comforting.' She tapped the bone on the plate. 'We're just matter, part of nature.'

Two of the villagers stood by with builders' trowels and a bucket of cement to seal the stone slabs over the dark mouths of the niches. Julia's mother was staring, her mouth open, eyes tearful and a crumpled handkerchief in one hand, ever-histrionic as if an intimate lover was being immured, not the ghost of a memory from a long-ago childhood.

A press photographer wanted a picture of the relatives. Julia's mother, Jaime and a cousin of Evaristo, arm in arm and in dark glasses, were photographed in front of the cemetery gate. Then it was Julia who stared into a dark TV camera lens and spoke severely: 'We hope very much that today can bring a sort of closure to this village, which has experienced so much suffering, not just 70 years ago, but recently too. However, we should not forget there are tens of thousands more people in unmarked graves throughout the Spanish state. It's a disgrace and a blight on our democracy that so many families are continuing to suffer, while the Government refuses to take decisive action on the question.'

She smiled at the end. She thought perhaps Arturo Folches would watch the interview on the local news. Her words might give him a jab of pain in his temple where Xavi had knocked him cold with a stone. She smiled and flexed her shoulder, where she could still feel her own wound. She thought she might even be learning to relax.

Pilar and her staff, hired for the day, had laid out a long trestle table in the square. Julia had driven up to see her two weeks before. It had been a cloudy day and in still-early spring there was a nip in the breeze.

'*Buenos días, señora*. What will you have?' Pilar made no sign that she recognised Julia.

'A beer today, why not celebrate? Have one yourself. And congratulations.'

Pilar nodded then, even smiled. 'Thank you.' In the elections for Mayor held a couple of months before, Pilar had been returned unopposed.

Later, Julia had asked the new Mayor to sit with her at one of the corner tables.

'I see the notice has been taken down.'

'Paris and London?'

'The new mayor agreed to your terms?'

'Absolute agreement.'

They both grinned.

'But tell me, Pilar, why did no-one else stand?'

'*Señora* Carmela wanted the unity of the village and stepped down because she thought she was inevitably identified with just one faction.'

'But you? I thought you had enough work here.'

The Mayor shrugged. 'Always asking questions. Look, this village needs more people. My bar needs income. We need the new estate. I decided that if I stood, I'd get the estate, people and income. Simple as that.'

'And goats' droppings.'

'Goats?'

'Yes, you need sheep and goats' droppings, not bye-laws against them. The stressed-out German tourists will love to see flocks.'

'OK, goats too, and what's it to me if someone wants to rebury their dead? I'm not Carmela with a grandfather to remember.'

'But you know, Pilar, the murder of Enrique Jurado was never solved.'

'You were wrong,' the new Mayor said.

'Wrong?'

'You kept going on, didn't you, about how we had to solve the murder of Enrique before you and *El Moreno* could bury your dead. Well, we haven't solved it, have we? But you're burying them now.'

Julia shrugged.

'So you were wrong.'

Julia nodded. 'You know, Pilar, who killed Jurado.'

'So. Everyone knows. You know. But no-one wants to know, do they?'

'So that means it's possible to commit murder, be discovered, but not go to jail because it suits everyone not to have the bother of a trial.'

'Ah,' said Pilar, with an irony Julia had not anticipated in her, but perhaps this like her confidence in conversation came with her new job, 'I see you are beginning to understand something of how politics works in this *comarca*.'

They had agreed terms for the funeral lunch. Now, after the speeches and the interment, the crowd had come back down to the square for the crisps, olives and nuts laid out in earthenware dishes on the long trestle table. Drinks were being served in the shade under the arcade. As the villagers arrived, plates of chicken, potato omelettes and pork ribs were carried out from the café. Julia saw an unshaven old man with a military crease in his trousers bite into a chicken leg, juice running down his chin. He jumped when Julia tapped him on the shoulder and said: 'Remember, Pinochet, this is about justice and anti-fascism, not murderous dictatorship.'

'Today is a day of re-concili-ation.' And he made a half-bow, chicken flesh hanging in strings from his brown teeth. One of the lean young anarchists, in a purple t-shirt and a pony-tail, caught her arm: 'Did I hear right? Is that his name, that old guy? Pinochet?'

'It's what he likes to call himself.'

'He's a fascist?'

'He's a poor devil worried what's going to happen to him when he's too old to wipe his own arse.'

She sat in the shade of the arcade, a plate of lamb and rice on her lap, beside Xavi, her mother, Jaime *el Moreno* and Aurelia the *golondrina*. She was sure it was one of those intense days in life, whose images would remain imprinted on your brain, never to be forgotten for as long as you lived.

'You'll come and visit us again?' Jaime asked.

'Why not?' Julia grinned. Though she already knew she wouldn't. In Valeria she had learned how to pursue the rest of her life. She had released the past. On this funeral day she hadn't smiled so much since..., since before Anna died. And now she kept on smiling at the memory of her beautiful daughter. Gone, but not forgotten. *Why should I cry when I think of her?*

On a day like this, of ceremony, of celebration, you talk to a lot of people and later only jagged memories remain, like driftwood sticking up half-buried from the sand of a storm-swept beach. Of all the exchanges of the day, one conversation stuck in her mind. At a point in the lunch and chit-chat, she loaded a plate with chicken, potato and green peppers, slipped away from the party and walked down one of the streets to a tin door painted red.

'Good morning, Anacleto,' she said to the old man who opened to her knock. 'We've missed you. I brought you your lunch.' He took the plate and set it down inside the door.

'*Buenos días, señora* Julia, and thank you very much. Very kind. I came to the ceremony, but then I felt tired. My legs aren't what they were.'

'I saw you there, Cleto. Look, I wanted to thank you for your support.'

'Me? Oh no. Really, I should apologise.'

'What for? You're innocent! One of the few.' She was a little drunk with the lunch and the excitement of the day.

'Step inside, out of the sun. I meant I should not have told you that you couldn't win this burial.'

'Sometimes you have to be a little crazy and have a lot of luck.' She thought that was a smart answer, though Cleto didn't seem to have heard her. Her eyes were growing accustomed to the cool dark and she saw that the inside of the house was quite different from the gaudy front door. There was a long, smooth wooden table on the beaten earth floor and a large domed clay oven set into the bricks of the back wall. She realised with a shock they were standing in the village's old bakery. Her mood shifted from euphoria. It was as if you had only to step out of the sunlight and at once you were hurled into the dismal past. This was where the women had gathered to knead and chat in the comforting warmth of the oven, smelling of pine branches, gorse and fresh-baked bread. And one of the odious Dúrcals had violated that space and hacked off a young woman's hair. Julia leaned her hand against the table. 'Cleto?'

'No, I was thinking, *señora* Julia, you risked your life and it should have been us villagers. What I said may have contributed to your desperation. Thank God you weren't killed.'

'What you said? No, you're quite wrong. When I met you by the bridge after getting nowhere with Carmela, it was your story of what had happened here, in your house, that made me determined to carry on.' The old man was looking at the ground and rubbing his eyes. 'Look, Cleto, what can I say? I'm convinced no-one has to feel guilty because they were victims of fascism.'

'Fine words.'

'Well, what could you do? Get yourself killed?'

'I kept my head down too long. We all did. You were persistent.'

'The time was ripe, Cleto, and I was ignorant and lucky. I just wanted to say thank you for your support.' She stepped towards him and kissed the old man on both cheeks. They were damp and she realised she too was crying.

As she walked back up the slope, Cleto's flattery reminded her of Xavi's reaction when she told him of her conversation with Teodoro Pérez. He'd laughed out loud.

'My God! You cunning sod! You went to bargain with the devil in his den. And I'd thought you were going to get yourself killed, like Juanita the absolutist.'

'I nearly did.'

As they were getting into the car to leave Valeria, she noticed a man with a thick, black beard and dark glasses across the other side of the square. A pipe was clenched in his teeth and a peaked cap shaded his eyes. He was sitting on the ground against one of the pillars of the arcade. He held a shotgun across his lap and was staring towards their car. While the others chatted, still excited and relaxed by the success of the day, Julia's eyes were drawn back to the lone figure. He had stood up and was still staring at her.

With a real shudder, one that ran a sudden pain through her shoulder, she saw it was the man who had nearly killed her. Who had killed her dog. It was Arturo Folches, still staring at her. *He can't shoot me now.* She thought of pointing an imaginary gun at him with two extended fingers, like children did, and saying *'bang-bang'.* But that would be quixotic, carried away by her momentary success. Triumph was temporary and partial, she knew.

She looked again at the killer with the real gun and suddenly he seemed no longer threatening. Trying to look ferocious, Arturo Folches succeeded only in looking like Captain Haddock, his pipe clenched between his teeth in harmless parody of his real rage.

Instead of shooting him, Julia got into the car. Her mother was going on about what a fine man our uncle Rogelio was. Julia nearly told her to just shut up for once in her life, there was nothing particularly fine about *our* Rogelio. He was just an ordinary man who loved, struggled to understand and committed murder. Then she wanted to be kinder and said nothing.

Acknowledgements

It's often a heavy responsibility to read friends' books. I am very grateful to the following who read with grace part or all of *The Bones in the Forest*. Every one of them helped me to improve it:

Marisa Asensio, Alba Dedeu, David C. Hall, Eugene Ludlow, Judith Ravenscroft (1947-2023) and Richard Zimler.

My heartfelt thanks too to Kathryn Phillips-Miles and Simon Deefholts of The Clapton Press for accepting the novel and then making the publication process so easy and enjoyable.

All characters in this novel are fictitious. Any resemblance to an actual person is fortuitous. There is one curious exception: the most improbable character, the village drunk who called himself 'Pinochet', is based on someone real.

Valeria too, is fictitious, both in its layout and its deliberately vague geographical location. If it seems familiar, that's because it's a composite of many such mountain villages.

The theme of people murdered during and after the Civil War and abandoned in unmarked graves is lamentably all too real. The details in Chapter Seven on the Association for the Recovery of Historical Memory were all taken from its web site (www.memoriahistorica.org.es).

BY THE SAME AUTHOR

Barcelona: The City that Reinvented Itself
Five Leaves Publications, 2006

Triumph at Midnight of the Century:
A Critical Biography of Arturo Barea
Sussex Academic Press, 2009

La Transició: moviment obrer, canvi polític
i resistència popular
L'Heura, 2009 & 2016

Con el muerto a cuestas: Vázquez Montalbán y Barcelona
Al Revès, 2011

Sails and Winds: A Cultural History of Valencia
Signal, 2019

A People's History of Catalonia
Pluto Press, 2022

Triunfo en la medianoche del siglo
Renacimiento, 2023

Antoni Gaudí
Reaktion Books, 2024

https://michaeleaude.com/books-by-michael-eaude/

MEMORIES OF SPAIN SERIES
AVAILABLE FROM THE CLAPTON PRESS

A Gypsy and a Rebel: Lillian Urmston in the Spanish Civil War
—Linda Palfreeman & Alicia García López

Perfidious Albion: Britain and the Spanish Civil War—Paul Preston

Forged in Spain—Richard Baxell

Never More Alive: Inside the Spanish Republic—Kate Mangan

The Good Comrade: Memoirs of an International Brigader—Jan Kurzke

In Place of Splendour—Constancia de la Mora

Firing a Shot for Freedom—Frida Stewart & Angela Jackson

The Fighter Fell in Love: A Spanish Civil War Memoir—James R Jump

The Last Mile to Huesca—Judith Keene & Agnes Hodgson

Struggle for the Spanish Soul—Arturo & Ilsa Barea

Hotel in Spain + Hotel in Flight—Nancy Johnstone

Behind the Spanish Barricades—John Langdon-Davies

Single to Spain & Escape from Disaster—Keith Scott Watson

Spanish Portrait—Elizabeth Lake

British Women in the Spanish Civil War—Angela Jackson

Boadilla—Esmond Romilly

My House in Málaga—Sir Peter Chalmers Mitchell

The Tilting Planet—David Marshall

Hampshire Heroes: Volunteers in the Spanish Civil War—Alan Lloyd

Remembering Spain: Essays, Memoirs and Poems on the International
Brigades and the Spanish Civil War—edited by Joshua Newmark/IBMT

288

TALES FROM THE SOUTHERN CONE
AVAILABLE FROM THE CLAPTON PRESS

Translated into English:

Brutal Tales by Ernesto Herrera

Mysteries of the River Plate by Juana Manso de Noronha

The Yocci Well by Juana Manuela Gorriti

Our Native Land by Juana Manuela Gorriti

An Oasis in Life by Juana Manuela Gorriti

Burnout by Patricio Jara

In Spanish:

La Tierra Natal por Juana Manuela Gorriti

Su Majestad el Hambre: Cuentos Brutales
por Ernesto Herrera

Los Misterios del Plata por Juana Manso de Noronha

Oasis en la Vida por Juana Manuela Gorriti

Lucía Miranda por Rosa Guerra

Memoirs in English

Rough Notes, Taken During Some Rapid Journeys
Across the Pampas and Among the Andes
by Captain Francis Bond Head

What One Man Saw, Being the Personal Impressions
of a War Correspondent in Cuba
by Harrie Irving Hancock

MODERN SPANISH CLASSICS
IN TRANSLATION

The Alligator's Trap by Antonio Soler (Clapton Press)

Soldiers in the Fog by Antonio Soler (Clapton Press)

Sur by Antonio Soler (Peter Owen/Pushkin Press)

The Gap Year by Cristina Fernández Cubas (Clapton Press)

Nona's Room by Cristina Fernández Cubas (Peter Owen)

Wolf Moon by Julio Llamazares (Peter Owen)

Inventing Love by José Ovejero (Peter Owen)

Yerma by Federico García Lorca (Clapton Press)

The Clairvoyant by Gervasio Posadas (Clapton Press)

Take 6 Spanish Women Writers —
Short stories by Emilia Pardo Bazán, Carmen de Burgos,
Carmen Laforet, Cristina Fernández Cubas, Soledad
Puértolas & Patricia Esteban Erlés (Dedalus Books)

www.theclaptonpress.com

www.ingramcontent.com/pod-product-compliance
Ingram Content Group UK Ltd.
Pitfield, Milton Keynes, MK11 3LW, UK
UKHW022324170125
453762UK00010B/448